...archway, she wished her mother were here to test its magical properties. If anyone deserved a long and happy life, it was Patricia Bentley. Tears filled her eyes.

"Allison?" Colin was suddenly beside her, blue eyes filled with concern. "Are you all right?"

She nodded, blinking rapidly, her throat working as she tried to regain control of her emotions. She couldn't burden this man with her problems. He'd had enough tragedy in his own life....

"Allison," Colin repeated, a husky note in his voice now. Before she knew what was happening, he had gathered her into his arms, cradling her head against his shoulder. His embrace felt wonderfully comforting. Safe. Right.

ABOUT THE AUTHOR

A trip to Bermuda served as inspiration for
Rosalind Carson's latest Superromance.
Fascinated by the history of the islands, she
decided to blend fact with fiction. Alys Thornley
didn't really exist, Rosalind points out, but she
might have. Ros's fans should watch for *The
Forever Love*, a story about reincarnation,
published by Worldwide Library in May under the
name Margaret Chittenden.

Books by Rosalind Carson

HARLEQUIN SUPERROMANCE

HARLEQUIN TEMPTATION

Don't miss any of our special offers. Write to us at the
following address for information on our newest releases.

Harlequin Reader Service
901 Fuhrmann Blvd., P.O. Box 1397, Buffalo, NY 14240
Canadian address: P.O. Box 603,
Fort Erie, Ont. L2A 5X3

Rosalind Carson

THE MOON GATE

Harlequin Books

TORONTO • NEW YORK • LONDON
AMSTERDAM • PARIS • SYDNEY • HAMBURG
STOCKHOLM • ATHENS • TOKYO • MILAN

For my friends, Joan and Karl Berg,
because they were there

First printing April 1988

ISBN 0-373-70310-4

Copyright © 1988 by Margaret Chittenden. All rights reserved.
Except for use in any review, the reproduction or utilization
of this work in whole or in part in any form by any electronic,
mechanical or other means, now known or hereafter invented,
including xerography, photocopying and recording,
or in any information storage or retrieval system, is forbidden without
the permission of the publisher, Harlequin Enterprises Limited,
225 Duncan Mill Road, Don Mills, Ontario, Canada M3B 3K9.

All the characters in this book have no existence outside the
imagination of the author and have no relation whatsoever to
anyone bearing the same name or names. They are not even
distantly inspired by any individual known or unknown to the
author, and all incidents are pure invention.

® are Trademarks registered in the United States Patent and
Trademark Office and in other countries.

Printed in U.S.A.

Allison's Family Tree

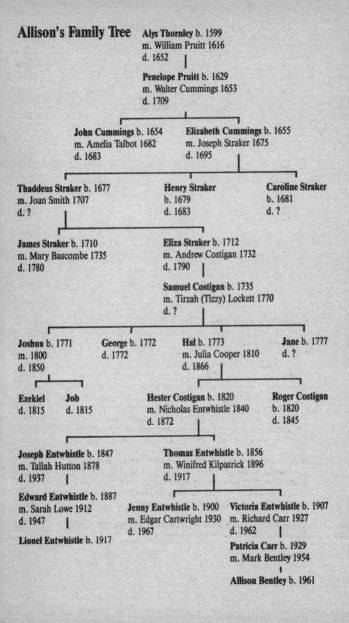

Alys Thornley b. 1599
m. William Pruitt 1616
d. 1652

Penelope Pruitt b. 1629
m. Walter Cummings 1653
d. 1709

John Cummings b. 1654
m. Amelia Talbot 1682
d. 1683

Elizabeth Cummings b. 1655
m. Joseph Straker 1675
d. 1695

Thaddeus Straker b. 1677
m. Joan Smith 1707
d. ?

Henry Straker
b. 1679
d. 1683

Caroline Straker
b. 1681
d. ?

James Straker b. 1710
m. Mary Bascombe 1735
d. 1780

Eliza Straker b. 1712
m. Andrew Costigan 1732
d. 1790

Samuel Costigan b. 1735
m. Tirzah (Tizzy) Lockett 1770
d. ?

Joshua b. 1771
m. 1800
d. 1850

George b. 1772
d. 1772

Hal b. 1773
m. Julia Cooper 1810
d. 1866

Jane b. 1777
d. ?

Ezekiel
d. 1815

Job
d. 1815

Hester Costigan b. 1820
m. Nicholas Entwhistle 1840
d. 1872

Roger Costigan
b. 1820
d. 1845

Joseph Entwhistle b. 1847
m. Tallah Hutton 1878
d. 1937

Thomas Entwhistle b. 1856
m. Winifred Kilpatrick 1896
d. 1917

Edward Entwhistle b. 1887
m. Sarah Lowe 1912
d. 1947

Lionel Entwhistle b. 1917

Jenny Entwhistle b. 1900
m. Edgar Cartwright 1930
d. 1967

Victoria Entwhistle b. 1907
m. Richard Carr 1927
d. 1962

Patricia Carr b. 1929
m. Mark Bentley 1954

Allison Bentley b. 1961

PROLOGUE

July 1609

THUNDER ROARED AND CRACKED across the turbulent sky. The wind screeched and howled like a hundred demons set loose from the gates of hell. The ship that ten-year-old Alys Thornley had thought so large and sturdy when passengers and crew set sail from Plymouth seemed small as a child's toy as it rolled and tossed in the raging sea. No division could be seen between water and sky; it was as though the mountainous waves were arrogantly demonstrating their tumultuous power to a frowning heaven.

A woman near Alys was praying aloud, calling on God's mercy to save her. Possibly God could not hear, so loud were the frightened cries of the women and children, the squeals of the pigs and the shouted orders of the officers. "Even seven men aren't enough to hold the whipstaffe in this storm," Alys's uncle had shouted to his wife before he went off into the howling darkness to lend his great strength to the task of keeping the *Sea Venture* upright.

"She's going to split asunder," Alys's aunt screamed close to Alys's ear. "We have lost the rest of the fleet, did you hear? And we are blown off our course. We should never have left England. My babies will die."

Her twin sons, normally vexatious, oftentimes obstreperous six-year-olds who refused to mind Alys when in her charge, shrieked with terror at this and held on even tighter to their mother's neck, coming nigh to strangling the poor hysterical woman.

Alys hung on to a wooden rail with hands long since bereft of feeling. Wordless prayers formed in her mind but could find no outlet on her bitten tongue. As hour followed hour and the ship heaved and dropped, rolled and pitched, her small stomach rebelled again and again though it had long since emptied itself and she could only retch painfully. To distract herself, she tried to recall her mother and father, gone to heaven so long ago. Was she to join them this terrible night? Should she not rejoice at the prospect? Why pray for deliverance and cling so hard to life? Was her life truly worth living? Would it not be as well to die and get the entire struggle over with?

No, she *wanted* to live. She wanted to see Jamestown. She wanted to find out if the New World was any kinder than the Old to a penniless ten-year-old female orphan. She wanted to grow to womanhood. She wanted to marry, if any man would take such a plain and gawky country wench to wed. She wanted to make a home, a place, her own place.

All the same, when word ran from mouth to mouth that the ship's hold was filling with water, Alys tried to compose herself for death. The people of Jamestown, she remembered, were desperately awaiting supplies the fleet was supposed to bring. Would the other ships of the fleet survive, or were they all doomed?

Men crept all over the ship with candles, searching every corner, plugging leaks with beef or whatever else came to hand. But it soon became clear that their efforts were wasted—the biggest leak could not be found.

All the passengers and crew took turns manning the pumps and bailing with buckets, some of them gentlemen who had never labored in such a fashion, but who now worked without sleep or food as if their very lives depended upon their labors, which indeed they might. Alys, weak and frightened as she was, ran all over the ship, helping to tend those who suffered injury. Any action, no matter how dangerous, was surely preferable to crouching in the dark dank sleeping quarters waiting to die, listening to the ship's dog whimper so pitiably and her cousins and aunt moan and sob.

For three days and nights the hurricane continued. Men passed full buckets from the hold upward and empty buckets back, pumps worked hour after hour, yet still the water in the hold increased and still no light showed in the eternally black sky.

And then on the third night since the storm had begun, Sir George Somers, who had barely left his watch for an instant, called for all to see the light that had suddenly appeared, dancing from shroud to shroud, leaping along the main yard.

Alys was dressing a seaman's rope-burned and blistered hands with some herbal ointment from her own recipe. "The light means naught," the man said when she raised her drenched head and exclaimed with hope, thinking the light a sign from God that they would be saved. "Such a light often appears in storms. It will not help a whit to save the ship. Naught will save this ship."

And so indeed it appeared. Even when the crew unrigged the ship and heaved overboard trunks and chests and hogsheads of oil and cider and wine, as well as all the ordnance on the starboard side, the ship still took on more water than the weary voyagers could pump or bail. There was no relief in sight from the boiling sea and raging wind.

"Only a miracle from God can save us," the injured seaman muttered to Alys.

But a few hours later, the miracle came, along with a brightening of the sky. "Land," Sir George cried.

Men who had slumped in sheer exhaustion into corners gathered their feeble spirits together and struggled to their feet. Pulling herself upright on the deck, Alys stared wide-eyed at the shadowy gray outline on the horizon, afraid to blink, thinking that whatever the shadow was it must surely disappear in the next roll of the ship. But it stood firm. As the waterlogged ship moved closer, passengers and crew bailing and pumping with renewed enthusiasm, the clouds lifted and the seas abruptly calmed. Alys could see trees swaying in the wind. It was, it truly was...*land*.

"Bermuda," Alys heard Sir George Somers say.

Alys had never heard of Bermuda before, but the name echoed in her mind like a familiar song. She was quite suddenly and completely convinced that she had found her place, the place above all others where she belonged.

"The Devil's Islands," someone else exclaimed, but Alys paid no attention to the man. Later, years later, she was to wish she had.

CHAPTER ONE

The Present

"I WANT YOU to go to Bermuda before I die," Allison's mother said.

Getting up abruptly from the side of her mother's bed, Allie went to look out of one of the condo's tall windows at the rain-blurred lights of downtown Seattle and the dark glimmering of Elliott Bay beyond. She blinked rapidly, banishing the sheen of moisture in her eyes, which she could see reflected in the rain-splashed window. No matter how many times she told herself that she had accepted her mother's inevitable death—*she could cope, she wasn't going to waste the precious time they had left together in what Patricia Bentley called "anticipatory grieving"*—her stomach still contracted as though recoiling from a blow whenever Patricia brought the subject up.

Swallowing hard, she turned back to look at her mother and forced a casual note into her voice. "Why on earth would I want to go to Bermuda? Just because it's been raining in Seattle for forty days and forty nights doesn't mean I should desert you and run after the sun. I thought you needed me to manage the store. Besides, didn't we agree we wanted to spend as much time as possible together? Who else would give you such sensational back rubs?"

"Dr. Sotero has given me the name of a live-in nurse," Patricia informed her. "I'll be well looked after. And Linda and Marty are perfectly capable of taking care of the store."

"I'm not so sure about that," Allie said worriedly. "Linda's going through a difficult time right now. You know she just broke up with Tony."

"And you've been letting her cry all over your shoulder every lunch hour, haven't you?" The affection in Patricia's voice took any possible sting out of her words.

"She needs to talk it out," Allie said defensively. "Besides, Marty needs me, too. It's not easy being a single parent. At least when I baby-sit the girls he gets out once in a while."

Patricia sighed audibly. "You don't think Marty can afford a paid sitter? We certainly pay him enough. And Linda will have a new man quicker than it takes to say, 'Do you come here often?'"

Allie laughed. "People don't use that line anymore, Mom."

"I don't see why not. It always worked for me before I met your father. Anyway, stop ducking the issue here. Marty and Linda can probably muddle along without you for a while. As for us spending time together," she added brightly, "look at it this way. We've probably spent as much time with each other in the past seven months as we have in the past six years, what with me running the store and you trotting around the globe with a video camera glued to one eye."

As Allie opened her mouth to protest this cavalier description of her job, Patricia went on, "You would hardly be deserting me, darling, when it's my request. Perhaps my last request," she added in a deliberately lugubrious voice. "How many last requests have I made now? Twenty?"

"I'm not about to let you pack me off to Bermuda," Allie said. "I know exactly what you're up to, and it won't work."

Patricia's dark eyebrows arched in mock indignation. Then she smiled and patted the place on her bed where Allie had been sitting. "Okay, smart one, come back here and tell me what I'm up to."

Allie studied her mother's face in silence as she obediently settled herself. People had always commented on the similarity between mother and daughter. They were both tall—five feet nine inches. Neither of them could be called great beauties, but they had *something*—a brightness, a warmth—that seemed to reach and attract other people. Allie had inherited her mother's strong features, dark curling hair and lustrous brown eyes flecked with green. Also, as long as Allie, now twenty-seven, could remember, they had shared a tendency to gain weight at the drop of a chocolate-filled croissant. A fine figure of a woman, Allie's father had said about Patricia many times, declaiming, teasing her, thumbs hooked in the imaginary pockets of an imaginary vest. But now Patricia's facial bones showed starkly beneath her sallow skin and her body scarcely raised the covers of her bed. "Hell of a way to lose weight," Patricia had grumbled earlier as Allie gave her a sponge bath. "Beware of wishing for something, Allison, darling...you might get it. I always wanted to be skinny. I thought skinny people never had problems. Now look at me."

"Well?" Patricia prompted. "Aren't you supposed to be reading my mind?"

"You just want me out of the way so I won't have to see you..."

"Fading away?" Patricia's illness might have dimmed her hair and stolen the healthy flush from her cheeks, but it hadn't diminished the incandescence of her smile. "Come off it, kid. One, I'm not the martyr type. Two, I have no intention of fading. I'm going to fight the Big C as long as I have breath left in my body. Anyway, this new medicine looks promising. Maybe I'll surprise everyone and last out the year."

"Mom," Allie protested.

"Black humor is my way of handling this situation, remember?" Patricia said lightly, but her glance was level. "Don't let me down," she had ordered Allie with just such a glance soon after they'd learned the devastating truth about her condition. "You have to help me keep my sense of humor. I absolutely refuse to go mewling and moaning to my death. Not my style."

Before this they had both gone through the usual stages of reaction to tragedy, just as they had when Allie's father had died several years ago. Shock, denial, anger, grief and, finally, acceptance. Acceptance, Allie reminded herself, swallowing hard. Could she be any less brave than her mother?

"Okay," Allie said with mock resignation. "I give up. Why am I going to Bermuda?"

"To solve a mystery for me." With a smug grin, Patricia settled herself back against her pillows and tugged her Ski Hawaii nightshirt into place. "Do you remember my Aunt Jenny Entwhistle Cartwright? My mother's sister?"

Allie laughed. "How could I forget anyone with a name like that?"

"Do you remember the story she used to tell about our long-ago ancestor, Alys Thornley, the relative I named you for?"

Allie frowned. "Vaguely. I wasn't all that old when Aunt Jen died. Anyway, I wasn't as patient with Aunt Jen as you were. You always loved all her stories, but I..." She raised her eyebrows. "Aha, the plot thickens. As I recall, Alys Thornley lived in Bermuda."

Patricia nodded. "She was shipwrecked there when she was ten years old. In 1609." She took a deep breath and a faraway look came into her eyes. "The name of the ship was the *Sea Venture*, and it carried one hundred fifty men, women and children," she continued in the voice of one telling a much loved story. "They were bound for Jamestown with supplies for the settlers there, but the *Sea Venture* ran into a hurricane."

She was silent for a moment, then she shook her head slightly and went on. "Luckily the captain was able to run the ship aground in Bermuda and everyone survived. They found the country totally uninhabited except for wild hogs and turtles and birds and fish. Sunshine and balmy breezes. A paradise. Not even an angry native to object to their landing."

She grinned. "Bermuda was one of the few colonies that didn't get pinched from the natives—there weren't any natives. Apparently the islands had a pretty bad reputation. The Devil's Islands, they were called, because of the rocky barrier reef, I guess—ships were wrecked fairly often. Anyway, a few sailors had visited involuntarily, but as in the old joke about New York, nobody wanted to live there."

"Didn't the survivors of the *Sea Venture* build another ship out of the wreckage?"

The corners of Patricia's eyes crinkled with amusement. "You *were* listening to Aunt Jenny, after all. Yes. They built two ships, the *Deliverance* and the *Patience*. Took them nine months. Then everybody sailed for Jamestown, including Alys, her aunt and uncle and two little cousins, all of whom died of unnamed fevers shortly thereafter. Alys was left alone."

"I don't remember that part," Allison said when her mother paused for breath.

"I don't know much more myself," Patricia said. "Unfortunately, Alys didn't write anything down for posterity. Perhaps she couldn't write—she was possibly one of what a certain Mr. Endicott calls 'the commoner sort.'"

There was such a note of sarcasm in Patricia's voice that Allie shot her a curious glance, but she shook her head and went on before Allie could question her.

"According to Aunt Jenny, Alys charged her daughter to remember the story of her arrival in Bermuda and to make sure her descendants learned about it. Curious, don't you think, that she'd be so insistent? In any case, her daughter did pass the story on to her children, who did likewise. The story was repeated to generation after generation for almost four hundred years. Which in itself is fairly remarkable. It became a sort of ritual in the family, which is why I'm passing it on to you."

Before Allie could comment, Patricia smiled nostalgically and went on. "I heard Alex Haley speak at Mills College in California a few years after *Roots* was published. He was wonderful! He started *Roots*, you remember, on just such a family story. He inspired me so, that I decided I was going to write a book about Alys. It might never be published, but you could give it to your children. If and when you ever have any," she added tartly, looking sideways at Allie. She sighed. "Anyway, after your father died I needed something to occupy my mind."

She paused to sip cranberry juice from a glass on her nightstand and Allie found herself remembering how shattered her mother had been by her father's automobile accident six years earlier. Allie had feared for her health and sanity, but Patricia had always been a strong woman and she had eventually found enough strength to go on . . . until seven months ago.

Patricia returned her glass to the nightstand. "I did some research at the library, knowing that oral history gets distorted over the centuries. I wanted my version to be as accurate as possible. I even meant to go to Bermuda myself eventually, but then I got so busy with the store. I didn't have time to spare until my own shipwreck took place."

She was silent for a moment, but soon continued in a stronger voice. "We know that somehow at some time Alys returned to Bermuda. We don't know when or why, but the story was passed down that she did go back. She even married there, though we don't know her married name. And she gave birth to a daughter, Penelope.''

"Penelope was in Aunt Jen's story," Allie contributed.

"So was Alys's philosophy," Patricia said.

Allie looked at her questioningly.

"Alys passed her philosophy on to her daughter, who in turn passed it on to her children. Alys believed that every human being has a place where he or she belongs. Unless the person finds that 'place,' he or she cannot find happiness." Patricia had turned to look beyond the windows, but Allie had the feeling she was not actually seeing the rain-drenched buildings.

"I used to think about that philosophy when I was a little girl," Patricia said softly. "I used to dream that one day I would find *my* place. And I did, though my place was with your father, rather than a physical place. We were so very happy...."

Allie touched her mother's hand, then took hold of it tightly. Patricia returned the grip, and for a moment they were both silent. Then Patricia went on briskly. "Anyway, that's why I get so furious with Colin Endicott."

Allie frowned. "Where does *he* come in? You did say there was a mystery, but..."

"Colin Endicott is a Bermudian writer." Patricia turned to wrestle a large padded envelope out of the nightstand drawer, opened it and dumped several papers and magazines and a notebook with a floral fabric cover in a pile on her lap.

"A couple of years ago, I took out a subscription to this magazine," she said, holding up several copies of a magazine called *The Bermudian*. "Colin Endicott wrote an article about the *Sea Venture* that was published last year. A few weeks ago, I decided to write to Mr. Endicott. According to the bio that follows his article, he was working on a comprehensive history of Bermuda. His own ancestors were early settlers, so I thought he'd be interested in Alys. I wrote down everything I knew about her and asked him to find out anything he could that would confirm the story. His reply came yesterday."

With some curiosity, Allie took the paper Patricia was holding out and read the fairly brief letter.

Dear Mrs. Bentley:
There is no record extant of your ancestor Alys Thornley. However, not all of the *Sea Venture*'s survivors are known by name, especially those of the commoner sort. It is possible therefore that such a person did exist and sailed on to Jamestown with the other survivors. I regret that I am unable to be of more assistance. My history of Bermuda, about which you also inquired, is not yet completed.

                                        Colin Endicott

"'The commoner sort,'" Patricia snorted. "Can't you just see the old curmudgeon who wrote this? 'Such a person,' indeed."

"He really got your goat, didn't he?" Allie murmured. Her mother's color was higher than it had been in weeks, her eyes shining with anger.

A sheepish expression appeared on Patricia's face. "I guess I'm still mad at him. I don't know if I can even explain to you why his letter upset me so much. Alys's story was always important to me, you see. I was a lonely child—well, you'll remember how strict your grandparents were. I was a daydreamer, a loner, a romantic. I *liked* the idea of having this adventurous ancestor."

"You don't suppose Aunt Jen made up the story about Alys Thornley."

Patricia shook her head. "She wasn't exactly an imaginative woman, was she? Anyway, when I was little my mother used to talk about Alys, too. She and Aunt Jenny got the story from their father. And the historical details matched exactly when I read Mr. Endicott's article."

"Isn't there a historical society in Bermuda? A library?"

"That's where you come in," Patricia said. "I can't check them out myself, so . . ."

"We could write."

"And have another terse communication come back? No, Allie, I couldn't bear that. I want you to go look at the records yourself. I lay awake most of last night thinking about it. The thing is, you see, sometime after everyone went on to Jamestown, Alys went *back* to Bermuda. She married there, gave birth there, died there. It was her *place*. There must be records. A tombstone even. I guess Mr. Endicott couldn't be

bothered to look into it for me, so he just wrote poor
Alys out of existence.''

"He certainly wasn't too helpful,'' Allie agreed.
"But this whole thing could just be a wild goose
chase.''

"You could do one of your videos on Bermuda
while you're there,'' Patricia suggested, as if her
daughter hadn't spoken. "You haven't done Bermuda.''

Allie made most of her living by making videotapes
of special attractions, festivals and unusual events in
the world's most exotic places. The edited videos were
then sold through travel magazines, tour wholesalers
and that particular region's stores. Tourists loved them
because they were practical and specific rather than
arty. They could either view them before taking a trip
and pin down what they wanted to see, or take them
home to show friends and neighbors where they had
been.

Originally, after majoring in communications at the
University of Washington, Allie had worked in the
family business. Mark Bentley had owned a camera
store in downtown Seattle since before he and Patricia were married—in fact, they met when Patricia had
gone to work for him there. With the boom in de-
mand for video equipment they had expanded the
company considerably. Besides selling the equipment, Northwest Video now offered full services, including tape duplication, titles, music, special effects
and complete production facilities.

Though Allie had enjoyed working with her father
and mother, she'd hated being tied to a schedule and

she'd gradually felt a need to be more independent. She'd wanted a job that would take her outdoors, give her a chance to travel. Video Vacations had worked out very well. In between trips she helped out at Northwest Video, mostly in the editing suite. She probably wasn't ever going to make a fortune, but she had seen more of the world than most women her age, and was constantly meeting interesting people.

"I have to do a lot of research before I go to a place, Mom," she pointed out. "I was all set to go to Rio de Janeiro next. Claudio and Denise invited me to stay with them while I—"

"How long does it take you to do the preliminary work?" Patricia interrupted. "Could you be ready in a month? I have a lot of material here already." She patted the pile on her bed. "Travel brochures, maps, that sort of thing."

"It's my birthday next month," Allie protested. "I want to spend it with you."

"In May then. Suppose you went in May? The season's just getting going then. The weather should be beautiful." She looked at Allison fondly. "I know you hate to make instant decisions, darling. Even as an infant you always wanted plenty of time to think about things, plan things . . . you walked around the furniture for months before you took off across the room. You've never been an impulsive person. I remember countless occasions on which I had to place my hand in the middle of your back and give you a shove and say, 'Go for it, Allie.'" She sighed. "I do wish, this one time, you'd just say yes and not worry about it."

Allie studied her mother's thin face for a long moment. How could she leave her? What if her condition worsened even more rapidly than Dr. Sotero had warned? What if she died while Allie was away?

"Please, Allison," Patricia said softly.

Her face had retained some of its pretty pink color. She looked wistful, sweet, irresistible.

"You really want this, don't you?" Allie said.

Her mother nodded. "When I read Colin Endicott's letter, it was as though my whole heritage were suddenly in doubt." She sighed. "Did you ever read one of those time travel stories where someone travels back in time and somehow messes up history so that someone isn't born who should have been? I felt like that, as though I hadn't really been born, hadn't really existed.

"I want it done right, though," she added, sitting forward abruptly. "I don't want you dashing over there and skimming the surface so that you can rush back. I want you to do your usual, thoroughly researched documentary. And, of course, I want you to find out everything you can about Alys. So you'd better plan on staying for a month or more."

"That's much too long," Allie protested.

"Isn't that how long it usually takes you?"

Allie nodded. "But I don't want to..."

"I know you don't, but I want you to. And I'm your mother."

Allie laughed and held up her hands in surrender. "Okay, you don't have to pull rank. I'll go. And I'll do a proper job."

Patricia smiled brilliantly, then leaned back, suddenly looking exhausted.

"Do you need a pill?" Allie asked softly.

Patricia moved her head gently. "Not just now." She smiled faintly, nostalgically. "Do you remember when you were seven or eight, you went through a period of being afraid of the dark? You wouldn't admit you were afraid, of course, not you. But you'd leave your bedroom door open and once in a while you'd call out. 'Are you okay, Mom?' I'd say I was just fine thank you and you'd say, 'You're not scared or anything, are you, Mom?' And I'd say no, I didn't have anything in the world to be scared of and neither did you. And then you'd go right off to sleep." She smiled again. "I think of that almost every night lately—I don't know why." Her eyes fluttered closed. "I'll rest for a while now, darling. Maybe I'll drift off. Thank you for agreeing to do this for me. You've made me very happy."

Allie leaned over and kissed her mother's cheek, then got to her feet. "That's what it's all about, Mom," she murmured huskily.

She had been blessed with a wonderful daughter, Patricia thought as Allison switched off the bedside lamp and left the room. Loyal, loving, compassionate. Too compassionate—if that was possible. Sometimes people took advantage of Allie. She had dropped practically everything to be with Patricia when she became ill.

Patricia sighed. She was worried about her daughter. One of the things she—and Mark when he was alive—had been most pleased about was that Allie, an only child, had always been outgoing, warm, gregarious. Yet lately she rarely saw her friends. And she looked . . . wan. Tense. Usually at this time of the year she was glowing with health from skiing, or else she was off journeying in some tropical paradise. She had even broken up with Curtis Yost, the young engineer she had liked so well. No explanation. During the past few months she had hardly left the apartment except to work at Northwest Video. She was developing permanent worry lines on her young forehead. Earlier Patricia had been afraid she was going to break down, and if Patricia was to have the strength to manage her life—and death—with dignity, she could not . . . absolutely could not bear to see Allie break down.

Yes, Patricia felt well satisfied with her strategy. She really did want very badly to prove that Alys had existed and had lived in Bermuda, but she had initially conceived this plan as a way of getting Allison away from her sickbed for a while. As Allison had so shrewdly guessed.

CHAPTER TWO

THERE WAS ENOUGH CHOP to the waves in St. George's Harbor to make the deck of the tender unsteady, even though the big boat was anchored securely. But in spite of the wind, the May weather was as glorious as Patricia's travel brochures had promised. Sunshine glinted on the vivid blue water and the tossing whitecaps and on the pastel limestone houses that crowded the hillside of St. George. The sloping terraced roofs—whitewashed to purify the rainwater they collected and delivered to tanks in the cellars—gleamed like the sugar icing on a large assortment of wedding cakes.

Allie loved all of the British colony of Bermuda that she had seen so far, but she especially loved St. George. It was a fascinating little town. Between the houses and the ancient historical buildings she had explored a couple of days earlier, steep narrow streets wound in and out, bearing wonderfully evocative names like Featherbed Alley, Shinbone Alley and Old Maid's Lane.

In the foreground, on the other side of Ordnance Island, the unrigged masts of the *Deliverance II* were outlined sharply against the cloudless sky. This *Deliverance* was not, of course, the original ship made from the wrecked *Sea Venture*, on which Alys Thornley had reportedly sailed to Jamestown. It was a replica, built by the Bermuda Junior Service League and "launched" as a tourist attraction in 1971.

Allie had found a secluded spot to set up her video camera on its tripod, between one of the tender's lifeboats and the rail. She was out of sight of the three hundred or so tourists on board, and could shoot the Bermuda Day dinghy race without being interrupted.

She was having some difficulty keeping her camera trained on the dinghies. For one thing, there were dozens of sight-seeing vessels—from humble outboards to luxurious yachts—between the tender and the shore, and every one of them wanted to keep up with the dinghies as they raced back and forth across the harbor. The dinghies themselves were only fourteen feet long, making them difficult to pick out from among the other boats. It was the wildest boat race Allie had ever seen—the dinghies were outrageously overcanvased and required an acrobatic brand of seamanship to keep them afloat. A great deal of bailing seemed to be one of the main features. Two of the small craft had already capsized, one with a broken boom.

She became aware that Celia Jordan had come up next to her and was waiting for an "okay to speak" signal. She glanced sideways through her wildly blowing hair at the slender young black woman. "Mike's off," she told her, then added, "does this race ever end?"

"This should be the last lap," Celia answered as she braced herself against the rail, sunlight glinting on her cropped blue-black hair.

She looked very colorful and boyishly slender in a yellow polo shirt and scarlet Bermuda shorts. Allie felt dull by comparison in her khaki linen shirt and the white cotton shorts she'd bought at Frangipani's in St. George. As she continued recording, Allie thought how lucky she had been to find this friendly and energetic young woman on duty at the Visitors' Bureau when she arrived three days ago. To make ends meet, Celia had accumulated a variety of jobs—she babysat, she shopped for senior citizens, she cleaned a couple of houses and she worked part-time at the Visitors' Bureau. "A woman's gotta do what a woman's gotta do," Celia had explained, playing on John Wayne's famous maxim. She had readily agreed to act as Allie's assistant and had already guided her around Hamilton, Bermuda's capital, where the library, historical society and colonial archives were located. And where, unfortunately, Allie had so far found no mention of Alys Thornley.

Actually, "guided" was a relative term. Allie had originally expected to rent a car as she usually did, but she had discovered in Patricia's brochures that there were no car rental agencies in the islands. "We've only got about twenty-one square miles altogether," Celia pointed out when Allie had grumbled about this. "We'd have chaos if we provided cars for all the tourists. It's hectic enough as it is, even though we're only allowed one small car per family."

Buses were frequent, cheap and fairly comfortable, Celia had continued, and there were plenty of taxis. Or Allie could rent a moped. Celia owned one herself and would be delighted to lead Allie safely along Bermu-

da's narrow highways and byways at the regulation
twenty miles an hour. Mesmerized by the younger
woman's earnest dark eyes, Allie had agreed with her
suggestion, though occasionally, chugging along on
the "wrong" side of the road behind Celia's bike during rush-hour traffic, finding herself crowded by a
large pink bus against a stone wall on a treacherous
turn, trying to figure out Celia's hand signals—which
were original to say the least—she had wondered if she
had been out of her mind to trust this latter day Pied
Piper.

Today Celia was working. This Bermuda Day
Cruise, Picnic and Jazz Festival had been sponsored
by the Visitors' Bureau. Tourists should have something special to do on Bermuda Day, someone had
decided. Everyone in Bermuda, Celia had told Allie,
recognized the fact that tourism was the islands' life-
blood. Almost all residents were either official or un-
official ambassadors of goodwill.

After watching the race for a few seconds, Celia
straightened, touched Allie's shoulder and pointed
toward the dinghies. "In the second boat there," she
said. "The team in blue shirts."

Allie zoomed in on the small boats, which were
rapidly approaching the buoy that marked the end of
the race. "What am I looking for?" she asked.

"You were asking about Colin Endicott, remember?" Celia said. "He's the one bailing."

At first, Allie could see little of the man in question, beyond a blur of white shorts and blue polo shirt.
But then he joined the rest of the crew on the wind-
ward rail, all six men crowded together, hiking out to

balance the small craft, bodies paralleling the water. Now she could see him more clearly, and she exclaimed with surprise. Here was no old curmudgeon. He didn't look at all like the image conjured up by the word "historian." He was built like an athlete, in a way that indicated an active life-style, rather than one where he worked out deliberately. Mid-thirties at most. His face was tanned, his hair blond, straight but unruly. His eyes were hidden behind aviator sunglasses, but he had a stern mouth, a jaw that meant business. A strong and attractive man, if a frustrating one.

So near and yet so far. She almost wished he would fall overboard. She'd dive in after him, rescue him, tow him back to the tender, take him below and keep him captive until he answered her questions about Alys Thornley.

Even as this wild scenario titillated her imagination, the blue team's dinghy sped past its chief competitor and sprinted for the finish, seconds ahead of the other boats. All the dinghies were immediately surrounded by sight-seeing boats, with much honking of horns and cheers and applause.

Allie switched off her camera, powered down the recorder that was slung over her left hip, then grinned at Celia. "I'm astonished. From all I'd heard about Colin Endicott in the past three days, I'd formed this picture of some crusty old gentleman with a long straggly beard. I imagined he probably lived in a cave. Devin Summers at the *Royal Gazette* told me he's practically a hermit. A woman librarian in Hamilton told me he didn't attend social events. He certainly hasn't returned any of my calls. Some character with a pronounced Scottish accent always answers the phone and says he's unavailable. I thought it was probably Mr. Endicott himself."

Celia grinned. "Sounds like a brush-off to me. What do you want him for, anyway? You need a man to star in your film? Perhaps I can find a substitute. Want me to try?"

"It's not for the video..." Allie began, but then broke off and started fumbling around in the case that held her recorder and battery packs, pretending that something needed checking. She hadn't told Celia her primary reason for coming to Bermuda. Not that searching for an ancestor was anything to be ashamed of, but she was afraid she'd find herself talking about her mother and she just didn't feel able to confide in someone she barely knew, even if Celia was a sympathetic and sensitive young woman. When she had talked to her mother on the phone yesterday, Patricia had sounded bright and confident. She was getting along just fine, she had said. She liked her nurse-companion. Aided by the new medicine, she was feeling strong enough to do a little more each day. She and the nurse had even gone for a slow walk through Pike Place Market and she'd bought a wonderful herbal wreath she knew Allie would adore. Superstitiously, Allie was afraid that if she talked about Patricia's illness it might worsen again.

She glanced up to find Celia looking at her curiously.

"I was told Colin Endicott knew a lot about Bermuda's history," she said hastily. "I thought I could maybe interview him for background stuff."

Celia shook her head. "I haven't seen any interviews with Colin Endicott since his wife died last year. Actually, your sources are correct...he's become a bit of a hermit. He doesn't live in a cave, though. He has this lovely house he and his wife bought and restored." She sighed. "I envy anyone who lives in a house. Sharing a one-bedroom flat with two other girls is not the best—"

She broke off, shrugging. "Colin Endicott goes to work at his furniture factory, I guess. They restore antiques and manufacture replicas," she explained when Allie looked puzzled. "Anyway, according to local gossip, which is usually pretty reliable, he doesn't have much of a social life. For all intents and purposes, when Diana died, he simply shut himself away. He adored her, people say."

"He must have," Allie murmured sympathetically. She hesitated. "Nobody told me he was a widower. For that matter, nobody told me he was gorgeous. What was she like, his wife?"

"Very much a socialite. No children. She played a lot of tennis. And golf. She was involved in several charities. Always in the newspapers. I never met her, just heard about her and saw her around. You ever see old movies of Grace Kelly? That's what Diana Endicott looked like. Ladylike. Blond, tall and slim.

Allie sighed. "Slim" was an adjective she admired and constantly strove to deserve.

Celia helped Allie fold the tripod, then they edged out from behind the lifeboat. "The elusive Colin Endicott aside, are you having a good time?" Celia asked.

"I certainly am," Allie replied. Her mother had been right to send her away for a while, she conceded. She was feeling stronger, much more relaxed. She looked around at their fellow passengers. They were an intriguing mixture, representing several countries and cultures. Now that the race was over, a few couples were dancing vigorously to the exuberant jazz band that had come aboard in Hamilton. Others were sitting around in groups, eating enormous hero sandwiches and drinking "dark and stormies." Celia had already introduced Allie to this Bermudian concoction of black rum and ginger beer, a deceptively mild-tasting drink, and her head was still slightly woozy from the experience.

"Looks as if everyone's having a good time," Allie commented. "Congratulations. A day like this must have taken a lot of putting together."

"As long as we come out even, we'll be satisfied," Celia said.

She grinned at a slight young black man who was approaching them with a stressful look on his lean features. "Z'appening, Michael?" she asked cheerfully.

"We're running a bit short on ginger beer, Celia. People don't want punch...they want dark and stormies. And they want 'em now."

Allie enjoyed the local speech, a mellow mixture of BBC English and slangy American flavored with expressions that were uniquely Bermudian.

"No problem," Celia said at once—the usual Bermudian response to any request. "I've a bin or two in reserve. Listen," she added to Allie, handing her the tripod, "I'm going to have to relieve the girls at the buffet for a while, and I'll be working on cleanup after we dock, so why don't we arrange to meet later? Somewhere between Hamilton and St. George's."

"The Swizzle Inn?" Allie suggested.

"Okay."

Allie sighed as she stowed her video camera in its cushioned carrying case, wishing that by some miracle Colin Endicott would walk into the Swizzle Inn this evening and offer to help her with her research. Everyone she had talked to so far had told her he was her best bet. He had a collection of diaries and letters that were the envy of the Bermuda Historical Society and he probably knew more about Bermuda's history than anyone now living on the face of the earth. He might not have finished his history of Bermuda, but if anyone could track down Alys Thornley it would be Colin Endicott. Which was all very well, except that no one could tell her how to beard the reclusive literary lion in his den.

USUALLY WHENEVER HE entered his house, Colin Endicott felt its serene atmosphere fold around him like welcoming arms. He loved the house he and Diana had bought and restored to its full eighteenth century glory. Wandering through room after golden room, straightening a painting here, running a finger over the carving on a cedarwood cabinet, he would feel himself mellowing, relaxing, nerve ends unwinding.

But on this particular evening, after the day's unusual activities, the anodyne didn't work. He felt restless, jangled. The race had been exhilarating, no doubt about that. He'd enjoyed taxing his body to its limits...and he'd certainly enjoyed winning. But all the same, he had looked forward to returning home, and it distressed him that the usual "cure" hadn't immediately taken hold.

His houseman, Macintosh, was in the kitchen, polishing the already spotless porcelain sink and tile counters. "Heard on the wireless that you won the race," he said. "Congratulations. You want some dinner?"

So much for glory, Colin thought with wry amusement.

Macintosh was a tall wiry expatriate Scot with grizzled hair and eyebrows and a spare way of speaking. A former sailor, he had kept house for Colin since before Colin and Diana were married. In many ways he had taken over as a father figure when Colin's mother developed a heart condition and she and Colin's father decided to retire to England.

Colin shook his head and leaned against the doorjamb, jangling the keys in his shorts pocket, still feeling restless. "Later, perhaps. I had a few beers. Better let them settle. Go ahead without me, Mac."

"Already did. I'll warm yours when you want it. Nice bit of chicken curry." Macintosh rinsed his dishcloth and folded it neatly. "Thought you might eat somewhere else," he added in a voice that was evidently supposed to sound casual.

"I had a few invitations. Several parties going on, as usual. Pamela Barrett asked me to tea, but I didn't trust the look in her eye."

"You could do worse. Don't know as I signed on to work in a monastery."

Colin sighed. It was a bone of contention between them that Colin kept turning down invitations. He was a rarity in the islands—a so-called eligible man—and the local hostesses didn't seem inclined to give up on him. Neither did Mac. The old man hadn't been as enchanted by Diana as most people, though he had certainly shared Colin's grief when she'd died. However, it was his opinion, expressed far too often in recent months, that life had to go on. He himself had a lady friend in St. George, whom he visited every Friday evening through Sunday noon. A creature of regular habits, Mac.

Colin straightened and turned to leave. "I'm in dire need of a shower and a change of clothes."

"Cuppa tea?"

"Later. I'm going to work for a while."

Though Colin always insisted on overseeing the production of his company's furniture, from the initial design consultation to delivery, business was so good and administrative duties took up so much of his time that he was rarely able to be as closely involved in the actual crafting as he would have liked. Also, in addition to handcrafting furniture, he was skilled in restoration and repair work. Quite often, then, partly because he found the work soothing, partly to keep his hand in and practice the skills his father had taken pains to teach him, skills he had later refined at an American Industrial Arts school, Colin would bring a project home from the Endicott workshops to work on in his spare time. Recently someone had unearthed an eighteenth century Queen Anne highboy from an attic and donated it to the Bermuda National Trust, whose chairman had asked Colin to restore it. The chest had been woefully mistreated, so much so that Colin had had to strip off the entire finish. The piece had even required a new leg.

After his shower, he went down to his cellar workshop, a comfortable well-equipped room that featured a red brick floor and open beamed ceiling, and began working carefully with folded cloth and stain at the painstaking but pleasurable task of refinishing the elegant old highboy.

After a while he began to feel more relaxed, but still not quite as contented as usual. On the edge of his consciousness was a distinct feeling of unease. Several times he caught himself listening, as though there was something to hear. He even found himself wondering if he should have accepted Pamela's coyly worded invitation. No doubt about it, he admitted to himself at last, just lately he had begun to feel lonely. That was why he had agreed to participate in today's race. Someday, he supposed, he was going to have to emerge from his self-imposed seclusion. But not yet. He wasn't quite ready yet.

BECAUSE SHE ALWAYS WANTED her videos to show the ''real'' place, when she traveled Allie tended to avoid the glossy restaurants in the large American-style hotels, which were about as intimate as Chicago's O'Hare Airport. She preferred to find the small out-of-the-way places that local people and less-wealthy tourists frequented. The Swizzle Inn had quickly become one of her favorite stopping-off places in Bermuda, though she had decided early on that the rum swizzles that gave the eighty-five-year-old tavern its name were too strong for her. Usually she ordered a beer, but tonight she settled for a mineral water, aware that she'd taken on too many calories already today.

The Swizzle Inn was a unique place, with tourists' business cards pinned all over the heavy ceiling beams and fascinating graffiti scrawled on the walls. Tonight the jukebox featured Bruce Springsteen singing "Born in the USA," which wasn't much for local color but was certainly lively. That's what she liked about the Tavern, she decided . . . it was always lively, noisy with high-spirited talk and laughter, life affirming. It was also casual, so she could wear the cool khaki linen shirt and cotton shorts she had worn all day.

She heard Celia before she saw her. "Z'appening, Barbara?" the girl called to someone in her usual cheerful voice. Allie turned to see her coming in with a handsome young black man who was about Celia's own height and just as skinny. A dead ringer for Michael Jackson. The young white woman Celia had addressed was sitting on a bench against the wall with a group of friends. As Allie watched, she raised her glass in the direction of the young man with Celia. "Hey, Si," she called. "I didn't know you were out."

Out? Allie's mind echoed.

She studied the young man curiously as he and Celia parked their safety helmets alongside hers under the table and sat down. Celia had spoken of her boyfriend several times, declaring her love for him while at the same time complaining that he'd been in trouble from the day he was born. He certainly was goodlooking. Huge dark liquid brown eyes. Fairly long curly hair. A slightly moody look to his mouth. He and Celia had known each other since they were children, she remembered.

"Allison Bentley, Simon Leverett," Celia announced, then grinned. "I brought Si along because I heard you needed a star for your video."

Allie smiled at Simon. "Are you applying for the job?"

His answering smile was on the shy side. "Celie likes to talk," he said.

Allie laughed. That certainly was true. "Maybe I could shoot you and Celia under a moon gate," she suggested. "I have to get some tape of a moon gate sometime." The moon gate was a Bermudian tradition, a circular archway formed of slabs of limestone and often used as the entrance to a garden. The idea had supposedly been imported from China by a clipper ship captain.

Celia started listing possible moon gates in the area and Allie made notes, noticing as she did so that almost everybody, black or white, on the way in or out of the tavern, greeted both Celia and Simon. Bermuda was a very small world. Everybody knew everybody's business, Celia had told her.

"Si has a new job at the Botanical Gardens," Celia said excitedly as Simon called a waiter over and ordered a couple of beers. "He's a horticultural assistant."

Simon shook his head at her. "I'm a gardener's assistant, Celie. Don't you go puttin' on airs."

Into the silence that followed this conversation stopper, Celia asked, "Did you ring Mr. Endicott again?"

Allie sighed. "He's still unavailable."

"*Colin* Endicott?" Simon asked.

Celia stared at him, looking surprised. Then her face cleared. "That's right," she said excitedly. "You know him, don't you? I didn't remember..." She turned to Allie. "Si used to work for Colin Endicott." Her dark eyes were sparkling.

"He did?" Allie stared at the young man, hardly daring to hope that he could help her.

"Mowing grass, weeding, my usual garden stuff," he said. He was frowning at Celia. "So what?" he asked.

"Allie wants to meet him," Celia explained. "You could set it up for her, couldn't you? He won't even talk to her. She can't get past someone with a Scottish accent."

"His houseman, Macintosh," Simon said. "I don't know, Celie, I don't really..."

"Did you work for him recently?" Allie asked.

He shook his head. "Not since his wife died. She was the one who hired me. He was, well, when she died, he didn't seem to want me to..."

"Could you call him up for me?" Allie asked. "Would you?"

"Of course he would," Celia said.

"Oh, now, I don't know," Simon said, looking uncomfortable. "That's going a bit—"

"Why not?" Celia demanded.

"Come on now, Celie."

"Don't you cut your eyes at me, Si Leverett. You told me he thought you were a terrific gardener. He liked you, you said. Those were your exact words, Si."

"Well, he *was* nice to me all right, but . . ."

"Then give him a ring, all right?"

Simon's mouth took on a slightly sullen twist. "I suppose you're going to nag me all night if I don't."

"I am. Allie needs help and—"

"Look, Simon," Allie interrupted hastily. "If you'd rather not call him, I'll understand. I don't want to put you on the spot."

"I do," Celia said firmly.

Si stood, glowering at his girlfriend. "I'm going, I'm going."

"I should think so," Celia said.

"Tell me," Allie said carefully when Simon was out of earshot. "Does 'I didn't know you were out' mean the same in Bermuda as it does in America?"

Celia sighed. "You heard, did you? I was afraid of that. Yes, Simon was just released from prison a couple of weeks ago. He served a month for breaking and entering. He's not really a criminal, Allie," she said earnestly. "When he was a kid, he was always in trouble for nuisance stuff—graffiti on the Alexandra battery, a little shoplifting, though nothing valuable.

More recently it's been speeding tickets, which in Bermuda you can get for going twenty-five miles an hour.''

She sighed again. "Simon did well in school, better than me, actually. He *liked* school, which I never did. But somehow he hasn't quite made a go of life since he graduated. He's a hard worker, but he doesn't last long in most of his jobs. He gets bored, drinks too much beer with his friends, starts acting up. The breaking and entering thing—he wasn't stealing anything. His dad had thrown him out again—he's an awful man, drinks—and Si needed a place to sleep. He was afraid he'd get picked up for vagrancy if he slept in the park. There's no room at my place...three of us...and the house was just sitting there empty and he jimmied the lock. He didn't do any harm—he even scoured the bath and the toilet. They were disgusting, he said, mildew all over." She sighed. "Well, anyway, Simon just never quite fits in anywhere."

"He hasn't found his place," Allie murmured sympathetically.

Celia frowned. "His what?"

Allie smiled. "Something my mother says. She believes all of us have a place we're meant to be in. We just have to find it. Her place was with my father. They were very happy together and—" She broke off.

"'All of us have a place,'" Celia echoed thoughtfully. "I like that." She looked at Allie curiously. "Have you found your place, Allie?"

"Not yet."

"Too liberated, are you? None of you American women want to get married, do you?"

Allie ran a finger around the damp ring her bottle of mineral water had left on the table. "Oh, I expect I'll marry someday. I'd like to have children." She laughed shortly. "Sometimes in the middle of the night I hear my biological clock ticking away like a time bomb. I'd like to start a family before I'm thirty. Which is only two years off. Unfortunately I haven't yet met a man I'd want to marry and have children with."

That wasn't exactly true, of course. There had been a couple of men who seemed to qualify. One had been too long ago, when she was too young to tie herself down. Curtis Yost, her last boyfriend, had dropped her without warning four months earlier. It was bad enough that she was always flying off somewhere, he'd said; now she was spending too much time with her mother and not enough with him. She had really thought Curtis might be the man she would marry. She had loved him, had thought he loved her. It still hurt dreadfully when she allowed herself to think about Curtis's leaving her when she was at her most vulnerable. It would be a long time before she could bring herself to trust another man.

"Perhaps you haven't stayed in one place long enough to meet the right man," Celia teased.

"You sound like my mother," Allie said.

"Thanks very much. I'll have you know I'm seven years younger than you are. Mother, indeed!" Celia laughed, then sighed deeply. "I'd get married tomorrow if Si would ever settle into a job. I hope he sticks to this new one. All these jobs I have...I get worn thin sometimes. What I'd really like to do is keep house and cook and have babies. Si's babies. I loathe living in that poky little flat. My roommates are awfully messy. I have this thing about being tidy. Simon has, too. Who else would clean up a house he'd broken into? But we just can't afford to get married."

"I'm sorry, Celia," Allie murmured.

Celia sighed. "It'll work out," she said without much confidence. She turned her head. "I wonder what's taking Si so long."

"You think he'll have any luck?"

She turned back. "Of course he will," she said, with real conviction this time. "Mr. and Mrs. Endicott really liked him when he worked there. The way Si talked, they were almost ready to adopt him." A small frown marred her smooth forehead. "Mind you, Si does tend to stretch the truth sometimes. He's awfully insecure. But all the same..."

"All fixed," Simon said from behind her.

Allie stared up at him, openmouthed. "You mean he agreed to see me? When? What time?"

In her excitement, her voice had risen. Simon looked embarrassed. She forced herself to speak more quietly. "He really said he'd see me?"

"No problem," Simon said, sitting down. "Tomorrow at six sound all right?"

"More than all right," Allie said warmly. "Thank you, Si."

Celia hugged him. "You did it. You really did it. You're my ace boy, Si, you really are. What did you say to him? What did he say?"

Simon shrugged. "What's the difference?"

"Give me your map, Allie," Celia ordered, then marked an X on it. "This is where he lives. It's fairly easy to find. The house is called End Court. There's a sign at the end of the drive. Okay?"

Allie nodded, then stood and pulled her crash helmet out from under the table.

"You leaving already?" Celia asked.

Allie nodded. "I have to get my questions ready... work out my strategy. I'm shooting at the Crystal Caves tomorrow, remember, so I won't have time then." She looked at Simon and held out her hand. "I really am grateful, Simon. This means a lot to me."

He looked a little uncomfortable again as he stood up and shook her hand. Maybe gratitude embarrassed him, Allie thought. She grinned at Celia. "I'll call you, okay?" She could feel excitement rising. She was going to see Colin Endicott. He must be willing to help her if he'd agreed to see her. Her mother's wish was going to be granted, after all.

CHAPTER THREE

"END COURT" was set in the woods, mid-island, down a long winding driveway lined with tall hibiscus and oleander bushes. When Allie switched off her moped, she could hear only the sound of the warm breeze rustling in the trees that closely surrounded the clearing. After a moment a kiskadee sounded off nearby, cheerfully chirping his own name.

The house was not exactly the mansion she'd envisioned, but it was beautiful, gracious, built of native limestone, two-storied, with the usual wedding-cake roof, an upper and a lower veranda and tall mullioned windows covered with the push-out louvered blinds called jalousies. From the research she had done before coming to the islands, Allie recognized that the house was traditionally Bermudian, probably built in the early eighteenth century. "Welcoming arms" steps, wide at the bottom, narrow at the top, with a solid stone railing at either side, led up to the entrance, symbolizing Bermudian hospitality. There was a walled garden, which she could see through the moon gate at the right of the house. A moon gate. Great. Maybe Mr. Endicott would give her permission to tape it.

Still straddling her moped, Allie kicked the stand into place, pulled her video camera from the bag slung over her shoulder, then hooked it up to the recorder in the front basket. First focusing on the fanlight above the massive front door, she panned across the front of the house to the moon gate, then back again. And stopped.

Colin Endicott, wearing a blue-and-green striped rugby shirt, white chinos and boat shoes, was glowering down at her from the top of the "welcoming arms" steps. His arms were folded in a very unwelcoming way across his muscular chest. He looked like the lord of the manor confronted by a troublesome peasant. Just the sort of attitude she might have expected from someone who'd refuse phone calls, write a terse unhelpful letter and upset her mother.

Steeling herself for a tough interview, Allie placed her camera with the recorder in the moped's large and sturdy basket, unfastened the chin strap from her safety helmet and eased herself off the bike. "Hello," she called, approaching the foot of the steps, smiling tentatively.

Colin Endicott came down to meet her, looking very tall and fair, very handsome, very strong, very annoyed. "Isn't it customary to request permission before photographing private property?" he asked.

His voice was British accented, well modulated...wintry enough to freeze the blood in her veins and wipe the smile off her face. She had been prepared to dislike this man when she read his letter; she saw no reason to change her mind so far. But she did need his help. Swallowing the hostile response that sprang to her lips, she said, "I'm sorry, Mr. Endicott," and held out her right hand. He showed no inclination to shake it and she dropped it awkwardly. His own hands were in his pants pockets now.

He was one of the handsomest men Allie had ever seen—she had to grant him that. His straight blond hair had been streaked lighter by the sun and it was untidy, as though he were in the habit of running impatient fingers through it. His eyes were as night blue and stormy as the sky over the ocean during a major squall.

"I'm sorry if my camera offended you," Allie began, "I was just—"

"First," he interrupted, looking down at her with a wrathful expression on his face, "first you shatter my eardrums riding in on that infernal machine, then you have the unmitigated nerve to photograph my house without..."

What a voice he had. An actor's voice. Good projection. Every syllable precise. Lost in admiration, it was a moment before Allie realized what he had said. "I did *not* photograph your house," she burst out. "I'm a professional videographer, Mr. Endicott. I *never* tape private property or people without the proper releases. I was merely admiring your house and I automatically looked to see how it would appear on camera. It's a sort of reflex action. I *wasn't* recording."

His mouth was still set in an unforgiving line. "Have you as glib an explanation for driving onto private property without permission?" he demanded. "Or is trespassing another reflex habit of yours?"

Shocked, she stared at him blankly, then blurted out, "But I did—do have permission, Mr. Endicott. I was supposed to be here at six o'clock and it must be exactly—" About to check her wristwatch, she realized to her horror that she hadn't even introduced herself. She shook her head. "I'm sorry, Mr. Endicott. I should have told you my name right away. I'm Allison Bentley—" She broke off as he stiffened, his eyes narrowing.

"The woman who's been hounding me all week?" he demanded. "What made you think you could—"

"I have not been 'hounding' you," Allie retorted. "I telephoned exactly three times. If your man says I called more than—"

"My man did what he is supposed to do. He informed you that I was unavailable. Nothing has changed, Miss Bentley. Good day." He turned on his heel and started up the steps, leaving Allie absolutely dumbfounded.

"You can't mean to just walk away," she said indignantly as he reached the veranda. "What kind of man reneges on an appointment?"

Colin stopped on the threshold of his front doorway and turned around. The damn woman wasn't going to be easy to get rid of, obviously. "Now look here, Miss Bentley—" he began, then broke off. She had pulled off her ugly safety helmet and a mass of curly dark hair had sprung out in all directions. He was suddenly aware that she was an attractive, vital young woman. In the strong sunlight her golden skin showed nary a flaw. She was obviously furious—her eyes were blazing—yet at the same time her mouth was soft, tremulous, vulnerable.

He felt a sudden urge to go to her and put his arms around her and tell her everything was going to be all right...he would guarantee it himself. The spurt of emotion astonished him. What on earth were his hormones up to? "If it's that important to you," he said in a kinder voice, descending the steps once more, "I suppose I shall have to hear you out."

She smiled gratefully, dazzlingly, and he felt as though he had been drenched in sunshine. She was wearing snug faded blue jeans and a nylon windcheater that exactly matched the green flecks in her eyes. She was certainly shapely. The word "lush" came to his mind, followed by "voluptuous." A sexual reaction that had been long dormant surprised him with its sudden urgency. It had been so long since he touched a woman. *Diana.* He winced from the familiar twisting pain and hastily searched his mind for a distraction. She wasn't wearing a wedding ring. Why had he even looked? Casting his thoughts back over their conversation, if it could be called that, he seized on an apparent inconsistency. "Did I hear you say you had an *appointment*?"

She nodded eagerly. "Simon set it up for me. Simon Leverett. He called you, telephoned you last night. He told me to be here at six o'clock and..." Her voice trailed away as he continued to look blank. Quite suddenly she was remembering how uncomfortable Si had seemed when she'd expressed her gratitude. "He *didn't* telephone you?"

He shook his head.

Si had a tendency to stretch the truth, Celia had said.

"I don't suppose you even know who he is, do you?" she added resignedly. She was going to kill Simon Leverett. If Celia didn't kill him first. He must have pretended to call just to get Celia off his back. Of all the irresponsible...

She took a deep breath, put her crash helmet back on her head, then fastened the chin strap. "I'm sorry, Mr. Endicott. I really thought you had agreed...I won't take up any more of your time."

Her dignity impressed him, and she had the most direct, honest gaze. "Simon Leverett?" he queried. "The gardener?"

"He said he'd done some yard work for you and your wife at one time, yes."

"He was a good worker, as I recall. But something of a rascal? Always in trouble of some kind. He actually told you he'd spoken to me? You believed I was expecting you?"

"Yes."

"The young scamp!" He ran his hand through his thick hair in a distracted way. At least she had been right about that habit.

He sighed audibly. "You must excuse me, Miss Bentley. We Bermudians have a reputation for hospitality and I've hardly...I had no idea, of course, that you had been deceived. Please, come in and let me try to make amends. Some tea, perhaps...." As she stepped forward, he looked irritated again. "Would you mind taking off that ridiculous helmet? I feel as though I'm addressing a visitor from outer space."

Obediently Allie hung the offending item from the moped seat. She would have stripped to the buff if he'd asked her to, so grateful was she that he'd turned into a human being.

"I take it you don't exactly approve of mopeds, Mr. Endicott," she said as they walked up the steps.

He snorted. "A lot of Bermudians lobbied exhaustively to keep automobiles off these islands altogether," he informed her. "They didn't give in until after the Second World War. I wouldn't go so far as to ban cars, I appreciate their convenience, but in my opinion mopeds are noisome, noisy intruders that should be buried ten feet deep with stakes through their hearts."

Well, at least he had a sense of humor, Allie thought.

She was soon lost in admiration again as she accompanied Colin Endicott into his house. The wooden floors were lustrous with polish, the colors in the flower-bordered area carpets discreetly muted. The rooms on either side of the foyer were high ceilinged, beautifully proportioned, furnished with English antiques. Or replicas, maybe, she thought, remembering the business he was in. The whole atmosphere spoke of restrained good taste. The house was well cared for, too. She couldn't even see any dust motes floating in the bars of sunlight that were slanting in through the lower windows. Only their footsteps disturbed the serenity of the place. She was almost inclined to tiptoe.

"In here," Colin Endicott murmured, touching her elbow lightly, turning her toward an open door beyond a gleaming staircase. The small contact startled her. Blinking uncertainly, she moved quickly inside, away from him.

The room held enough books to qualify as a mini-library. On every wall floor-to-ceiling shelves held countless volumes. An enormous desk took up most of the middle of the carpet. Obviously this was Colin Endicott's study. It was no less intimidating for the fact that it was smaller than the other rooms they had passed. Was that a real marble floor under the carpet, she wondered. Yes, of course it was. Likewise the fireplace. Above the mantel hung a lifesize portrait of a woman wearing English riding clothes. Tall, blond, ladylike, blue eyed, very slim. As cool and elegant as her house. "Diana Endicott" was printed in gilt on a small plaque at the frame's base. She and her husband must have looked magnificent together.

Allie sat carefully on the edge of the carved, stiffly upholstered chair he'd indicated, suspecting it to be priceless, hoping she didn't have any grease on her jeans.

"This used to be the powdering room," Colin Endicott said. "The ladies and gentlemen of the household came in here to have their wigs powdered."

She could imagine him in a powdered wig. Knee breeches. An embroidered satin coat. He would look superb. To the manner born. Standing with his back to the ornate fireplace, he looked elegant even in a rugby shirt and chinos. "Your ancestors?" she asked.

To her surprise he laughed spontaneously, which made him look boyish and much more approachable.

She felt herself warm toward him. A lot. Without the scowl he was fantastically attractive. More than attractive. Sexy. *Steady on there, Allie,* she warned herself. *He may be the most gorgeous man you've ever seen in your entire life, but you're here on family business, nothing more.*

"I'm sorry," he said at last, with laughter still evident in his voice. "That struck me as funny because my wife was never quite sure I fitted in, yet you thought—" He broke off, shaking his head. "I come from a long line of hardworking carpenters, Miss Bentley," he explained. "Not a powdered wig in the lot. My grandfather was the first Endicott even to have his own shop. My father and I took it from there to build up Endicott Design. I acquired this house when the family that originally owned it died out. It had fallen into a terrible state of disrepair."

He was looking at her enquiringly now, but mildly. The scowl had been banished. She just might be able to deal with this man, after all. "What precisely can I do for you?" he asked.

"My mother wrote to you," she began, nervously pulling the notes she'd jotted down the previous night out of her jacket pocket. "Her name is Patricia Bentley," she added. "We live in Seattle—Washington. She asked you for information about our ancestor, Alys Thornley."

He nodded, taking the papers from her and scanning them. "I remember. As I recall, I couldn't find any trace in the records of anyone by that name."

"You did look, then?"

"Of course."

Allie frowned. "Your letter was rather . . . terse. We weren't sure. And you said you hadn't finished your history book. I thought perhaps you didn't want to give out details . . ."

He averted his eyes. "I abandoned that project, Miss Bentley."

Why? she wondered. And why did he look so hunted all of a sudden?

"As for my so-called terseness," he went on stiffly, "you must realize that if as many ancestors as are claimed to have sailed on the *Sea Venture* had actually done so the ship would have foundered in Plymouth Sound. I receive countless letters asking me to trace coats of arms or some such nonsense. . . ." He shrugged. "Now if you'll excuse me while I find Macintosh, I'll see about that tea I promised you."

"I don't need tea, Mr. Endicott," Allie said firmly. "But I evidently need to straighten something out. My mother and I are not snobs. We would not make a claim that wasn't true. The story of Alys Thornley and the wreck of the *Sea Venture* is part of our family history. We merely wish to find out more about Alys, and perhaps trace other descendants. The story was handed down that Alys came here on the *Sea Venture* and left on the *Deliverance*. But she wasn't *just* a survivor. She came back to Bermuda from Jamestown after the rest of her family died. She married here, gave birth to a daughter, and died here at the age of fifty-two or three. Is it really possible that there's no record at all of her existence?"

"Our early records do have many gaps in them," he admitted in a milder tone. "It would help if you knew

Alys's married name. It might be possible to trace her then, but as it is..."

He hesitated for a second, looking at her, then put her notes down on his desk and nodded as though he'd reached some kind of decision. "I keep all my research materials here," he said, going over to a large oak filing cabinet next to the desk. He touched the key set in the upper drawer but didn't turn it. Then he opened one of the lower drawers, which was stuffed with papers, but didn't take anything out. He looked nervous suddenly; his jaw tensed as though something about this task were annoying him. Or upsetting him? "I hadn't expected to—" he began, then broke off.

"Is anything wrong?" Allie asked, going to stand beside him. "You seem so—"

"I'm perfectly all right," he said firmly. Was he trying to convince her or himself? He was acting as though he were faced with Pandora's box, about to loose all the evils of the earth upon the world.

But when he finally opened the upper drawer she saw only harmless ranks of manila folders. Still, it seemed to cost him an effort to lift out one of the files and riffle through it. "These are copies of lists of the *Sea Venture*'s passengers and crew," he said, laying a sheaf of typewritten pages with many alterations and scribbled notations on them on top of the cabinet. "You may keep them if you like."

Studying the papers, she recognized a reference to John Camden Hotten's "The Original Lists of Persons of Quality who went from Great Britain to the American Plantations—1600-1700."

"I saw lists like this at the library," she told him, scanning them quickly, disappointed that this was all he had come up with. There were only about sixty to seventy names on the list of people who had landed in Bermuda, though the *Sea Venture* had carried one hundred fifty people. No Thornley. No Alys.

He was standing quite close to her, looking over her shoulder. She was suddenly very much aware of the silence of the house and a sort of clean, woodsy smell emanating from her host that wasn't from any after-shave. The hand that turned the papers for her was tanned, strong looking, callused. Golden blond hair glinted on the back of it.

She glanced up. His face was fairly close to hers as he read along with her, his mouth still stern, eyes guarded, jaw firm. "I suppose Alys wasn't a 'person of quality,' whatever that is," Allie said. "In your letter to my mother, you referred to Alys as possibly one of the 'commoner sort.' Does that mean you don't think ordinary people have a right to some history?"

He stepped aside and ran his hand through his hair, frowning. "If I thought that, I would have had to leave my own ancestors out," he said tartly. He smiled rather ruefully. "I'm truly sorry if I offended you and your mother, Miss Bentley."

"Apology accepted," she said crisply, then hesitated and added, "I'm not much for formality. My name is Allison."

"Allison," he echoed gravely.

She liked the way he said her name. "My friends call me 'Allie,' " she told him.

He frowned as though considering that, then held out his hand. "I'm Colin."

His fingers were definitely callused. But steady as a rock. Had she imagined his former nervousness? To her amazement, some kind of feeling seemed to arc from his hand to hers. Sexual feeling. Sexual *tension*, immediate and strong. From the surprised look on his face, he was aware of it, too. Feeling slightly stunned, she scurried back to the uncomfortable chair, carrying the papers with her as though she wanted to study them further, conscious of a distinct weakness in her knees.

"I'm not really a prig," he said, a little defensively. "I was probably just quoting from the records. Most of what we know about Bermuda's early days come from an account of the *Sea Venture*'s shipwreck written by William Strachey. He was a Cambridge scholar and secretary-elect of Virginia, and he spoke frequently of the 'commoner sort.' Such class distinctions were the norm then. I'm opposed to them myself, and I didn't really realize how awful my letter sounded."

He closed the cabinet and locked it with an almost palpable air of relief. Then he turned to look at her, still frowning. "I'll check into this further for you, I promise."

Why not now? she wanted to ask, but managed not to. "I won't be in Bermuda very long," she said, instead, hoping he'd take the hint.

"Where can I get in touch with you?" he asked.

"I'm staying at Mrs. Tolliver's Guest House in St. George. Do you know it?"

He nodded. "Everyone knows practically everyone else in Bermuda, Allison. And Mrs. Tolliver—" He broke off. "I'll telephone you if I come up with anything. As you can see, there's a lot to go through, so I can't promise how long... I have your notes and your mother's letter is still in my desk. I'll do what I can."

He managed a smile. He certainly had charm when he chose to exert it. "I'm truly sorry you thought I was...looking down on your ancestor. I truly didn't intend..." He glanced away from her as an elderly man in white slacks and a short-sleeved white shirt came into the room.

"Dinner," the man said without preamble.

"Macintosh," Colin said. "This is Miss Allison Bentley."

"Aye. I saw her come in."

The man nodded at her and she stood and held out her hand to him. "I'm pleased to meet you, Mr. Macintosh. We've talked on the phone."

"Aye." From the glint in his gray eyes she guessed he was remembering his curt responses to her calls. But his handshake was warm. "Seems you got in, anyhow," he said.

Allie laughed and he nodded approvingly. "It's nice to see a pretty lass between these walls. Welcome to End Court, Miss Bentley. I admire perseverance."

Colin gave him a surprised look but didn't comment. "Allison's in Bermuda to trace her family's roots, Mac," he said. "One of her ancestors might have come here on the *Sea Venture*. I've promised to go through my records and see what I can find out."

A long look passed between the two men, which Allie found impossible to interpret, then Macintosh looked over at the filing cabinet and nodded. "That will be a good thing, I'm thinking." He smiled warmly at Allie. "Genealogy's a fascinating study, unless you've a family like mine. A dull lot, I'm afraid, nothing distinguished about any o' them."

Colin was frowning. "Is that your sole purpose here? Tracing your family?" he asked Allie.

He must be remembering the camera. "I'm also making a movie," Allie told him. "As I said earlier, I'm a professional videographer."

"What kind of movie?" he asked, rather suspiciously.

"A travel movie. But not the arty kind. I'm not . . . well, I don't make movies that show the sun sinking slowly in the west, or sea gulls circling the wake of a boat. Nor do I show how the rich and famous live, if you're worried about that. I make practical movies for practical tourists. Movies that show them what they can do and see in the place, help them decide if they want to go there. Enjoyable activities for ordinary people."

Colin glanced at Macintosh. "Miss Bentley wants it clearly understood that she's not a snob," he murmured.

"Quite right, too," Macintosh said.

Allie supposed she *had* sounded defensive. She smiled ruefully and Macintosh winked at her.

"You make these movies all by yourself?" Colin asked.

"I shoot the tape and do the editing, yes," she answered. "I usually hire someone to help me lug the gear around, though—it weighs a ton—and I have a lot of help with the production side of things." Briefly she explained about the family business.

"Dinner," Macintosh said again when she was done. "I took the liberty of setting a place for the young lady."

Colin looked so taken aback that Allie hastened to say she was just leaving.

Macintosh fixed her with a withering look. "You'll no be turning down a chance to sample my fish chowder?"

Allie suddenly remembered she hadn't eaten much breakfast and she'd skipped lunch entirely. It was always easiest to diet at the beginning of the day. She'd try again tomorrow. "*Bermuda* fish chowder?" she queried. "The kind with sherry peppers and black rum in it? Like they serve at the Hog Penny Pub in Hamilton?"

"Better."

"I'll no be leaving," she said in a reverent tone of voice. They both laughed. Colin was looking very suspiciously at his houseman, but Macintosh was ignoring him.

"You've evidently made a good impression on Mac," Colin murmured when they were seated in the dining room, eating tossed salads, and Macintosh was ladling their soup into bowls in the kitchen. "I've never seen him so hospitable."

Allie was feeling inexplicably nervous. Because she was alone with Colin Endicott again? There was such an awareness between them, so strong it was almost palpable. "He seems a nice man," she said lamely.

"Salt of the earth. Like a father to me, but not always pleasant to strangers. As you found out on the telephone. Apparently you've captivated him."

He insisted Macintosh join them at the table. Was he nervous, too?

The old man turned out to be an entertaining raconteur, telling Allie stories about his childhood in Scotland in the shadow of Edinburgh Castle and of the scones his mother served him with stew on Sunday mornings. "No one worked on the Sabbath you see, so we had whatever was left from Saturday." He shook his head. "Those scones of Mum's were the heaviest things. We used to joke you could sole your boots with them. I became a good cook in self-defense. That's what I did in the navy...cooked."

He went on to talk about the Perot Post Office in Hamilton, where the first Bermuda stamp originated. "He was a distinguished gentleman, Mr. Perot," he told Allie. "When he delivered the mail, it would have been beneath his dignity to carry it openly, so he secreted letters in the crown of his top hat."

Colin seemed content to listen to Macintosh, commenting only rarely. Once in a while his eyes would meet Mac's and he would arch an eyebrow, evidently still surprised at Macintosh's friendliness toward Allie. But often there was an air of melancholy about the man. Loneliness? she wondered. In repose his eyes and mouth looked shadowed.

After dinner, Macintosh suggested Colin take Allie on a tour of the house. He agreed at once, but not without another suspicious glance at the old man, who responded with an expression that couldn't possibly be as innocent as it looked. Obviously there was some kind of byplay going on between the two men, but Allie had no idea what it meant.

To her surprise she didn't enjoy the tour of the house as much as she would have expected. She had always loved old houses, but more and more as Colin led her through the gracious rooms, pointing out old treasures, a Georgian mahogany table, a Grinling Gibbons carving in a limewood mantelpiece, dated 1705, a huge Chippendale bed, she felt as though she were viewing a museum rather than somebody's home. Or perhaps a shrine, she thought, remembering the huge portrait of Diana Endicott that hung in the study. She had always felt that houses retained the impressions of people who had lived in them. Some houses "felt" happy, some unhappy. This one felt terribly sad, and somehow suffocating. She wished she could open all the windows and let the flower-scented breeze blow through.

It wasn't until they entered Colin's basement workshop that she felt she could speak above a whisper. "Now this is really nice," she said, looking around at the red brick floor and open beamed ceiling.

"The brick was brought in as ballast on clipper ships," he told her. "These cellars were the slave quarters in the 1700s." He glanced at her sideways. "No, not my family's slaves, Allison. We were usually slaving away for somebody ourselves."

He had a collection of hand tools, arranged neatly on shelves or hanging on pegboard fixed to the walls.

A group of cabriole legs hung in a corner, looking like a complex still life.

There was another large picture of his wife on the wall behind a workbench. A photograph this time. Diana in front of a lighthouse. Gibb's Hill Lighthouse, Allie recognized. Strangely, the treetops were blowing in the breeze but not a hair on Diana's head was out of place. In her tailored slacks and bow-tied blouse, she looked slimmer than ever. Allie wondered jealously how she'd managed that with Macintosh cooking for her.

"We started with this room when we began work on the house," Colin said. "I kept it as a workshop because I occasionally bring projects home."

The workshop was surprisingly well equipped with power tools. "I'd have thought in your line of work you'd use only hand tools," she said.

He smiled. "Don't you think the early woodworkers would have used machines if they'd had them? I do use hand tools when necessary, but I'm more interested in the results than the method, so I've no objection to using a power saw if I think it will serve my purpose better."

Allie nodded, then sniffed appreciatively, recognizing the scent as the one she'd noticed hovering around Colin. "The air smells wonderful in here, like the inside of a hope chest."

"Cedar," Colin said. "We use a lot of it in the factory, too. It's traditional in Bermuda." He sighed. "Unfortunately I have to import it. At one time cedars were indigenous to Bermuda. They forested the islands down to the water's edge. According to my grandfather, the trees were huge enough to yield planks over twelve feet long and a yard wide. But then in 1943 *Carulaspis minima* showed up—scale insects that devoured the cedars and left only skeletons of trees in their wake. Casuarinas were imported from Australia to replace the cedars, but they don't compare—'' He broke off abruptly. "Sorry, I didn't intend giving a lecture."

He showed her the Queen Anne highboy he was working on, one hand caressing the scrolled pediment as he talked. "Someone actually painted this piece," he told her. "A sort of dirty red-orange. Can you believe that people would put paint on such lovely wood? It took me hours of careful work to get the paint off."

Delicately his fingers followed the curves of the carved shell ornamentations. His hands might be callused, Allie thought, but they were beautiful. Strong, yet graceful.

"I have this idea," he said softly, "that wood has a soul. I can feel it sometimes, working with the bare wood, like a presence...."

She was moved by the sensitive concept he was describing, as well as by the sincerity in his voice. There was substance to this man beneath the arrogance and the strange nervousness he had displayed earlier. Here was a man she could like and admire. Here was a man she would like to have as a friend.

She realized he had once more broken off, and was looking embarrassed. "Sorry again, Allison," he said with a sheepish glance her way. "There must be something about you that makes the men of this household so talkative. Excuse me, please. I'm not used to entertaining anymore."

As though involuntarily, he glanced beyond her at the photograph of his wife, then hurriedly looked away. The shadows had returned to his face.

Allie felt a swift rush of sympathy and spoke without thinking. "I understand your wife died some time ago."

His eyes met hers and for a moment she thought he was going to say something about his wife, but then he averted his gaze and said only, "Yes."

Though he hadn't elaborated, she had the feeling he could have told her precisely how many months and weeks and days and minutes had passed if he wanted to. There was so much pain in that one word!

"She must have loved working on this house," she said warmly. "It must be very difficult to—"

"I would rather not talk about my wife," he interrupted, sounding very clipped and British.

There was a brief awkward silence, then he headed for the staircase, saying briskly, "Yes, well, perhaps we should go outside now. You mentioned to Mac that you'd like to see the walled garden, I believe."

"This is lovely," Allie said a couple of minutes later, though again she wasn't sure she really thought so. The flowers in the walled garden were beautiful and there were lots of them . . . the air was heavy with their perfume. But the beds were laid out formally, looking like pictures she had seen of the grounds of great English houses. Too stiff, too geometrically symmetrical, for someone's home.

She glanced at Colin, who was standing alongside her, still with that shadowed look around his eyes and mouth. Because she felt concerned about him, she said quietly, "It isn't always good to keep feelings locked away inside you, you know. Maybe if you did talk about your wife a little, you might feel much better about everything."

His eyes met hers again and again she thought he was going to confide in her. But then his gaze shifted and he said in a very even voice, "Women always feel such a need to interfere. Why is that, Allison?"

Just when she'd begun to like him, too. "That's a very chauvinistic remark," she told him hotly.

"You'll admit most men don't poke their noses into other people's lives."

"There's a difference between nosiness and compassion. You're a sensitive man. I'd have thought you'd recognize it."

He shook his head. "You must realize I've lost count of the women who've told me I have only to confide in them to have all my little griefs neatly healed up and put away in safekeeping." He looked her in the eye, his own eyes stormy, belying the stiffness of his speech. Then he turned away. "Didn't you say you wanted to photograph the moon gate?" he asked in a voice devoid of expression. "There's still some light."

"I didn't mean to..." Allie began as he stalked off ahead of her, but he didn't slow down. When was she going to learn to mind her own business, she wondered despairingly. She had obviously offended him.

"I really didn't mean to belittle your grief," she said carefully after she'd gathered her gear together and joined him at the moon gate. "Sometimes I speak without thinking first. And I tend to interfere. It's one of my major faults. Please forgive me. No offense was intended."

He took a deep breath, then turned to face her with a smile that was so obviously forced it tore a piece out of her heart. However, this time she forced her sympathetic response down and concentrated on setting up her tripod. He didn't want her poking around in his psyche; he'd made that pretty clear.

She tried for a lighter note. "I thought you were going to call me 'Allie.'"

He hesitated, then smiled ruefully. "I just can't, I'm afraid. It makes me think of Ali Baba and the forty thieves. Do you suppose you could allow me to be more formal and call you 'Allison,' instead?"

Formal, she thought, feeling flattened. Formal, like his house and garden.

"No problem," she said, and he gave her a dazzling smile that unnerved her all over again.

Taking advantage of his restored good humor, she managed to persuade him to pose under the moon gate for her, though she had to promise first that the shot wouldn't be included in the finished movie. "I value my privacy," he said seriously, as though she wasn't well aware of that by now. He gestured at the moon gate. "If you walk under it, you will supposedly live a long happy life," he said as she taped the shot. "Very popular with honeymooners," he added in a rather cynical tone as he came toward her. "And tourists, of course. Mostly, moon gates are a tourist attraction. Nothing more."

"Well, I'm a tourist," Allie said challengingly. "Do you mind if I try it?"

"Not at all," he said courteously.

She paused under the archway and looked up at the sections of stone, suddenly wishing she could bring her mother here to walk under the moon gate with her. If anyone deserved a long and happy life, it was Patricia Bentley. If only there were something...anything. But there wasn't, there wasn't...

"Allison?" He was suddenly standing right next to her. "Are you all right?" he asked.

She nodded, blinking rapidly, her throat working as she tried to regain control of her emotions. Sometimes a wave of despair for her mother struck unexpectedly, sharply, and she was helpless to combat it. It just didn't seem fair that the breeze could blow so warmly, the flowers smell so heavenly or that birds should continue to sing....

"Allison," Colin repeated, a husky note in his voice that hadn't shown up before. Compassion showed in his face. When word of her mother's illness got out, Allie had of course received sympathy from her many friends and business acquaintances. She had managed to acknowledge it with dignity, holding back the tears that wanted to fall, afraid if she let them go once there would be no stopping them. But now, when Colin Endicott's hand touched her shoulder, she felt as though she were dissolving. Before she quite knew what was happening, he had gathered her into his arms, cradling her head against his shoulder. His embrace felt wonderfully comforting. Safe.

"What is it, Allison?" he murmured. "What's wrong?"

She couldn't possibly answer without falling apart. Her whole body was shaking. Moving her head from side to side against his shoulder, she squinched her eyes tightly against the tears that were building up behind her eyelids, but for once she couldn't seem to prevent them from spilling over and making a damp stain on his rugby shirt. Never in living memory had she permitted a man to take her in his arms on the first occasion of their meeting, or even on the second, but just now, right this moment, she couldn't possibly pull away, not possibly. There was so much tenderness and comfort in this man's embrace.

"Allison," he murmured again, and then as though the sound of his own voice had awakened him to the knowledge of what he was doing, he straightened and set her away from him. "Sorry," he said gruffly. "You looked so terribly sad and Lord knows I'm aware of what sadness is like. I couldn't . . ."

What must he think of her? Collapsing against him like that. Crying on his shoulder.

Embarrassment engulfed her and fresh tears welled up. Taking a deep breath, trying desperately not to sniffle, she called upon all the dignity she could scrape together. "I think I'd better go," she said thickly. His features were blurred by the rainbow effect the last of the sunlight was having on her tears, so she couldn't tell what expression might be on his handsome face. Probably one of alarm, she thought. No man appre-

ciated a woman weeping all over him, especially when
he didn't even know the woman. What on earth had
possessed her? This man was a stranger to her, yet he
had aroused so many differing emotions within her in
the space of a couple of hours. And all she had wanted
in the first place was some help with a little piece of
history, unimportant to anyone but her and her
mother. Hurriedly packing her video gear while he
watched in silence, she took her leave as quickly as she
could, thanking him gruffly without looking at his
face again.

She had acted like an idiot, she acknowledged as she
chugged away on her moped up the winding driveway
through the long shadows of evening, dashing one
hand against the tears that were still slipping down her
cheeks. It was bad enough that she'd let Colin take her
in his arms, but then to compound her foolishness by
running away like a frightened schoolgirl... Probably she'd blown any chance of Colin Endicott helping her with her search for Alys Thornley.

CHAPTER FOUR

ANNUALLY, Endicott Design Limited hosted a group of carpentry students from the local technical institute, hoping to persuade some of them to join the firm as apprentices. The students were always courteous, but few of them wanted the responsibility that a master craftsman had to accept.

This year there were two students who had expressed an interest in learning to handcraft fine furniture and Colin took pains to explain to them his company's philosophies. "Building beautiful furniture is an exacting, maddeningly slow process that uses traditional methods of joinery, inlaying, carving and finishing," he told the boy and girl who had accompanied him to his office after touring the factory. "New handmade furnishings should have the same strength and elegance and lasting appeal as their antique counterparts. We look upon our finished products as the antiques of the future."

Kenneth Stroud, a handsome young black man, nodded as though in agreement, but was apparently too shy to voice an opinion. The young woman, Maria Foster, was more outgoing. "You take a great deal of pleasure and pride in your work, don't you, Mr. Endicott?" she said forthrightly.

Colin smiled at her. Of this year's group, she appeared to him the most intelligent, the most likely possibility for future employment. He had enjoyed talking to her, explaining things to her, answering her courteous but very pertinent questions.

After the students left, he stayed in his office awhile, thinking about the morning and Kenneth and Maria. He would really like to train more Bermudian young people instead of relying on expatriates from England or Europe. He hoped these two would work out; especially Maria. . . .

He caught himself up. The young man was just as intelligent, just as interested, if less vocal about it. Why did the girl intrigue him so?

Because she had long dark curling hair and lustrous brown eyes, he admitted to himself with an inward groan. She had reminded him of Allison Bentley. During the tour, the way her eyes had shone as she challenged him with questions had reminded him forcibly of Allison standing at the foot of the steps outside his house, informing him that she did indeed have an appointment.

It was only a breath from that image to the memory of Allison Bentley's firm fragrant body in his arms. Allison had moved him in a way he had never been moved before. What great sorrow had engulfed her as she walked under the moon gate, he wondered. He had automatically offered comfort, but he hadn't expected to feel as if his heart had separated from its arteries and was floating around in his body. He had never felt anything quite like that before. Diana, yes, he had always wanted Diana. She had excited him, stirred him, even thrilled him, but he had never experienced such a heartbreaking feeling of tenderness when he held her.

Why hadn't he called after Allison when she'd run off? Embarrassment? Lord knows he wasn't normally so impulsive.

Was he afraid of the alarming symptoms she had generated in his body as she'd wept in his arms?

Perhaps.

More to the point, was he going to see her again? So far he hadn't found the courage to go through his records for her. Which was stupid of him of course . . . he'd *promised* her he would help. Why was it so impossible for him to face reading through all that material?

He slumped back momentarily in his large swivel chair. He knew the answer to that question, of course—he didn't require a psychiatrist to tell him his reluctance was bound up with his feelings of guilt over Diana's death.

He was relieved when his secretary buzzed him on the intercom and told him a client was on the phone from North Carolina. He would *make* himself dig into his long neglected research papers, he decided as he waited for Loretta to put through the call. If he found something about Alys Thornley he would decide then whether to send it to Allison by messenger, or if he could risk his hard-won peace of mind by meeting with her again.

"I WOULD NEVER HAVE BELIEVED even you could be so awful, Simon Leverett," Celia said for the fourth

or fifth time since she and Allie had arrived at the Hog
Penny Pub in Hamilton.

All day Allie had debated ignoring the stupid trick
Simon had played on her, but had finally decided that
when she met Celia she would have to explain what
had happened. Celia deserved to know what her boyfriend was capable of and Si really shouldn't be allowed to get away with such nonsense. Unfortunately,
when she'd met Celia outside the Visitors' Bureau
earlier and had accepted her suggestion that they eat
dinner here, she hadn't realized Simon was going to
join them.

Now she was beginning to regret telling Celia that
Simon had lied about his call to Colin Endicott. Evidently Celia was going to go on about it all evening
and Allie was beginning to feel swamped with embarrassment every time the pretty young black woman
raised her voice. "Look, Celia," she interjected when
Celia paused for breath. "It all turned out okay. I did
get to see Mr. Endicott."

"That's not the point," Celia said, and she was off
again.

So Allie wouldn't see Simon squirm, she mostly
kept her attention on her dinner, with occasional
glances at a couple of female tourists who were
perched on high wooden stools at the bar. The young
women were preening without noticeable success for
the benefit of a trio of handsome young men dressed
in what seemed to be Hamilton's male business uniform: Bermuda shorts worn with dark knee socks and
polished shoes, white shirt and dark tie and well-cut
blazer. One of them was tall and blond and reminded

her of Colin Endicott. She had to concentrate for a while on fighting the image of herself crying her eyes out in Colin's arms. She hadn't heard a word from him all day and she was damned if she'd allow herself to think about that whole embarrassing experience.

Allie and Celia were seated on a bench at one side of a booth, Si on a chair at the other. Between Celia's angry outbursts and Si's apologetic responses, they had somehow managed to order a delicious steak and kidney pie for Allie and fish and chips for themselves.

The popular English-style pub was crowded and several of the tourists seated nearby were quite obviously eavesdropping, smiling at Celia's dramatically charged statements and Simon's lame excuses. Allie was beginning to feel sorry for Si. He appeared mortally crushed, and kept giving her wounded looks from under his absurdly long eyelashes as he sprinkled vinegar on his chips. She had begun to feel she was the one at fault here.

"It was such a rotten thing to do," Celia said, also for the fourth or fifth time.

Simon smiled wistfully, looking like a small boy who'd been caught with his hand in the cookie jar. "Sorry, Celie," he said softly. "I wanted you to be pleased with me."

"Pleased with you!" Celia exploded, her round young face set in unusually grim lines. "Pleased with you ... !"

"Hey, did I tell you I saw the whistler?" Si said abruptly, sitting forward.

He had successfully distracted Celia at last. "Chingas!" she exclaimed, which seemed to be the Bermudian equivalent of "Wow!" "How is he? Where did you run into him?"

"In the Botanical Gardens," Simon told her, obviously relieved to pursue this new subject. "The garden for the blind. He was just sitting there in the sunshine. Listening to the birds, he said."

The whistler, it seemed, was a blind man. He had been a teacher of theirs. From the way they talked about him, it was evident they both regarded him fondly.

"Is he a college professor?" Allie asked.

"Are you kidding?" Celia said. "*We* didn't go to college." She shook her head. "The whistler doesn't even teach anymore. He's retired. But we had him in elementary school. He could make you *want* to learn just for the sake of learning. He was terrific really. Half the time I'd forget he was blind."

"College," Simon snorted. "Only snobs go to college."

Allie looked at him curiously. Why did he sound so defensive?

"Not so," Celia argued. "Look at my friend Anna Tobley. I wouldn't call her a snob."

"I would," Si said.

Allie spoke hurriedly before they could get into another argument. "Why do you call him 'the whistler'?" she asked for want of anything else to say. "Does he have a gap in his front teeth or something?"

Celia laughed. "No, Allie. It's a play on his name—Entwhistle."

Allie stared at her. "Entwhistle?" she echoed.

Celia nodded, giving her an inquisitive look. "Lionel Entwhistle. He lives on the south shore. Have you met him?"

Allie shook her head. "Entwhistle. I can't believe it. I never thought of looking under Entwhistle. Do you suppose it could possibly be..."

She realized Celia was staring at her, very puzzled. "I'm sorry, I'm not making much sense, am I?" she murmured. "I just can't get over..." She looked at Celia apologetically. "I haven't told you—one of the reasons I came to Bermuda was to check on my family's background. It's possible one of my ancestors came here on the *Sea Venture*. Alys Thornley. I've been trying to find some record of her name—so far without luck. Entwhistle is my grandmother's maiden name. My great-grandfather was Thomas Entwhistle. Do you suppose your Mr. Entwhistle could possibly be related?"

Simon was sitting back in his chair and watching Allie with his shy smile. "You do have dark hair, Allie, and I'll grant you it's pretty curly," he said. "But all the same..." Suddenly he leaned forward, reached across the table and picked up one of her hands, turning it over so that he could see the palm. "Nope," he said. "You don't look black to me."

Allie stared at him for a moment, uncomprehending, then felt herself flush. "Your Mr. Entwhistle is black?"

"Six out of ten Bermudians are," he said.

"You must think I'm awfully dumb," Allie said. "How stupid of me to think—it's just that Entwhistle is a fairly uncommon name, isn't it?"

"That's why you wanted to see Colin Endicott?" Celia queried. "You wanted him to help find your ancestor?"

Allie nodded. "He's promised to look into it for me," she said, noticing that Simon appeared uneasy again. Probably he didn't want Celia reminded of the trick he'd pulled on Allie. "I'm sorry, Si," she said. "That was pretty stupid of me. All the same I would like to meet your Mr. Entwhistle. If he was a teacher he must know something about Bermuda's history. Call it a hunch, but I have this strong feeling... Could you take me to his house, do you suppose?"

"Now?"

She nodded, then flushed again when Simon twisted his wrist around to show her his watch. It was almost 10:00 p.m.—hardly a good time to go visiting. "Tomorrow then?" she asked.

"Some of us peasants have to work," Si said, then relented and smiled at her. "I'll write his address down for you." He was a charmer when he smiled. She could see why Celia couldn't resist him.

THE NEXT MORNING Allie ate breakfast on the patio at Robertsons, sharing her toast crumbs with a host of cheeky sparrows and a pair of ducks. She had decided she wouldn't telephone Lionel Entwhistle, as she had no idea what she would say to him. She'd leave the guest house about ten, she decided, reasoning that by the time she found Lionel Entwhistle's house it would be late enough for even the latest riser to be up. But after she returned to Mrs. Tolliver's and changed into Bermuda shorts and a white cotton sleeveless blouse— the day was turning into another humid scorcher—her landlady knocked on the door to tell her Colin Endicott wished to speak to her on the telephone. He had called, after all. Had he found something? Her heart started knocking against her ribs as she ran up the stairs to Mrs. Tolliver's drawing room. Was she out of breath because he might have stumbled on some fact about Alys, she wondered, or out of breath simply because he had called?

For want of a hotel in St. George, Allie had arranged to stay with Mrs. Tolliver, a somewhat eccentric woman who owned a huge, coral-pink Bermudian house in the hills above the town. According to one of the maids, Mrs. Tolliver's family had been very wealthy clothing manufacturers, but Mr. Tolliver, now deceased, had squandered his wife's inheritance with wild investment schemes. Mrs. Tolliver, however, refused to acknowledge her reduced circumstances and treated her paying guests as though she had specifically invited them to stay with her. Her housekeeper, a blunt-spoken Yorkshirewoman named Freda Long, handled all financial transactions.

A vaguely pretty woman who wasn't exactly fat or exactly thin, her body's contours a shapeless mystery within the loosely draped, wildly flowered cotton she seemed to favor, Mrs. Tolliver had almost aggressively gracious manners and a predilection for psychic matters. Allie had lived in Bermuda in a previous life, Mrs. Tolliver had insisted on her very first day. She often read tea leaves for her guests, she had added with a hopeful glance upward through her long mascaraed eyelashes. Allie had not taken the bait.

In order to maintain the fiction of herself as a gracious hostess, Mrs. Tolliver had installed only one telephone in the entire guest house. It stood on a small antique table in her drawing room, where she also served tea every morning and afternoon. She presided over the tea table while Allie talked to Colin, which made communication a little difficult.

"I thought I might take some French leave this afternoon," he said without preamble.

"French leave? Oh...you mean play hooky?"

"I wondered if you had explored the *Deliverance* yet. That's the replica of the ship the survivors of the *Sea Venture* built from the wreckage and sailed in to Jamestown. It's moored at Ordnance Island, near King's Square."

"I shot some tape of the outside, but I haven't gone aboard yet," Allie said. "I've been concentrating on the Hamilton area."

"Perhaps we could go and look it over then."

She wanted to ask if he had found any clue to Alys yet, but there was Mrs. Tolliver, her rather pert little nose quivering almost imperceptibly as she poured tea into Spode cups.

"Are you all right, Allison?" Colin asked when she didn't answer at once. "I've been very concerned about you. I wanted to ring you up yesterday, but I was afraid you might still be annoyed with me. I didn't handle things well, I'm afraid. I wasn't quite sure what was wrong and—"

"I wasn't annoyed," she interrupted, then broke off as Mrs. Tolliver glanced sideways at her from the sofa. "Thank you, yes, I'm fine," she substituted. Hurriedly she considered postponing her visit to Mr. Entwhistle, then decided she didn't want to appear *too* eager to see Colin. "I'd like very much to go with you," she said, "but I have to go to the south shore today. Can we make it tomorrow?"

"No problem. I'll meet you at Mrs. Tolliver's, shall I? I'll drive you, so you won't need your infernal machine. Around half-past two? You might like to bring your camera." He had evidently decided to be helpful in all areas.

"Yes. Thank you. I'll do that. Tomorrow at two-thirty then." She was afraid she sounded terribly stiff, but she was still conscious of Mrs. Tolliver's watchful presence.

"How fortunate for you that you were able to meet Colin Endicott," Mrs. Tolliver said after Allie had replaced the telephone receiver. Without asking Allie if she would like some tea, she handed her one of the exquisite cups and indicated a sofa opposite her chair. It was a very soft sofa. Allie thought she might never be able to get out of it.

"Did someone introduce you to Colin?" Mrs. Tolliver asked.

"In a way," Allie replied ambiguously, unable to come up with an excuse to refuse the tea.

"Such a charming man."

"Isn't he."

"Such a shame," Mrs. Tolliver said, aimlessly pleating the ruffle on the front of her colorful dress, ambiguous in turn.

Torn between curiosity and reluctance to snoop, Allie smiled politely.

"His wife," Mrs. Tolliver added.

Allie sipped her tea. "I heard he was a widower."

"He is, indeed." Mrs. Tolliver smoothed her permanently waved brown hair on either side of its center parting, then fingered her large flat pearl earrings. "Diana," she offered.

Allie set her cup down on the table between them. "I should be getting along," she said, preparing to pry herself out of the cushiony softness that surrounded her.

Mrs. Tolliver picked up Allie's cup and studied it closely, an air of drama around her. "Just as I thought," she said immediately. "Your soul *has* lived in Bermuda before. And you are going to make your home here again. I wonder..." She glanced at Allie in a strangely conspiratorial way. "He was devastated, you know," she said slowly. "Colin, I mean. When Diana died. She was flying to England, you see. To visit her family supposedly. The plane crashed into the ocean. Several local people were on board, including Colin's best friends, the Perry twins. And Johnny Barlow's nephew. Such a tragedy."

There was a note in her voice that seemed to attach some special significance to what she'd said, but Allie hadn't allowed herself to read between the lines. Diana Endicott was none of her business, alive or dead.

"I always travel by ship myself," Mrs. Tolliver added. "It's so much safer, don't you think?"

Allie quelled an insane impulse to mention the *Titanic*.

"I knew Diana socially, of course. Absolutely." Mrs. Tolliver's emphatic tone of voice left no doubt that she and Diana Endicott had moved in the same circles. "She was English, you know." Again the odd note in her voice. Something less than admiring. "Colin met her in England on a business trip. She was a blade."

Allie was surprised into responding, though she'd vowed to herself she wouldn't. "She was a what?"

"A *Blade*." This time Allie could hear the capital letter. "One of the Sussex Blades. A very old family."

"Oh." In spite of herself Allie couldn't help asking. "What was she like?"

"Quite the beauty," Mrs. Tolliver said in a rather acid way. "Exquisite manners. On the surface, anyway. Actually, she was a terrible snob, but Colin worshipped her. I remember their wedding. He had eyes only for her. It seemed to be a perfect marriage. At first." She leaned forward. "He hasn't recovered from her death, you know. He probably never will. That's why I think someone ought to tell him."

"Tell him?" As soon as the words were out Allie regretted them. She hadn't meant to encourage Mrs. Tolliver's gossip. She certainly didn't want to hear whatever Mrs. Tolliver had to say about Diana and Colin Endicott.

"She was having an affair, you see," the older woman said all in a rush, as though she suspected she was about to lose her audience. "With one of the Perry twins. I don't know which one—never could tell them apart. Anyway, the two of them were going off to England together, with the other brother for camouflage."

"Mrs. Tolliver, I don't really think—"

"Several of us knew about it," the woman went on as if Allie hadn't spoken. "Colin didn't, though. He still doesn't. We kept it from him." She paused dramatically. "A conspiracy of silence."

"He doesn't know? He still thinks—" Allie broke off, remembering those large portraits of Diana, the air of a shrine about the Endicott house. That poor man, grieving, not knowing he had been betrayed. Leaning forward and pushing down hard with both hands, she managed to get to her feet. "Look, Mrs. Tolliver," she said. "I wish you hadn't told me all this. It's none of my business. I hardly know Mr. Endicott and I certainly—"

"Ah, but you are *going* to know him," Mrs. Tolliver predicted, still gazing into Allie's cup. "It's quite clear here, the pattern, the weaving of two bodies—"

"Mrs. Tolliver!"

Obviously hearing the outrage in Allie's voice, Mrs. Tolliver finally set down her cup, but she certainly didn't look at all repentant. In fact, judging by the dreamy, thoughtful expression on her round face, she was about to make another prediction.

"I have an appointment, Mrs. Tolliver," Allie said hastily. "If you'll excuse me."

Mrs. Tolliver inclined her head graciously. "I want my guests to feel free to come and go at will," she said. "Do drop in again tomorrow for tea. When Colin calls for you. He is meeting you here? Yes? How nice. I haven't seen him for a long time. Two-thirty you said, I believe?"

Poor Colin, Allie thought as she rushed down the stairs. She had the feeling Mrs. Tolliver would be lying in wait the next afternoon.

MR. ENTWHISTLE'S house looked more Victorian than Bermudian. It was a larger home than either Mrs. Tolliver's or Colin's. Stately, set in glorious grounds, with a wide view of the coastline and inshore reefs, it was the same shade of coral as Mrs. Tolliver's guest house—a popular color in the islands. Closer observation showed Allie that the gardens were beginning to run to seed and the house itself was also a little on the neglected side. The stepped roof gleamed white as did all roofs in Bermuda, but the rest of the house seemed to need a new coat of paint. A huge poinciana tree shaded the entrance.

No one answered the doorbell, even after the third ring. Allie was turning away, feeling disappointed, when she noticed a face at a nearby window. An elderly man was standing inside, looking at her. "Mr. Entwhistle?" she called, then broke off, feeling foolish. The man was white. For a minute longer he stood looking curiously at her, then he nodded as though he'd reached some solemn conclusion and disappeared.

"Hello," Allie said when he opened the door.

He was a very old man, short and skinny, with a mane of untidy gray hair that made him look like a mad professor. Wrinkles radiated around small brown eyes that were as bright as a bird's and bristly gray eyebrows gave him a bad-tempered expression. He was wearing a blue cotton shirt and blue jeans that seemed a little too large for him, cinched at the waist with an overlong belt.

"I don't have any money," he said loudly. "My roommate's the rich one, not me. This is his house. He lets me stay here out of charity. I don't have any charity to give. You have to be rich to give out charity."

At a loss, Allie stared at him.

"Aren't you collecting for something?" he asked. "Or are you a religious person?"

"I'm looking for Mr. Entwhistle. Does he live here?"

"Of course I live here. Do I look dead? State your business, young miss, and be off with you."

Allie tried again. "Mr. Entwhistle. Lionel Entwhistle."

"*I'm* not Lionel Entwhistle."

"I know that." She took a deep breath and hung on to her sanity. "I just want to know if Mr. Entwhistle lives here."

"Who?" He scowled at her. "You'll have to speak up, miss. I'm ninety years old and deaf as a post."

"Lionel Entwhistle?" she yelled.

"What about him?"

"Is he at home?"

"What?"

"Is Mr. Entwhistle here?"

"You'd better come back later," he said. "My roommate's not here."

"Your roommate is Mr. Entwhistle?"

"I know. I know. He's black and I'm white. I suppose you think something's wrong with that?" He gave her a fierce look.

Allie spread her palms in a gesture she hoped would seem pacific rather than hopeless. "I came to see Mr. Entwhistle," she yelled at the top of her voice.

"Why didn't you say so then," the old man asked. And closed the door in her face.

Totally frustrated, but certainly able to see the funny side of the situation, Allie retreated to her moped, climbed on and tried to decide whether she should just return to the guest house and call again later. She didn't really want to do that. On the map Lionel Entwhistle's house didn't seem too far from St. George, but Bermuda's winding roads made the distance a fairly long one.

Finally she decided to shoot some tape of the shoreline while she was there. For several hours she drove around, shooting pink beaches from various angles and trying to capture the true color of the sea, which was extraordinarily turquoise in this area. She enjoyed watching the graceful white longtails, soaring skywards at the ocean's edge, and, of course, the ubiquitous and vociferous kiskadees.

Just about the time her stomach started telling her it wanted to be fed, she found a lunch wagon parked at the side of the road and enjoyed a wonderful calorie-laden hot dog with chopped onion and cheese and tomato in it.

Around three-thirty she stowed her video gear in the moped basket and returned to Lionel Entwhistle's house. Nobody answered the doorbell. No face appeared at the window. Feeling frustrated again, she walked around the side of the house and stood staring at the ocean view through some banana trees. Moving closer to study a cluster of bananas, she suddenly remembered Simon's saying he'd run into the whistler at the Botanical gardens. It was worth a try.

A short time later she entered the gardens by the west gate, parked her moped and located the garden for the blind. A sign on a stone pillar at the entrance said This is a Garden Designed for Those Not Blessed with Sight. May Those More Fortunate Use It with Respect.

Directly opposite, beyond a small pond with a statue of a little boy at its center, a portly, dignified-looking black man with tightly curled gray hair was sitting on a bench beside a pomegranate tree as though fate had left him there for her to find. He was wearing a white shirt and tan trousers. Dark glasses covered his eyes and he held a white cane between his knees. Loaded down with her video gear, Allie walked around the pond. "Mr. Entwhistle?" she said.

He had the sweetest smile.

"Could you spare me a moment?" she asked.

"I don't know your voice, young lady, but you smell very pretty. I would be happy to have you sit with me awhile. I have an appointment with my dentist soon, but in the meantime we could share the lovely odors of the rosemary and sweet marjoram and broadleaf sage."

"Thank you." She was relieved he wasn't deaf like his roommate—walking toward him, she'd had visions of herself yelling at the top of her lungs and scaring all the birds away.

"Simon Leverett and Celia Jordan told me about you," she said.

"Two of my more memorable students. Especially young Simon." He sighed gently. "Simon has a good mind. If he would just apply it properly. He was a delightful student, but some of his friends weren't so delightful, and since he graduated..." He moved his head slightly to one side. "I understand Simon works here now. He isn't with you, listening to all this, is he?"

"No. I came alone. I went to your house first."

"Ah, then this is not a casual encounter. You have business with me."

"In a way." How to begin?

He chuckled softly. "Did you meet Taylor?"

"If Taylor's your roommate, yes, I sure did."

"Taylor Rossiter. I don't suppose he was wearing his hearing aid?"

"Not noticeably."

He shook his head and chuckled again. "That stubborn old man. I do apologize. Taylor used to work as a chef at the Hamilton Princess. He's a widower like myself. He and I are a strange pair, but we have a symbiotic relationship that works well. I hear the doorbell and telephone—he sees visitors coming. He cooks—I wash dishes. Most of today, I was visiting with a sick friend in Hamilton, which Taylor could

certainly have told you. But at least he suggested you
might catch me here. He's not always so obliging."

About to tell him she'd guessed his whereabouts,
Allie decided to let Taylor have the credit. "My name
is Allison Bentley, Mr. Entwhistle," she began. "I'm
in Bermuda for two reasons."

She went on to describe Video Vacations. He was
most intrigued and drew her out skillfully, all the while
handling her camera with great interest and running
his fingers over the recorder buttons. "Isn't this a lot
of weight for one young woman to be carrying
around?" he asked.

"I'm strong," she told him. "There is lighter gear
available, but I don't want to sacrifice quality for
convenience. With the equipment I have I get broad-
cast quality pictures and sound. Anyway, I'm riding a
moped while I'm here, which is a big help—it has a
good roomy basket. When I have to walk I drape a bag
on each hip and carry the tripod. I look like a pack-
horse, my mother tells me."

He chuckled, handing the camera back to her. "You
said there were two reasons for your visit?"

"I guess you could call it a search for my roots,"
Allie began, packing the camera into its padded bag.
"Supposedly one of my ancestors came here on the
Sea Venture." She hesitated, then decided because she
liked him so much to share with him the story of her
faux pas. "When Celia first mentioned your name I
had this wild idea you and I might be related. My ma-
ternal grandmother's maiden name was Entwhistle."

"What a delightful possibility," he exclaimed. "I
should certainly welcome some relatives. I thought I

was the last of my line." He had spoken lightly, but there was pain in the quick tightening at the corners of his mouth and in the drawing together of his eyebrows.

"I'm the last of my line, also," Allie told him, touching his arm.

He smiled and patted her hand. "What made you decide we *couldn't* be related? After all, if Adam and Eve really did begin the human race then all peoples of the world belong to one giant family. A quarrelsome one, unfortunately. But, then, most families have their differences."

She felt herself grow hot. He hadn't seen her, of course. He didn't know... "Well, I'm white," she said awkwardly.

"Ah."

He stood. Had she offended him? He was smiling at her, holding out his right hand, so she didn't think she had.

"I heard a car horn, Allison," he told her as she shook hands with him. "That must be Taylor. One of his many virtues is punctuality. I believe I told you I have an appointment with my dentist." He sighed. "I would much rather sit in this lovely garden and talk to you, but my dentist is almost as crotchety as my roommate. He gets cross if I'm late and I don't want a cross dentist poking around in my new cavity." He held her hand gently between both of his. "Will you come to see me again, please?" He cocked his head to one side. "Tomorrow around 7:00 p.m.? I may not be fit for visitors this evening."

She hesitated. "I'm meeting someone tomorrow afternoon and I'm not sure how long... Perhaps I could bring him with me... Colin Endicott?"

He nodded. "He wasn't a student of mine, but we have met briefly on occasion. Bring him along, by all means. And you and I shall have a good long talk. Your search intrigues me. Who knows, we might find out we are related, after all. Family trees have many branches, Allison. And my grandfather was an American, a white American. One of his ancestors was also shipwrecked on the *Sea Venture*. A child named Alys Thornley."

Before Allie could recover enough from this bombshell to make a sound, he had walked briskly away around the pond, swinging his cane from side to side. A few stunned moments later she heard a car door slam and a car motor start up.

It was a minute or two before she could pull herself together. Bemusedly she glanced at her watch. She had nowhere else she had to be. She might as well look up Simon, as long as she was here. Perhaps he could shed some light on Mr. Entwhistle's startling statement. Though on second thought, she wasn't sure she wanted to discuss Alys Thornley with Si. Not until she knew a little more.

After distributing her gear about her person, she questioned a nearby workman, who directed her to Cacti and Succulents. She found Si sorting flowerpots in a large greenhouse that was absolutely packed with prickly-looking plants. He was being helped, or hindered, by three very young children—a girl in a white blouse and navy jumper and two boys in khaki shorts, white shirts, dark ties and navy sweaters.

"That's *Opuntia microdasys*," Si said to the little girl when she asked a plant's name.

Her huge dark eyes gazed up at him uncomprehendingly and he smiled at her with obvious affection. How different he seemed without his usual shy and diffident attitude, Allie thought. He was radiating confidence as he talked to the children. Could this be the real Simon Leverett? "You can call it bunny ears, Holly," he said to the child. "It looks like a bunny, doesn't it?"

Holly nodded shyly, pulling at one of her cornrow braids.

"What's this one?" one of the little boys asked.

Si grinned at him. "What does it look like?"

The boy hunched his shoulders under his school satchel and studied the plant in front of him. "It looks like an old man's beard."

"Exactly." Si ruffled the boy's curly hair. "That's what it's called, old man cactus—*Cephalocereus senilis*. It comes from Mexico."

"Tell us some more, Si," the other boy said.

"Don't you have homework?" Si asked.

"We did it in detention," the boy answered. "We had to stay late for being rude to the teacher. Can I take a cactus home with me?" he asked, picking up a pot that contained an aloe plant.

"That's not a cactus," Si said, then pointed above the boy's head. "What does the sign say?"

"Anyone Removing Plants Will Be Prosecuted." The boy frowned. "What does 'prosecuted' mean?"

"It means you stay in detention for a long time," Simon said gravely. "It's not much fun, believe me." Glancing up, he caught sight of Allie and gave a half wave, half salute. "Off you go," he said to the children. "You're late getting home already. Your parents will be worried. Besides, I have a visitor."

"Is she your girlfriend?" the little girl asked, looking at Allie with great interest.

"She's my girlfriend's girlfriend," Simon said solemnly, and the children walked past Allie discussing what exactly that could mean.

"Can we come back tomorrow, Si?" the little boy who'd wanted the aloe plant turned to ask.

"If you don't have detention," Si answered.

"We won't," they chorused.

"You like children, don't you?" Allie said as Simon smiled after the children.

He nodded. "I've always watched out for my brothers and sisters. They're all teenagers now. Did you see the whistler?"

"Yes." It was too hot to go into an explanation of how she'd tracked Lionel Entwhistle down, she decided. "He didn't have much time, so I'm going to see him again tomorrow evening." She hesitated. "He certainly likes you, Simon. He said you had a fine mind."

"Much good it does me," Si said gloomily. He leaned against a rack of plants, pulled a cigarette from his shirt pocket, lit it with a match and blew out a plume of smoke.

"You don't like your job?" Allie asked.

He shrugged. "It's all right. I like being outdoors and nobody's looking over my shoulder. But I'm tired of menial work. I'm not getting anywhere." He dragged deeply on the cigarette, then dropped it on the ground and stamped it out.

There was a moment's awkward silence. Allie shifted the weight of the bags on her shoulders and said, "Well, you seem to know a lot about plants." She smiled nostalgically. "My dad used to be an expert, too. He was always talking about *Hypericum* and *Prunus ilicifolia* and getting blank looks from everyone."

"I don't know anything about botany," he said flatly. "There are labels on the plants and I just happen to have a photographic memory."

"Is that all? You make it sound as if everyone had one."

He grinned. "I used to think they did. It surprised me when I found out it wasn't that common."

"I should think so." She shook her head. "You should have gone to college, Si," she added without thinking.

"With seven brothers and sisters and a father who drinks?" he said bitterly. "You think I didn't want to go?"

"You said, well, something about snobs..."

"It was the truth. Only snobs get to go to college. Poor people can't afford it. They can't afford anything. If I hadn't been born here I wouldn't be able to live here." His smile was without humor, more like a grimace. "We have a two year college here," he added, "but you have to be able to support yourself while you go. And if you want anymore education than that you have to go off island for it. You have any idea how much that costs?"

"Scholarships . . ." Allie murmured.

"Full tuition and board and lodging? Not to mention air fair?"

"There must be some way." She looked at him curiously. "What would you like to do, Si, if you could do anything you wanted? If you had lots of money?"

He shook his head and started sorting flowerpots again. "You don't want to know about that."

"Yes, I do. I'm really interested." She hesitated, then plunged on. It was her way to be straightforward, even if sometimes people didn't respond. "I'd really like to be your friend, Simon," she said. "Is that possible?"

He flashed her a startled glance and she thought he wasn't going to answer, but then he said, "Okay," and after working in silence for a few more minutes, he added, "I'd like to be another whistler."

She was puzzled at first, but light finally dawned. "You want to teach?"

"I already told you I like children," he said defensively.

"They like you, too, Si. That was obvious. Do they come here every day?"

He nodded. "Little nuisances. There were half a dozen of them earlier. You wouldn't believe how many questions they can find to ask." The fond tone in his voice belied the impatient words, and his liquid dark eyes had taken on the glow of a man with a dream. Simon Leverett was okay, Allie decided impulsively.

Given the right kind of break and a boost to his self-confidence, he'd be a good citizen, a decent, law-abiding citizen, she'd be willing to bet.

"I wish I could help," Allie said softly.

He shrugged. "My dad says you take what life hands you and that's all there is."

"You surely don't believe that."

He started to nod, then looked at her sideways and shook his head. "I don't want to."

"Maybe I could do something," Allie said as a thought occurred to her.

The diffident expression had returned to Si's dark features. She didn't want to arouse any false hopes, but she did have an idea, possibly a foolish one, but an idea nonetheless.

CHAPTER FIVE

A LARGE AND FAIRLY rowdy party of American tourists, obviously off the *Bermuda Star*, the cruise ship moored in St. George's Harbor, was just leaving the *Deliverance II* as Allie and Colin boarded her. Allie heaved a sigh of relief when she descended the steps into the small sailing ship's interior and found it empty. Though she depended on tourists to buy her videos, the noisy variety were the bane of her existence and if she wanted to use a microphone she had to wait them out before she could start taping.

The light levels between decks were low, but high enough for Allie to use her camera. She switched on the taped commentary and began recording, fascinated by the roughly hewn timbers and fittings that seemed completely authentic, as did every last coil of rope and the palm frond baskets filled with fish, shells and berries. She had to keep reminding herself this was a replica of the ship, not the ship itself.

Scattered throughout the hold were life-size models of crew and passengers—women in long period dresses, white bonnets and Quaker collars, men in doublets or jerkins and breeches tucked into hose. They all looked eerily real, as though at any moment they would move and speak.

The whole atmosphere was eery, Allie thought as she packed her camera away and folded up the tripod. Now that the rowdy tourists had departed the area there wasn't a sound to be heard, but it seemed to her that if she listened really hard she'd be able to hear the timbers creak and the waves slap against the hull. Surely the lookout above was just about to call out "Land ho!"

Listening, she could hear herself breathing and Colin, too. She stole a glance at him. He was standing a few feet away, reading a notice pinned to a bulkhead, his hands on his slim hips. An errant bar of sunlight shining through the hatch outlined his athletic body and strong features and turned his hair to gold. No shadows in his face today. He was wearing the Bermudian gentleman's business uniform, but if he were to replace his short-sleeved shirt and striped tie with a doublet and his Bermuda shorts with baggy breeches tucked into his knee socks, he might pass for one of the courageous pioneers who had sailed in the original of this vessel. She remembered how at ease he had seemed on the racing dinghy, moving around without hesitation or fear, obviously at home on the sea.

Evidently feeling her gaze on him, he turned his head and smiled at her. He had a wonderful smile, she thought. The other side of dazzling. Once again, she felt the force of his charm. There was something about this man that affected her strongly.

He had returned his attention to the sign. She wondered what he was thinking. Though he seemed friendly enough, and certainly more relaxed than she'd

seen him so far, he hadn't said much since she'd res-
cued him from Mrs. Tolliver's clutches. Did he keep
remembering, as she did, that she had cried all over
him the last time they were together? Or was he still
reeling from the softly pedaled but no less direct third
degree Mrs. Tolliver had given him?

Allie bit back a smile, remembering how uncomfortable he'd looked in Mrs. Tolliver's drawing room
when she'd gone up to meet him after changing into a
cool tan cotton dress. Ensconced in her blue wing
chair, wearing one of her usual colorful dresses, Mrs.
Tolliver had been sympathetically plying him with
questions along with his tea. Wasn't he lonely at home
with only old Macintosh to keep him company? What
had he been doing with himself? Working? *All* the
time? Tsk. Wasn't it about time he accepted invitations to parties again, especially to *her* parties.

"What parties?" Colin had queried later. Allie
hadn't heard about any parties, but she had the feeling Mrs. Tolliver would be setting one up any day
now.

Sunk into the cushiony sofa with his legs sprawled,
balancing a cup of tea and a plate of tiny cookies on
his bare knees, Colin had looked as though he were
undergoing some refined type of torture. When the
old-fashioned anniversary clock on Mrs. Tolliver's
mantel struck three, Allie had finally stood up, pulled
her sunglasses from their perch on the top of her head
and put them on. "My goodness," she'd exclaimed
breezily. "I had no idea that was the time. We're going
to be late. Come on, Colin, we have to go."

The ploy had worked and had earned her a look of undying gratitude from Colin as he struggled upward. Mrs. Tolliver hadn't seemed to mind, either. When Allie looked back from the door, the older woman was avidly staring into Colin's discarded teacup, her lips moving soundlessly. . . .

"Those bunks are awfully small," Allie said to break the silence between them.

"The average height of a man in 1610 was five feet eight inches," Colin said.

She shook her head. "It's just as well they weren't any bigger. How on earth could so many people fit themselves into this small ship?"

"Most of them didn't even have bunks—they slept on blankets or hammocks. And remember that those steps over there weren't on the original vessel. They were built on this replica for the convenience of sightseers. The original passengers had to climb down through the main hatch. They were used to hardship, of course."

"I guess." She pointed at the figure of a small girl posed beside a crate. "Look, that could be Alys—she's about the right age." She sighed. "I had hoped something about the ship would speak to me, but so far nobody's talking. I keep wondering how the survivors felt about leaving such a beautiful country."

"A lot of the passengers wanted to stay in Bermuda," Colin said. "It seemed like paradise to them. But Sir Thomas Gates, who was to be governor of Virginia, insisted they had an obligation to the Virginia Company who had outfitted the ship. They were committed to go to Jamestown, he said, so they must go."

Allie decided Alys was probably one of those who had wanted to stay in Bermuda. Who wouldn't want to stay when the alternative was to get on board a small ship like this and risk another shipwreck? Alys wasn't given any choice, of course; women and children weren't given much choice about anything in that age. How cramped Alys must have felt, and the smell must have been fierce. Fourteen days and nights to reach Jamestown. Had Alys suffered from claustrophobia? Seasickness?

"When they arrived in Jamestown," Colin went on, "they discovered that the colonists were starving. There were only sixty people left alive out of the original five hundred, 'scarce able to crawl out of their houses to greet the newcomers,' according to one account. Some had been killed by marauding Indians, some died of unexplainable diseases or the 'prevailing fever,' which was probably yellow or scarlet." He glanced at her questioningly. "Am I boring you, Allison? My wife used to tell me I was inclined to lecture people."

Mrs. Tolliver had been right, evidently. All had not been fair sailing in the "perfect" Endicott marriage. Allie tried to close her ears to the memory of the rest of Mrs. Tolliver's gossip, wishing she'd never heard it.

Colin had obviously taken his wife's criticism very much to heart. She remembered his saying, "I didn't mean to lecture," when he'd talked about Bermuda's cedar, the way he'd glanced at his wife's picture when he'd apologized for talking about the "soul" of the wood. What kind of woman made a man feel that self-conscious?

"My sin is being too nosy," she said lightly. "As you've already found out. Anyway, I'm always trying to learn about everything under the sun, so as far as I'm concerned you can lecture away." She hesitated. "I was interested in what you said about diseases. According to my family story, Alys's aunt and uncle and two little cousins died of unnamed fevers after they got to Jamestown." She frowned, trying to remember the research she'd done. "Didn't Sir George Somers go off to get supplies for the Jamestown colony?"

Colin nodded. "He returned to Bermuda on the *Patience*—the other boat the survivors had built. And died here, sadly. The *Patience* returned to England with his body."

"Nobody stayed behind in Bermuda?"

"Oh, yes. Three men stayed, waiting for an expedition to come from England."

"Three men. No ten- or eleven-year-old girl."

"I'm afraid not, Allison. Alys must have returned at a later date. In 1612 Governor Moore arrived from England with sixty colonists on the *Plough* and founded St. George's Town. Maybe Alys came back at that time." He looked at her sideways. "Governor Moore was formerly a ship's carpenter," he added. "We carpenters have a tendency to get ambitious. Actually, my own ancestor was supposedly on board the *Plough*. I can't prove it, though. We have no list of those colonists at all. According to *our* family legend, he had returned to England on the *Patience,* but came back here just as soon as he possibly could.''

"Maybe he and Alys knew each other.''

"Probably.'' He glanced at her again, smiling this time. "I wonder if Alys had brown eyes with green flecks in them.''

Their eyes met. And held. Inside herself, Allie felt that a connection had been made. She had the sudden deep certainty that this man was going to become very important to her, not just for the information he could give her, but for himself alone. Made a little uncomfortable by this unexpected confirmation of Mrs. Tolliver's prediction, she started to ask a question, hesitated, then decided that if nothing was ventured, nothing would be gained. "Did you come across any clues to Alys in your records?''

Colin looked as uneasy as he had in the face of Mrs. Tolliver's questions. "I'm afraid I haven't had a chance to—''

He broke off, sighed and said, "No, that's not true,'' then worried his hair with one hand and looked at her with a determined air. "Look, Allison, I'm not good at lying. I have a confession to make and I'm not sure you'll understand....''

Just then, another group of tourists tumbled down the steps, activated the recorded commentary and then started talking over the top of it. Colin frowned.

"Why don't we drive up to the unfinished cathedral,'' he suggested. "It's pleasant there, and we'll get the benefit of any breeze there may be.''

Allie wanted to videotape the Gothic stone ruins that stood high above the town, so she was happy to agree, but when they got there, she found she was much more interested in hearing whatever Colin had to say. She shot only a few feet of token tape before going to sit next to him on a low stone wall, hoping the moss wouldn't stain the full skirt of her dress.

The townspeople had begun building the cathedral in 1874, Colin told her. It was intended as a replacement for St. Peter's, the town's original church, but passionate arguments among the parishioners slowed and eventually stopped the work. Finally the townspeople agreed to use available funds to restore their old familiar church, instead. Although open to the skies, the incomplete structure had a majestic feeling and the cacti and palm trees that had grown where the nave was intended gave a romantic air to the place.

Colin and Allie sat in the shade of a palm tree, looking down at the town and the harbor. The breeze was warm, smelling wonderfully of flowers, the sea in the distance incredibly blue.

How odd it was, she reflected, that in life you could meet so many people who didn't make any particular impression one way or another, and then you'd meet someone who affected you emotionally right from the start. Some people believed the phenomenon was due to auras complementing each other; others, like Mrs. Tolliver, believed it was due to the meeting of souls who had known each other in previous lives. Whatever the reason, she was disturbingly aware of the strong silent man at her side.

"Do you always use a tripod?" Colin asked, gesturing at it.

"Always," she said, glad of the distraction. "Even a videographer has to breathe, and when you breathe you move. Once in a great while there's a shot I can get only with a hand-held camera. I've got very steady hands—Stable Mabel, my dad used to call me—but it's much safer to use a tripod."

He nodded vaguely, as though he hadn't really been listening. "I'm sorry, Allison," he said after another short silence. "I have to confess that I haven't even looked at my records. I know I promised you I would, but..."

Allie waited, sensing that there was more to come.

He spoke slowly, as though every word were being dragged from him. "A year ago, I locked all my research materials in the filing cabinet you saw and swore I wouldn't touch them again."

When it became obvious he wasn't going to add to that surprising statement, Allie murmured, "When your wife died."

He nodded, his mouth drooping at one corner in a wry smile. "Aida Tolliver is quite a gossip," he said after a moment's silence. "I imagine by now she has acquainted you with the details of my wife's death."

"She told me she died in an airplane crash, yes."

His gaze was fairly penetrating as he looked at her. "Did she tell you anything more?"

She was carefully casual. "Only that some friends of yours—twins?—were also on board. And somebody's nephew."

Allie wasn't sure what he was expecting her to say, but the intensity of his gaze was making her nervous.

"She said Diana was very beautiful," she added. "And that you . . . worshipped her."

"That was all?"

She equivocated. "Should there be something more?"

He hesitated. "No. Not really. There was some talk about . . . I wasn't sure."

He wasn't as naive as Mrs. Tolliver thought then. But did he know the full story? It had nothing to do with her, she told herself firmly.

"The point is," Colin continued painfully, "I now find it almost impossible to go through my research material. Just opening the filing cabinet is difficult enough, as you probably saw for yourself. I know it's ridiculous to give in to such a foolish aversion, but all the same I can't bring myself to go back to work on my book. To be honest, I don't even like talking about it."

Her first reaction was one of frustration. How was she to track Alys down if he couldn't even bring himself to open his filing cabinet for her? Almost immediately she castigated herself for her selfishness. She would just have to find another way. No, that wasn't good, either. Colin needed to face his problem and deal with it. He *should* finish his history book, and if she was very careful in her approach, maybe her search for Alys Thornley could be the catalyst that would make him go back to work on it. She suddenly remembered his comment about women wanting to interfere, but decided to ignore the memory.

The tall trees that had grown up through the stone ruins swayed in the breeze, casting shadows over his face so that she couldn't read his expression. His jaw looked strong and stern. But she had a vivid awareness of his pain.

"When I was a little girl," she began, "I went through a period of being afraid of the dark. To cover up, I used to call out to my mother, asking her if *she* was afraid." She laughed softly. "I was completely convinced there were monsters in my clothes closet. My dad made me take everything out of the closet and inspect it, then put it back. It was always a good idea to bring things out into the daylight, she said."

He didn't look at her, but he covered her hand with his for a moment. "You're a very caring person, aren't you, Allison?"

"I suppose I am." She hesitated. "It's not always a good way to be. People tend to think you're interfering."

He laughed. "Touché." He turned toward her. "I'm almost afraid to look at you," he said. "You have the most amazing eyes. They absolutely radiate sympathy, compassion. Every time I look at you I'm tempted to tell you every problem I've had in my entire life, beginning with nursery school."

"I guess we may be here awhile then," Allie answered with a light laugh to disarm his intensity.

"I'm very strongly attracted to you, Allison," he said after gazing at her in silence for a while.

Her heart jumped. "I thought *I* was outspoken," she said, with what sounded to her ears like a very false laugh.

"I'm not sure what to do about it," he went on. "I've avoided personal contact with people for so long, I'm not sure I can overcome the mental barriers I've set up."

"I'm not sure anyone has asked you to overcome your mental barriers," she said hotly, furious at his assumption that he was the only one with a decision to make.

"And of course I don't even *know* how you feel about me," he continued apologetically, taking all the wind out of her brave sails. "For all I know you hate the sight of me. After the way I behaved when we first met I shouldn't blame you."

She met his gaze straight on, her heart pumping strongly now. "Let's just say I'm not exactly unaware of you," she said, equivocating because she really wasn't sure she wanted anything to happen between them. "I've got to tell you, though, I was dumped by someone a few months back and I'm not yet ready to risk that again. Dumping hurts."

He nodded vaguely, looking as though he knew nothing at all about dumping. The poor betrayed man. He needed someone to love him, there was no doubt about that, and she was certainly attracted to him. Her breathing was becoming erratic just thinking about the possibility of something sexual happening between them.

But if they did start something, then what? She was only in Bermuda for a short time. What if it turned out that they liked each other a lot? And then she had to leave. What would that do to him? And to her? She had never been one to give her love lightly, anyway. She had to know a man through and through before...

As she had known Curtis? Who had let her down so very badly?

"We don't have to decide anything now," he said, and she realized her confusion must have shown clearly on her face. "We could just start off as friends, couldn't we?"

She felt relieved and disappointed all at the same time. "Friends," she agreed.

He looked at her curiously. "Is that what you were crying about?" he asked. "The dumping, as you called it?"

She shook her head. "No, that was something else." She raised her eyebrows. "Aren't you avoiding the issue we started out with here?"

"Absolutely," he admitted, then sighed. "The trouble is, Allison, I'm not sure I'm ready to meet my monsters face to face."

"Try it," Allie advised. "It's the only way, believe me."

He took her hand again and held on to it this time. Once more, she was amazed at how much feeling could come through a hand. It was almost as though she could feel the blood pulsing in his fingers. Pulse points touching? she wondered. Or something a lot more emotional?

After a moment, he spoke quietly, almost as if he were speaking to himself. "I had neglected her, you see. Diana. We worked on the house together and everything was . . . wonderful, she loved the house so, but then after we finished, she didn't seem to know what to do with herself. She was very gregarious. She liked people, parties. Not that I disliked either, but I was always so busy. And then I got involved in writing the history. It was something I'd always wanted to do, and working on the house, researching that whole period, made me more eager than ever. So on top of all my other duties, I spent two or three hours every evening in my study, researching, collating, writing. For a whole year.''

He paused, turning away from the view to look up at the hollow remnants of the tower from which no bell had ever rung. "I was, of course, far too busy to take trips with my wife, apart from our annual pilgrimage to England. She was very homesick. She grew to hate the islands. They made her feel claustrophobic. 'Rock fever,' she called it. 'Stop the world,' she'd say. 'I want to get off.' She wanted to go home more and more often, and I kept refusing. When she went to England that last time...'' He stopped speaking, and Allie saw from his face that he didn't really want to say any more.

She wished she didn't know the rest of the story. She wished she knew for sure whether he knew it. Damn Mrs. Tolliver, anyway. Why on earth had she saddled Allie with the truth?

She saw that Colin was waiting for a comment and decided that just in case he didn't know about the Perry twins, it would be best to hazard a guess at what his interpretation of the facts might be—a busy husband, a restless wife.... "You felt guilty because you weren't with your wife when she died?''

He nodded without looking at her.

"So you put away your history book as some kind of expiation—to make amends for your wrongdoing.''

"Something like that, yes. It sounds pretty stupid when you put it like that, doesn't it?"

"Everyone has his own way of handling grief," she said gently.

He looked at her gratefully. "You do understand."

Damn Mrs. Tolliver. She had no right...somebody should have told him.

"As you said yourself," she continued carefully, "once you've experienced sadness you recognize it in others."

"You've lost someone?"

"My father. Several years ago. And my mother..."

He looked at her uncertainly. "Your mother? But I thought you said..."

"My mother is dying."

It took a moment for him to register what she'd said, then he frowned. "How long have you known that?"

"About nine months now."

"You mean that when your mother wrote me..."

"She knew. Yes. That's why she wanted to find out about Alys. She'd always wondered."

He abruptly got to his feet, walked away from her and stood gazing down at the view, obviously in the grip of some strong emotion. The sun lit his hair, turning it to burnished gold again. Allie waited.

After a minute or two, he came back, sat down on the wall and took both of her hands in his, looking down at them, rubbing the backs of them gently with his thumbs. "Your mother knew she was dying and I wrote her the way I did, as if I couldn't care less about her request."

He was obviously a man who was ever ready to take the blame for the results of his own actions. Which was okay to a point, but not if carried to excess. He must have suffered a lot in his lifetime with an attitude like his. "You didn't know she was dying, Colin," she pointed out.

"Of course I didn't, but that's no excuse. I was wallowing in my own selfish guilt, blocking out other people, other people's problems. I'm sorry, Allison. I'm truly, truly sorry."

Very gently he lifted her hands and kissed them, then looked at her searchingly. "What happened to Stable Mabel?" he asked, and she knew he was referring to the fact that her fingers were trembling.

Before she could think of anything to say, he cupped her face between his hands and touched his lips to hers, kissing her delicately. His mouth seemed to fit against hers perfectly. There was no awkward fumbling, no bumping of noses or tilting of heads, just a coming together that felt wonderfully right. Her heart danced against her ribs and she could feel her blood racing through her veins and arteries as a wonderful sweetness filled her. But then he removed his mouth from hers, put his arm around her shoulder and held her close to his side. "Tell me about your mother," he said.

He was very quiet while she talked. He didn't interrupt at all until she told how strongly Patricia had identified with Alys, how she'd felt her heritage had been taken away from her. "I'm so sorry, Allison," he murmured.

She shook her head and went on with her story, telling him she'd talked to Patricia only the previous day and she had sounded strong and happy. "She's a very brave lady," she concluded. "She's determined to fight this thing as long as she can. I've promised to be strong, too. But sometimes, like the other day in your garden..."

"We'll find Alys for her," Colin said firmly. He stood up and extended a hand down to her. "Let's go to my house now and you can start looking. I'll turn over my records to you. Just because I have this foolish aversion doesn't mean someone else can't work out the puzzle. I'll simply give you the keys and—"

"Oh, dear," Allie said as she got to her feet, brushing off the skirt of her dress. "I forgot to tell you. I'm going to visit Lionel Entwhistle tonight." Swiftly, as they gathered up the video gear, she explained how Lionel had come into her life and the amazing bombshell he had left her with the previous day. "Do you suppose he really could be related?" she asked.

"Anything's possible in Bermuda," he said. "I'm actually related to Aida Tolliver through some second cousin or other." He grinned unexpectedly, looking so boyish and carefree that she wished she could somehow make it possible for him to look like that all the time. "Don't let it get around," he cautioned. "I don't think Aida knows."

They began walking down to Colin's car, a neat little dark-blue Renault. "From what Lionel said, we do at least have confirmation that there really was an Alys Thornley and she did come to Bermuda," Colin said.

"It's certainly worth following up. Would you mind if I were to come with you?"

Evidently he was becoming enthusiastic about helping with her project, even if he was still determined not to dig into his own research materials. Who knows, Allie thought, one enthusiasm might lead to another. "I'd like that," she said as they stowed her gear in the car's trunk. "I was going to suggest . . ."

"I remember Lionel," he said thoughtfully. "We were on a couple of environmental protection committees together. He's a wonderful old man. I'd enjoy getting to know him better."

His hand was under her elbow now and he reached past her to open the car door, then paused. "Would you like to have dinner at the White Horse Tavern before we go to Lionel's house? It will be cool on the waterfront and we can sit and watch the activity in the harbor while we eat. They have what they call a Tavern Burger that you might like."

"Fruit salad," Allie said firmly, and he nodded and smiled vaguely as he walked around the car to the driver's side.

He was acting as though the kiss hadn't happened. Did he regret it, or had he simply forgotten it? It had affected her more than any kiss she'd ever experienced in her entire life. She had enjoyed Curtis Yost's kisses, but Curtis hadn't ever understood that the way to a woman's heart was paved with tenderness. More forceful behavior had its place, especially when it was playful, but not until later, when senses were aroused.

In the beginning, for the first touch, gentleness was everything. Colin's gentle kiss had filled her with a yearning, a yearning for something she had so far missed in life.

CHAPTER SIX

IT WAS LIKE a reprise of her previous visit. First Taylor's ancient face and wild hair appeared at the window and he studied both of them thoroughly through the branches of the poinciana tree. He took his time, as though to be sure he'd recognize them in a police line up, then finally ambled to the door. He looked at them questioningly. Didn't he know they were expected?

"We've come to see Mr. Entwhistle," Allie yelled at the top of her voice, making Colin jump.

Taylor assumed a pained expression. "No need to shout," he chided, and Allie belatedly saw he was wearing a hearing aid in each ear.

Lionel greeted them in a large, beautifully furnished but terribly cluttered Victorian living room with a breathtaking view of the ocean. His face wreathed in smiles, he rose from a huge reclining chair to shake hands with Colin and Allie. "Bring in the dessert and coffee, will you, please?" he asked Taylor.

"We just had dinner," Allie protested.

"There's always room for dessert," Lionel said comfortably as he seated himself. "You haven't truly lived until you taste Taylor's chocolate mousse."

Chocolate mousse! Allie groaned inwardly. She was going to go home with a bulge on each hip.

They indulged in small talk while they ate the sinfully delicious mousse. Allie told about her visit to the Crystal Caves a couple of days earlier and Colin tried to remember which were stalactites, which stalagmites.

"That's easy," Allie explained. "Stalactites grow from the ceiling, stalagmites from the ground. Just think of the 'c' and the 'g' and you've got it."

By the time they had finished their coffee, they were on first-name basis all around. Even Taylor had unbent enough to rearrange his craggy features in a frown that might have been a smile when Allie complimented him on the mousse.

After Allie and Colin carried out the dishes, including a few that had been left over from a previous meal, Taylor wandered out into the gardens muttering something about not being needed. Lionel turned his head toward Allie in an expectant way. "You wanted to ask me about the *Sea Venture*, I believe. Though why you think I can be helpful when you have access to Colin Endicott, I don't know."

He inclined his head toward Colin. "Taylor has read me some of your articles in *The Bermudian*. I thought them excellent. I'm eagerly awaiting publication of your book."

He smiled at Allie as Colin evidently searched for a comment. "Thank you for bringing Colin with you. I've wanted to know him better." His smile gentled at the corners of his mouth and became mischievous. "There is a good feeling between you two," he announced. "I always know when people are emotionally compatible. You'd be amazed at how jangly the atmosphere can get when the feelings between people are bad. You two now, you have a strong mix of pleasure and excitement and affection between you." His smile widened. "With perhaps a little fear mixed in to give it spice."

"You like dropping bombshells, don't you?" Allie said awkwardly on the heels of this unexpected remark. She didn't dare look at Colin to see how he had taken it. "You dropped one on me yesterday, you know."

Lionel smiled his sweet smile, obviously aware that he had embarrassed her, but not about to apologize for it. "I wasn't aware of any bombshell yesterday, my dear. I trust it wasn't too unpleasant."

"Not at all, only amazing. The ancestor of mine I told you about, you remember, the one I'm trying to trace? Her name was Alys Thornley."

"That is amazing." He chuckled delightedly. "How terribly dramatic of me to leave you with that. What wonderful timing. You must have been furious."

Allie laughed. "Frustrated, I must admit."

"Well, now, let me think. What do I know about Alys? That she was ten years old. That she was an orphan traveling with an aunt and uncle and two cousins—little boys she was taking care of." He pinched the end of his broad nose as if to jog his memory.

"Did she leave on the *Deliverance*?" Colin asked.

"Indeed, she did. But she came back—that was the surprising thing. According to my grandfather, who told me all about her, she came back when she was seventeen."

Colin nodded. "So that would be around 1616, a few years after Governor Moore brought colonists in."

Allie was scribbling like mad in the notebook she'd brought along. "I haven't been able to find any record of her," she told Lionel.

He rubbed his close-cropped gray curls, his wide and dignified brow furrowing. "There was a reason for that. Which escapes me, I'm afraid. Something to do with the man she married." He shook his head. "I haven't thought about Alys for years. When I was a boy the story fascinated me, but one gets busy, one forgets. My father and I did find her tombstone, I remember."

Allie could hardly contain her excitement. "Where?"

"St. Peter's churchyard, in St. George. To the west, I believe, near the slaves' burial ground. Let me think now. I remember tracing her name with my finger, but it was very faint, almost worn away... An *A* and an *L*, perhaps an *S*, then some of her last name. What was her married name?"

"We don't know," Colin said, leaning forward. "If we had that information we'd be much more likely to..."

"I can't quite remember... perhaps I'll think of it later if I don't try too hard."

"Your grandfather was an American, you said," Allie interjected.

"Joseph Entwhistle. Yes. He was a white American. Very wealthy. An investor who knew what he was about. He built this house in 1877 when he came to Bermuda."

"Where did he come from, do you know?"

He frowned. "I've an idea it was the Midwest somewhere. He didn't talk much about his past, my grandfather. He said he was a Bermudian now and one must live for the future. I remember thinking that was amusing, as he was around eighty when he said that, but he lived until ninety. I was twenty years old when he died."

"My mother's family came from Illinois," Allie told him. "Great-grandfather Entwhistle had a farm near Peoria. Thomas Entwhistle. Did your grandfather talk about his family at all?"

"He didn't have any family."

"Not at all?"

"Not according to him."

"But there must be some connection between us if Joseph Entwhistle's ancestor was Alys and Thomas Entwhistle's ancestor was Alys." Allie was puzzled.

Lionel nodded thoughtfully. "There was a family tree..." He turned his head toward the open window behind him. "Taylor," he called.

Taylor's head popped up so promptly that Allie was pretty sure he had been eavesdropping right outside. Judging by the fact that Lionel had known to call through the window, Lionel must have heard him out there. He might have been weeding, she thought more charitably.

Taylor looked as bad-tempered as ever. "What is it now?" he asked, as though Lionel had been nagging him all evening.

"Whatever happened to my family tree?" Lionel inquired.

"You expect me to remember everything?"

Lionel smiled. "Of course I don't *expect* you to. But you usually do."

Looking somewhat mollified, Taylor frowned in thought, then said, "I don't remember," and disappeared again.

Colin sent Allie a sympathetic glance and took hold of her hand, evidently realizing she was beginning to feel frustrated once more. They were sitting at a right angle to Lionel's recliner—side by side on a rather hard sofa with a medallioned back, Colin in his Bermuda shorts and shirt and tie, looking formal but relaxed. And very attractive. Whoever declared that Bermuda shorts and knee socks were de rigueur for the Bermudian male deserved Hall of Fame inclusion, Allie decided. She also loved the feel of Colin's hand holding hers. She felt protected, cared for, cherished. She also felt a lot of other more complicated sensations, but she was trying not to dwell on them right now.

Lionel sighed. "You've probably noticed this house isn't as tidy as it might be, Allison. It's not easy for two old men, who also happen to be pack rats, to keep track of things. We've had household help from time to time, but nobody stays long. It takes a special kind of person to deal with our particular set of problems."

His wide brow furrowed deeply above his dark glasses. "Let us examine this from the beginning again," he suggested. "Alys came back to Bermuda, married someone whose name I'm going to remember, and gave birth to a daughter."

"Penelope," Allie supplied, getting excited again.

"Penelope, indeed," Lionel agreed. "Now—as I recall the story—Penelope quarreled with her father, whose name we don't know, and *she* went to Jamestown. She was twenty-three when she emigrated to America and she married someone and raised a family... two children, I believe, a boy and a girl."

Allie was busily scribbling again. "I hadn't heard about the quarrel with her father," she said.

Lionel nodded solemnly, was silent for a minute or two, then said, "My grandfather, Joseph Entwhistle, was directly descended from Penelope."

"So was my great-grandfather Thomas," Allie said.

"All right then, let us think about dates. My Entwhistle, Joseph, was born in 1847."

Allie did some rapid calculations on her notepad. "Thomas came along in 1856. I remember Mom saying her grandmother was twenty years younger than her husband and I also remember that she was born in 1876, when the United States had its first centennial."

"Joseph and Thomas were contemporaries then," Colin put in. "Cousins, perhaps?"

"Or brothers," Allie suggested.

Colin nodded. "Nine years apart. Joseph must have come to Bermuda when he was thirty."

"He was thirty-one when he married," Lionel said.

"Thomas would be twenty-one when Joseph left then. Old enough to come with him if he'd wanted to." Colin looked at Allie. "Do you know anything more about Thomas, apart from the farm?"

She shook her head, then immediately remembered something. "He and my great-grandmother were very religious. Strict. So was my grandmother, and my great-aunt Jenny. I only vaguely remember Aunt Jenny. She died when I was a little girl."

"What we have to do is fill in the gap between Penelope going to America and Joseph leaving America to come here," Lionel concluded.

"A two-hundred-year gap," Allie said with a sigh.

Colin squeezed her hand lightly. "You're closer than you were before...you were trying to fill in three hundred eighty years."

She smiled at him gratefully. "That's true. Thanks for reminding me."

He smiled back and once again she felt some interesting sensations along her spine and in other more personal areas. His blue eyes were calm and clear this evening, not in any way as stormy as she had seen them on previous occasions, but there was something glinting there as he looked at her, his face stilled as though he were holding his breath. "Allison," he murmured, tightening his grip on her hand.

"Taylor," Lionel yelled abruptly, and they both sprang apart like guilty children, then looked at each other and laughed silently. Of course Lionel hadn't been watching them—he couldn't see them. Which didn't mean he had no idea of what was going on between them.

Taylor appeared in the doorway, carrying a huge book. "What now?" he demanded.

"Have you thought any about that family tree?"

"Hold your trousers on. I have it right here." He placed the book on Lionel's lap, shook his head and stomped noisily out of the room again.

"The family Bible, of course," Lionel breathed, his fingers tracing curlicues on the ornate cover. He raised his head toward Allie and Colin. "This Bible belonged to my grandfather Joseph. The family tree is in the beginning. If you'd care to look."

Colin jumped up and brought the huge book over to the sofa, setting it gently across Allie's knees. With fingers that showed a distressing tendency to tremble, she opened it. She was so anxious the writing seemed to jump around so that she couldn't make it out.

"Alys Thornley married William Pruitt," Colin said beside her, and her heart jumped.

"Pruitt. That's the name," Lionel confirmed.

"There's a memorial plaque to a Pruitt inside St. Peter's," Colin commented.

For what seemed like a long time, Allie couldn't take her eyes off the family tree. Her family tree. It had to be—the name Alys Thornley was written in a neat, forward sloping script at the top of the chart. Excitedly Allie scanned the whole tree, smiling over biblical names like Tirzah and Ezekiel, running quickly through simpler names—John, Walter, Eliza, Mary, Joseph.

"No Thomas Entwhistle," she said, feeling terribly let down.

"I didn't remember a Thomas," Lionel said. "My father used to read the names to me, like the begats in the Bible. I don't think he ever mentioned a Thomas."

Allie sighed, then looked back at the family tree again. "The tree shows a gap between Joseph's grandparents and Joseph," she said. "Yet he must have had parents."

"If he left out his parents, he could as easily leave out a brother," Colin said.

"A family quarrel?" Allie suggested. She was quivering with excitement again, Colin saw. Her lovely eyes were more green than brown when she was moved or excited. They were shining like polished jade now. "There's one way to find out," she said. "What's the time in Seattle now? Four-thirty, five o'clock? May I use your telephone?" she asked Lionel. "I have my charge card with me. I want to call my mother."

Esther Denham, Patricia's nurse companion, answered the telephone. Patricia was resting, she said. Should she disturb her?

"No, don't do that," Allie said, feeling very disappointed. "How is she?"

The nurse hesitated, which made Allie's heart race. Immediately she forgot her excitement over discovering Alys, her curiosity about Joseph Entwhistle's denial of his immediate family. "Is anything wrong?" she asked, her voice suddenly sharp.

"She's doing fine," Esther said soothingly. "She had a little nausea yesterday, nothing too bad. She's fine really."

"You'd tell me if she wasn't, wouldn't you?"

"Of course. Do you want her to call you when she wakes up?"

Allie thought for a moment. "No. I'm not sure when I'll get back to the guest house. Just tell her I called to see how she was doing. I'll call again later."

"Everything all right?" Colin asked, standing up when she came back into Lionel's living room. "I heard you exclaim..."

Allie had gone into the kitchen to use the phone. "Nothing to worry about," she said as she sat down.

"Are you sure?" he asked, obviously concerned.

She frowned. "I don't know. There was something in the nurse's voice. I had an uneasy feeling." She shook her head. "I'm sure she would have told me if anything was really wrong. Unfortunately Mom was sleeping, so I couldn't ask about Joseph."

Trying to suppress her uneasiness, she wrestled the heavy Bible back into her lap and studied the family tree again. "Your grandmother was named Tallah?" she asked Lionel.

He nodded. "You know the population history of Bermuda?"

She shook her head. "Not completely."

"Bermudians are mainly of African or British or Portugese descent," he explained. "The original Bermudians were English, like Alys. Intertribal wars in Africa led to various chieftains selling their prisoners to the Spaniards and Portuguese. A lot of them were taken to the West Indies to work the plantations. Many were also brought here to work in agriculture, but there were no huge plantations like there were in America. In many cases a reciprocal loyalty developed between the slaves and the families who owned them. American Indians and Irish people were sent here as slaves, also, and slaves were imported from Scotland—prisoners who had fought against Cromwell. Later the Portuguese came, farmers mainly, from the Azores, to help with agriculture. So we have a surprisingly rich ethnic mixture. Grandmother Tallah was born free—emancipation came here twenty-three years before her birth—but her ancestors were African slaves. I was told she was remarkably beautiful.''

''And she married Joseph Entwhistle,'' Allie said.

''When she was twenty-one.''

Allie frowned. ''If Joseph was related to my great-grandfather Thomas, I can't understand why my great-aunt Jenny never told my mother or me about him, or about Tallah. Jenny had a terrific interest in family history.''

There was a wry expression on Lionel's dignified face. ''How did your Aunt Jenny feel about black people, Allison?'' he asked gently.

When Allie hesitated, searching for a diplomatic reply, he said, ''There's your answer.''

''Taylor,'' he suddenly yelled again, causing Allie and Colin to jump.

Taylor appeared in the doorway once more, his grizzled eyebrows drawn tightly together, making him looking fierce. ''What the hell is it now?'' he asked.

Lionel ignored his roommate's impatience. They might be an odd couple, Allie thought, but they evidently accepted each other's flaws without wasting time in recriminations. ''Could you please bring me Tallah's jewelry,'' Lionel requested.

''It's upstairs,'' Taylor said.

"Hell and damnation, Taylor, I know that," Lionel said evenly.

Taylor glowered at him, but of course Lionel couldn't know that, so he just smiled his sweet smile and waited. After a moment Taylor turned on his heel and went out. Within a few minutes he returned carrying a velvet-covered box, which Lionel opened to reveal a gorgeous emerald-and-gold necklace. "This was Joseph's engagement present to Tallah," he told Allie, running his fingers over the stones. "There was a ring that matched, but it was buried with her."

With infinite care, Allie took the necklace from him, awed by the fact that it was over a hundred years old. Green light flashed from the emeralds as she spread the intricately set piece across the lap of her tan dress. "Put it on," Lionel urged.

The stones felt cold against her throat. Colin helped her fasten the clasp, then leaned back to look at her. "The emeralds make your eyes look really green," he said softly.

"She's big enough to wear them," Taylor told Lionel with one of his ferocious grizzled-eyebrow frowns that Allie thought might be meant as a smile. "She does them justice. She's a pretty girl. Dark haired. Striking."

"I could tell she was pretty," Lionel said. He smiled at Allie. "The necklace should be yours," he added in a casual voice. "Why don't you take it with you?"

Stunned, Allie protested at once. "I couldn't possibly do that." Hastily she started undoing the necklace clasp. "We don't even know yet if Joseph and

Thomas were related. Besides, it must be worth a fortune."

"It serves no purpose in my bedroom," Lionel pointed out, then tilted his head as though listening and nodded. "You truly are reluctant, I can tell. Perhaps you would feel better if we wait until the relationship is proven. Then you can take the necklace with you."

Allie carefully arranged the necklace in its satin-lined box. "You know nothing about me," she chided Lionel. "You can't go giving a small fortune in jewelry to people you don't know."

"Why not?" he asked with a laugh. "It's fun and I can afford it. Grandfather's investments are still good. He was a shrewd man. Besides, I pride myself on being able to sense honesty. And you radiate it, my dear, along with compassion and sensitivity."

Moved, Allie went over to his chair and kissed him on the cheek. "Thank you," she said simply.

"Thank *you*," Lionel replied with a wide and very white smile. "I don't receive many kisses these days."

"Don't deserve them," Taylor told him gruffly, looking moved himself.

"It's a shame those emeralds can't speak," Colin said, breaking in tactfully. "Perhaps they could tell us about Joseph's family."

Lionel frowned. "There was a box of papers. I can't think what ever happened to..." Still frowning, he handed the jewelry box to Taylor.

"I suppose you expect me to put this away again," Taylor complained.

"If you would be so kind," Lionel said.

There was another deep sigh from Taylor as he left the room.

Allie went back to her seat, hoping the emeralds were on their way to a safe of some kind. She wouldn't be at all surprised if the necklace was kept in a dresser drawer. But she could hardly ask without appearing to have some self-interest at heart. Of all things, to offer her the necklace as a gift—a family heirloom like that.

"Taylor," Lionel yelled again, and again Colin and Allie jumped. They exchanged amused glances as Taylor's footsteps on the staircase ceased abruptly.

There was a full minute's silence, then footsteps again, coming down. "You trying to wear me to a frazzle?" Taylor asked when he came back into the room.

"Of course not," Lionel said with an apologetic smile. "I just remembered we were going to go through the attic someday to sort things out. Did we ever do that?"

"What's this 'we' stuff," Taylor demanded. "Who's the workhorse around here?"

"I apologize," Lionel said. "I was trying to be tactful. Did *you* ever sort through the attic?"

"When would I have time to do that? It's all I can do to keep things tidy down here."

Allie and Colin exchanged a grin. Judging by the turmoil in this room—the piles of books and magazines and tape cassettes, the stack of mail on the open desk, paper wrappings left over from some earlier snacks—neither man had much idea of tidiness.

Lionel didn't answer, but continued to smile.

"No, I didn't clear out the attic," Taylor said at last. "I don't know what's valuable, what isn't. It's mostly your stuff."

"*Your* newspapers," Lionel said.

"Just a few."

Lionel sighed. "Would the box be up there?" he asked.

"What box is that?"

"The box with Grandfather Entwhistle's journal in it."

"Joseph kept a journal?" Allie asked excitedly.

Lionel nodded. "So I was told. My father would read me bits from it when I was a child. It was about the past, some of it about Alys. Grandfather wanted to write the whole family history. I don't know how far he got. And I've forgotten most of what I heard. I couldn't read it myself, of course. And I've no idea what it looks like. But I seem to remember it was put away in a box in the attic with other family memorabilia when my father died." He inclined his head toward Taylor, who was standing glowering in the doorway, still holding the jewelry box. "Could you take a look, do you suppose?"

"Are you mad?" Taylor asked.

"It's for Allison," Lionel said placatingly.

"I don't care if it's for the queen of England. There are limits, you know."

With that he stalked off, and a moment later they heard his footsteps on the stairs again.

Lionel sighed. "I'm sorry, Allison," he began, but Allie interrupted him.

"Could I look for the box?" she begged.

Lionel looked doubtful. "I think the attic is rather messy."

"I don't mind," she said eagerly. "It would be so wonderful if I could come across something, anything..."

"I'll help," Colin said, getting up. Allie flashed him a grateful glance.

A minute later they were standing at the entrance to a cavernous attic that seemed to stretch forever. It reminded Allie of the Crystal Caves, which she had explored a couple of days earlier, except that there was no tidal pool in sight. The floor was probably wood like the rest of the house, Allie thought despairingly, but it was impossible to tell. As far as she could see, boxes and stacks of paper and lamps and paintings and sculptures were piled higgledy-piggledy against and on top of each other. Long racks held clothing from various eras. The room looked as though some giant tidal wave had plucked the contents from three or four oceanside homes and dumped them all on shore. There was even a disused toilet sitting on top of a suitcase that had seen better days.

"Good Lord," Colin breathed.

Allie felt like crying. "I have less than three weeks left in Bermuda," she wailed.

Colin put an arm around her shoulders. "I don't think it's even worth starting to look today. It's already nine-thirty."

Allie crouched to look at the date on a yellowed newspaper. According to the large headlines, France and the United Kingdom had declared war on Germany. The date was September 3, 1939. She opened a nearby box labeled Christmas Ornaments. Inside were tinsel and glass balls and strings of old-fashioned lights. "Well, at least the label's correct," she said, feeling hopeful again.

"These over here aren't labeled," Colin said. He tilted a box toward her. Baby clothes, apparently. "Perhaps we could come back tomorrow evening," he suggested.

Allie nodded and stood. "We'll never get through all of this in time, Colin," she said, looking around. "I do still have to make a movie. I can only spare evenings."

They said their goodbyes to Lionel, Allie managing not to let her disappointment show. He assured her she was welcome to go through the attic at any time, as often as she liked.

"I figure it would take about six months," Allie said as Colin parked outside the guest house in St. George. Neither of them had said much during the drive. Colin must have been as overwhelmed as she by the sight of such chaos, Allie thought.

He smiled ruefully and worried his hair with one hand in his characteristic way. "I'm sorry, Allison," he said. "I don't know what to suggest. We might hire someone, but that would be even more of an intrusion on Lionel's and Taylor's privacy."

Allie nodded vaguely, not really listening, still seeing that overflowing attic in her mind's eye. They didn't even know for sure that Joseph Entwhistle's journal was in there. She sighed.

"At least we know Alys's married name now," Colin pointed out. "There may be some mention of

Pruitt in my research materials. If you'd like to look through tomorrow while I'm at work, you're certainly welcome."

Hope rekindled inside Allie. "I'd almost forgotten about Mr. Pruitt," she exclaimed. "Maybe I can track him down without worrying about Lionel's attic. And I can call my mother tomorrow and see if she's ever heard of Joseph."

She was looking happy again, Colin was pleased to see. What a wonderfully open face she had. It showed everything she was thinking. He felt a rush of warmth toward this vital, attractive young woman. More than warmth. Heat.

"You could come back with me tonight," he suggested abruptly.

She looked at him warily. "I don't think that's too good an idea," she said.

"Why not? I thought you liked me. I thought we had decided to be friends."

"I do like you. I like you a lot, Colin. That's the problem."

He looked at her directly for a long moment, then nodded gravely. "There's something very strong happening between us, isn't there? Are you afraid I'll try to seduce you?"

She met his gaze just as directly. "I'm afraid I'll want to be seduced."

He caught his breath. There was no guile in this woman. She came out with whatever she thought. "Then as long as it's mutual," he murmured.

She shook her head. "I've just recently recovered from a great disappointment over a man, Colin. I told you I'd been dumped, remember? Curtis let me down badly when my mother became ill. I loved him and lost him. I don't want to go through that again. Nor do I want to put you through it." She looked at him sadly. "Our timing is off, Colin. You're still tied to your past and I'm in single-minded pursuit of Alys Thornley. Once I've found out all I can about her I have to leave Bermuda and give everything I've got to caring for my mother. I can't handle anything else right now."

"Not even pleasure?"

"Not even that."

He sighed, then looked at her questioningly, teasingly. "Don't you ever let yourself get carried away with passion, Allison?"

She couldn't help laughing, but her answer was firm. "Never."

Her very insistence was a challenge. Rising to it, he leaned toward her, put his arm around her, pulled her close and brushed her lips with his. He had intended kissing her lightly, briefly, just to let her know she shouldn't make such challenging remarks, but at the first petal-soft touch of her lips desire coursed through him and he tightened his hold and deepened the kiss. She didn't struggle, but neither did she respond, at least not at first. There was a long moment when her lips remained immobile and her whole body stilled as though in surprise, then he felt a sigh go through her as her body relaxed. Her lips parted and he felt her breath against his mouth, warm and sweet as a baby's. Tenderness flooded him and he held back on the urgency that was pushing him to hold her more tightly, kiss her more roughly. "Sweet Allison," he murmured against her lips.

Her mouth was pliant now against his own, her body curved into his. She was responding to his kiss, moving her mouth against his, opening it to tentatively touch his lips with her tongue. His own restraint was driving him mad. It had been so long, so very long. Without conscious thought, he moved his hand across her back, feeling the smooth cotton of her dress with his fingertips, the warm firm flesh underneath, easing her closer, closer, until they were pressed tightly together. And for a moment, as he kissed her, just one short moment, the power of his passion erupted in a kind of wild elation over the fact that it had found a matching power. For the space of perhaps ten seconds, they were totally, breathlessly, completely in tune and nothing could have stopped them from continuing until they had consummated their love.

And then a car horn sounded somewhere nearby and he felt her stiffen again. Easing his mouth from hers, he gazed down at her face and took in a deep breath. By the lamplight outside the guest house gate, he could see that she was adorably flushed, her lips swollen from his kiss, her eyes dark and velvet deep as the night sky. Her dark hair tumbled to her shoulders, clinging to his hand. He didn't even remember tangling his fingers in the curling mass. He remembered how she'd looked wearing Lionel's emeralds. Like a queen, regal and gloriously self-confident. At the moment she didn't look confident of anything. She looked dazed. "That wasn't fair," she said softly.

He nodded. "I know."

"I have to go in, Colin," she murmured. "I just can't handle this. I really can't. It mustn't happen again."

"All right." He released her at once. Tomorrow was another day, he thought. Let her go now so she'd know she could trust him always to let go.

"You will come over and do some research tomorrow?" he asked as he opened the door on her side of the car and helped her out. "I'll be at work, so you won't have to worry that I'll attack you. Mac will be there. He can show you where everything is. Shall I tell him to expect you?"

She nodded shyly. "I appreciate..." Her voice trailed away.

He opened the Renault's trunk and helped her drape herself with her equipment, then held out his hand. She put hers into it without hesitation. "Good night, Colin," she said. "Thank you for all your help."

In the lamplight her hair shone like the purest silk. He felt a response to her that was almost painful, yet full of pleasure at the same time. "I enjoyed this evening very much," he said. "Lionel and Taylor are quite a comedy team."

Allie laughed softly. "What my father would have called a pair to draw to," she agreed. She took a deep breath. "Good night, Colin," she repeated, and he realized he was still holding her hand. Reluctantly he let it go.

"Perhaps we could go to the churchyard tomorrow evening," he suggested. "To look for Pruitt. If you'd care to wait until I get home from work, that is."

She studied his face gravely. "Do I look trust-worthy?" he asked.

She laughed. "No, but I'll wait, anyway. I need all the help I can get."

As Colin fastened his seat belt, he decided he would leave work early again the following day. He didn't want to leave her alone too long. Maybe if she got used to having him around she'd change her mind about holding him at arm's length.

He deserved some time off, anyway, he assured himself. In any case, if Allison Bentley was working at his house he wouldn't be able to get any work done for thinking about her.

He liked thinking about her. Allison in her space odyssey crash helmet standing at the foot of his steps, defying him. Allison radiant in emeralds. Allison loaded down with video camera and recorder and tri-pod, looking strong and vital and professional. Allison kissing old Lionel on the cheek, her face soft with affection. Allison in his arms, fragrant and soft yet firm, her mouth warming to passion against his.

He sighed as he started the engine, but it was a sigh of pleasure rather than sorrow. It seemed entirely possible to him that time had finally completed her healing work where he was concerned. It seemed en-tirely possible to him he was ready to love again. Which raised a question. Was Allison ready?

CHAPTER SEVEN

COLIN'S RESEARCH had obviously been meticulous. Allison was impressed by the neatness of his papers, his bold and legible handwriting, the typewritten pages that were without a single typo or spelling error.

Going through his notes, she learned that Bermudians had been faced with a division of loyalties when the American Revolution began. Their allegiance might belong to England, but most of their food came from America. On a dark and sultry night in August 1775 a band of brave souls broke into the powder magazine and stole one hundred barrels of gunpowder for George Washington. Bermudians in return received a large shipment of food, but still managed not to break with England. A practical people.

She learned that privateering and piracy flourished at the end of the eighteenth century. Some Bermudians even became wreckers, luring ships to destruction on the reefs so they could salvage the contents. Smuggling was taken for granted. Whaling was a mainstay, as was the salt industry. During the American Civil War, St. George's Harbor was chosen as a base for blockade-running ships. How wild the town must have been then! The Confederacy even set up an office in town. Decades later, rumrunners made a lucrative living during American Prohibition.

Bermuda, she marveled, had experienced a microcosm of world history. What a tough hardy bunch the people had always been. How hard they had fought for survival.

Ensconced in Colin's study, feeling intimidated whenever she happened to glance up at her elegant surroundings, aware at all times of Diana's portrait behind her, Allie read and studied assiduously. She was interrupted only once, when Mac served her a beautifully prepared salad in the kitchen at lunchtime.

"I'm very grateful to you, lassie," he said as they drank coffee together.

She smiled at him. "What have I done that's so terrific?" she asked.

"You've taken Colin out of himself. He was whistling this morn's morn while he dressed himself. It's been a long rare while since I heard him whistle. I was beginning to think this house was always going to be a tomb."

She looked at the old man curiously. "What do you think of this house, Mr. Macintosh?"

"'Mac,' please." He hesitated. "Cards on the table?"

"Right up front, Mac," she said with a grin.

"But between you and me?"

"My lips are sealed."

"Well, then, there's no doubt it's a beautiful house. Colin and Diana worked on it for four years. Almost nonstop. And they did a wonderful job of restoring it.''

"True. But . . . ?"

He sipped his coffee thoughtfully, studying her face from under blunt gray eyelashes. "But I'm always feeling I should be charging five dollars a head to guide tourists through it."

She laughed. "I'm glad it's not just me. I feel exactly the same about it." She frowned. "It's not funny, though. I have the feeling Colin would be better away from it."

"I agree. But all suggestions I make for a move fall on deaf ears. Yon's a stubborn man sometimes." He took a deep breath. "Do you think you might bring a little influence to bear, Allison?"

"How can I, Mac? It's none of my business."

"I'm thinking it could be."

"I'm not going to be in Bermuda long enough to influence anybody."

"A word or two wouldn't hurt."

She reached across the kitchen table to touch his gnarled hand. "If the opportunity comes up, I'll speak my mind," she promised.

"That's all I can ask."

He stood and began clearing their dishes away. It was time for Allie to go back to work. In the doorway she gave in to impulse and turned back. "What was she like, Mac? Mrs. Endicott. Diana."

There was a silence. Then the old man briskly rinsed out a coffee mug, set it in the dishwasher and turned to face her. "Cards on the table?" he asked again.

She nodded. "Between you and me."

"Well, then. I admired her, you understand, though she wasn't the type to get too close to anyone. But she was a fine lady and Colin loved her, and that was enough for me in the beginning. And she seemed just fine for the first few years, though a wee bit of a snob in many ways. She was always after Colin to 'mix more in society,' as she called it. She wanted to be number one hostess in the islands. Wanted Colin to run for political office, too, so she would have more power. Which was all fairly harmless. He's never had much patience with such maneuvers, so he was able to stand up for himself and keep her from running his life. But then—" He stopped abruptly.

"It's okay, Mac," she assured him. "I shouldn't have asked. I'm just curious, I guess. But I don't need to know."

"I'm thinking it would be best you did know, lass. Maybe you can help him pull his head out of the sand he's buried it in this past year. He's blaming himself for not going to England with her, for being too busy to take her home for a visit, for not getting himself killed with her. The truth is she didn't want him to go with her. She was traveling with her fancy man."

It was true then; it wasn't just Mrs. Tolliver's gossip. In any other circumstances the old-fashioned term Mac had used might have struck Allie as amusing, but the old man was intensely serious, righteously indignant on Colin's behalf. He could not have been more concerned if Colin had been his son.

"Somebody Perry," she murmured.

He flashed her an alarmed glance. "Where did you hear that?" His face cleared. "Aida Tolliver, no doubt. I wondered if she knew. Question is, why would Aida think *you* should know? Did she also think you might be able to help?" The question was evidently intended to be rhetorical. He didn't wait for an answer. "It was Bruce Perry. From long before Colin started working on his history of Bermuda. Maybe even from the beginning. And Bruce married, also, and not likely to change things, his wife being the one with the money. It was like an obsession with the two of them, Diana and Bruce. They couldn't let each other alone." He straightened away from the kitchen counter abruptly and looked her directly in the eye. "This is in confidence, you understand, Allison. It wouldn't do for Colin to know. He went to school with Bruce, played cricket with him. They were the best of friends. Colin truly loved Diana and he also loved Bruce. He'd be devastated if he knew."

"You're sure he doesn't know, Mac?" she said softly. "Bermuda is a small world. Several people have told me everyone knows everyone. I've an idea everyone knows everyone's business, also."

He shook his head. "People see what they want to see. And Colin was always working so hard. No, he doesn't know about Diana and Bruce."

"Mrs. Tolliver thinks he should know."

A smile took some of the worry from his lined face. "Aye, well, Aida Tolliver fancies herself as something of a psychologist, and she has her moments of wisdom, but in this case, I'm thinking she's wrong. My old grandmother used to say, 'When in doubt, do nowt.'" He frowned. "You'll be thinking I'm an old gossip, Allison, and a busybody, but I've never discussed any of this with anyone else. I want you to believe that.''

"Then why me, Mac?" she asked, spreading her hands helplessly. "I'm just passing through. What can I do?"

Again he studied her face, his pale gray eyes narrowed under eyebrows almost as bristly as Taylor Rossiter's. "I'm thinking it might come to you what you can do," he said.

She shook her head. "I'm sorry, Mac. I just can't take the responsibility—"

"Colin told me about your mother," he said abruptly. "I'm sorry as can be about that poor lady and what you must be going through. But I'm still thinking you might be able to help Colin, at least persuade him to move out of this house."

Again she shook her head.

"Will you consider it at least?"

She nodded reluctantly. What else could she do? She sighed as his face lit with relief. She could hardly tell him she'd stayed awake most of last night thinking about Colin Endicott, worrying about the excitement that had leaped into being between them. Like one of her videos running in her mind, the kiss they had shared had repeated and repeated. Not a movie she wanted to edit in any way, but one that worried her. What was the sequel going to be? She was trying to avoid getting too involved with Colin Endicott. But people and circumstances seemed to be dictating otherwise.

Later, she thought, as she returned to Colin's study and the piles of paper she still had to go through. She'd worry about Colin Endicott later.

By the time Colin came home, she had managed to push her conversation with Mac to the back of her mind. She had concentrated on research until her head felt as stuffed with facts as Mac's salad had been with sliced mushrooms. It seemed to her that the only fact she hadn't come across was any mention of Alys Thornley or anyone named Pruitt.

"I've got to go back and concentrate on the early years," she said to Colin as he drove her to St. George. "If Alys's daughter Penelope was the last of the family to live in Bermuda until Joseph Entwhistle returned, there's not much point in taking time to see what happened in Bermuda in between, interesting as it is. I got carried away, I'm afraid."

She was aware she had been talking nonstop ever since Colin had arrived home from work. As soon as he appeared in the study, she had wanted to feel his arms around her again. And yet she had been so very aware of Diana's portrait behind her. Even Colin himself had appeared constrained. Because of Diana, or because Allie had refused to go home with him the previous night? Whatever the problem, she'd deemed it best to erect a barrier of words between them. She suspected that if he ever kissed her again, neither of them would want to leave things at that. They were not children; they were not promised to others; there was no real reason for them to hold back. But that didn't mean she had no reason to be afraid.

"You're convinced Joseph was a relative?" Colin asked.

She stared at his profile blankly for a moment, realizing once more that he was an enormously attractive man, wonderfully masculine and marvelously put together. Looking at him, admiring him, feeling a literally breathtaking surge of attraction toward him, it took her a moment to absorb what he had said and a moment more to realize she hadn't yet told him her big news of the day. "I talked to my mother before I went to bed last night," she said triumphantly. "She remembers that her grandfather Thomas had a brother Joseph who made a million dollars on the stockmarket before he was thirty but then disgraced himself. He was disowned by the family for marrying someone 'unsuitable.'"

"Tallah," Colin said, smiling ruefully.

"Exactly. Aunt Jenny didn't ever talk about Joseph because as far as she was concerned he was beyond the pale. Mom had forgotten about him until I brought him up. She certainly didn't know he'd gone to Bermuda. She supposes he must have been interested in Alys's story, too." She laughed. "I called Lionel this morning. He's as delighted as Mom and I are." She hesitated. "I'm afraid I took advantage of his kind heart and told him about Mom. He says he'll persuade Taylor to go through the attic, but not to expect too much. Every time Taylor gets up there he starts reading his old newspapers and forgets what he's supposed to be searching for."

Looking out the car window, Allie saw that they had arrived in St. George and were on Duke of York

Street, approaching St. Peter's Church. Though built
in 1713, the church contained within its walls remains
of the church erected in 1619 after the original one of
timber and palmetto had been blown down in a hurricane. Had Alys entered those original buildings, she
wondered. Of course she had—the church had been
part of everyone's daily life in those days.

As Colin parked the car Allie studied the building.
It looked, she thought, like the kind of straightforward church a child would sketch if asked to produce
a drawing of one. Very simple, small, whitewashed,
with highly polished cedar doors, it stood at the top of
a flight of well-worn brick steps.

Colin and Allie wandered along the brick footpaths
between the ancient tombstones in silence for the most
part. Allie set up her camera and shot some tape, but
she was more interested in finding Alys than in working and she gave up quite quickly.

Some of the crumbling tombstones were marked
with only a first name; other names were invisible after long exposure to the elements. They found the
slaves' graves at the west side of the church. The ma-
jority of the tombstones there were small and oblong,
carved from local limestone. Some were partially faced
with pieces of slate, with names scratched into the
surface.

Colin found Alys's stone beyond this area, almost
hidden by a small palm tree. "Here," he called excitedly. He was bending down, trying to form a shadow
between himself and the tombstone.

Squinting, Allie could make out an *A* and an *S*,
followed by *PRU*... "It must be," she whispered,

crouching beside the small weathered stone. With gentle fingers she touched the grass-covered ground under which had been placed the earthly remains of her long-ago ancestor. Tears filled her eyes. She could not remember when she had ever been more moved.

Helping her to her feet, Colin put an arm around her to steady her, then provided her with a large cotton handkerchief from his jeans pocket. He had changed from a beautifully cut suit into jeans and a cotton knit sweater when he'd arrived home and discovered this was what Allie was wearing. She had felt relieved; when he was dressed in a formal suit and they were in his formal house she couldn't relax with him at all. He looked wonderfully handsome and successful in a suit, but his sweater was dark teal blue and exactly matched his eyes.

They stood looking down at Alys's grave for several minutes while Allie put his handkerchief to good use. "I'm sorry, Colin," she said between swipes at her eyes. "You're going to think I spend half my life crying. I'm not really as weak as I seem."

"I hadn't thought of you as weak at all," he told her. He continued to hold her close to his side. It was very quiet in the churchyard. The sounds of street traffic, including the ubiquitous mopeds, were muffled by the trees. Tourists had returned to their cruise ships or hotels to get ready for dinner. Only the ever present kiskadees disturbed the silence, and even they seemed more subdued than usual.

After a while Allie regained control of herself and handed Colin's handkerchief back to him. Then she set up her camera again and recorded Alys's resting place for her mother to see.

"I wish I knew what she died of," she murmured when she was done. "I'd like to know why she doesn't appear in any of the records, too. Lionel said there was a reason for that, but he doesn't remember what it was."

"Let's check on Mr. Pruitt," Colin suggested. He picked up the camera and tripod and led the way into the church, Allie following behind with the recorder, tethered to him by the camera cable.

The memorial tablets that lined the interior walls of the church glorified more prominent Bermudians than Alys. Doctors were represented, and a much admired governor, and Joseph Entwhistle, who had "acquitted himself with approbation in the several relations of life."

William Pruitt's plaque was written in old and very formal English, with an *f*-like letter taking the place of *s*, a practice that made reading difficult. According to whoever had arranged for the engraving on the marble plaque, William Pruitt had "endeavored to mitigate all evil" whenever he was confronted by it.

"Sounds ominous," Colin muttered.

Allie nodded, reading on as she videotaped the plaque. William was born in 1589—"Ten years older than Alys," she murmured—and died in 1660, aged seventy-one.

Then she read the bottom of the plaque where it said that William Pruitt was survived by his daughter, Penelope, and his beloved wife, Martha.

"Martha!" she exclaimed, startling a group of American tourists who were admiring the fifteenth century English ironstone font and the seventeenth century pulpit.

"A second wife, do you suppose?" Colin asked.

Stunned, Allie switched off her camera and recorder. "I guess she'd have to be. But what happened to Alys? Shouldn't she at least be mentioned?"

"It would seem William wasn't enamored of her."

Allie laughed. "You've been reading too many old epitaphs. Enamored, indeed." She shook her head. "I don't know where to turn now," she said despairingly. "The tombstone is great, but it's not really proof of Alys's existence. We can't be *sure* it's her name on there."

"Let's go home and think about it," Colin suggested solemnly, taking hold of her hand again.

She was suddenly aware that the ancient church smelled as fragrant as Colin's cellar workshop. Cedar rafters and pews. She studied his face for a long moment. He looked directly back at her, his dark-blue eyes totally clear.

"I wouldn't mind doing some more work in your study," she said lamely.

"What else would I have in mind?" he said, touching her cheek with a gentle finger.

NATURALLY SHE HAD expected Macintosh to still be at the house. It wasn't until Colin put a couple of wrapped dishes in the microwave and started pushing buttons that she realized they were going to eat alone. Mac visited a lady friend in St. George on weekends,

Colin told her. He would return on Sunday afternoon without a word to say, but with a broad smile on his old face.

Almost immediately Allie began to feel nervous. The two of them were completely alone. In Diana's house.

Colin orchestrated the evening beautifully. From the garden, he brought her a single rose, which she clipped to a three-inch stem and stuck in her hair. Then he served the filleted sole and vegetable mélange and a tossed salad in the dining room with great formality and much flourishing of white damask...all of which contrasted rather markedly with the casual way they were dressed.

The proper wines accompanied the dishes, finishing with a dessert wine that was a bit too sweet for Allie. By the time they drank coffee she was feeling just the least bit giddy, though she had barely touched any of the wine.

Colin hadn't drunk much wine, either. "I like the *idea* of wine with a meal more than wine itself," he said lightly as they carried the last of the dishes into the kitchen. "I'd really rather have a beer."

Allie wondered if Diana had allowed him to drink beer. Possibly not.

When she would have loaded the dishwasher, he took her hands in both of his and shook his head. "I'd rather look at you than wash dishes," he said. "For example, right now the sunlight is coming through the window behind you and making a halo around your head."

"I'm such a saintly person," she teased.

He looked alarmed. "I hope not." He was suddenly very serious. "Allison. Allie." He touched her cheek with the palm of his right hand and brushed her lips with his thumb. "It's possible to talk a relationship to death," he said softly. "Let's not do that. I want so much to make love with you and I think you feel the same. Couldn't we just be together for a little while without worrying about the consequences? Couldn't we just comfort each other?"

His use of the word *comfort* reassured her. It sounded nonthreatening and gentle—it didn't carry overtones of high expectations. In any case, her body's signals were already taking over from her mind's concerns. She had altogether forgotten how to breathe.

"I can't handle anything serious right now, Colin," she said tentatively, just to make sure he wasn't expecting too much from her. "I told you that already."

"Then we'll keep it light," he promised.

Was that possible, she wondered. She had never experienced a casual affair. But other people had. Why shouldn't she be able to enjoy some respite from all the serious concerns that had plagued her during the past few months?

She studied Colin's face. The last of the sunlight might be haloing her hair, but it was also lighting fires in his blue eyes and gilding the edge of his strong jawline...a line she had wanted to trace ever since she first laid eyes on him.

Lifting a tentative finger, she moved it gently along his jaw, from chin to ear and back again. She saw him swallow, saw his mouth move as though to say something, then close on the words as he silently gathered her against his chest. The contours of her body fitted the curves of his as though they were two halves of the same sculpture, crafted by a master hand.

Gently he turned her, his arm holding her close to his side. He was easing her up the stairs before she even realized she was moving, walking at her side, so that the journey was one of mutual desire rather than the macho pulling or pushing that Curtis Yost had preferred to indulge in.

No, she wasn't going to think about Curtis, or about the pain of loneliness that was so much worse after the experience of making love. Nor was she going to think about Diana.

Such brave assurances to herself. None of them any good. The moment Allie entered the huge paneled bedroom and looked at the enormous canopied bed, all passion died. She hesitated just beyond the threshold, panicked, not knowing what to do. What could she possibly do?

Forget Diana, she instructed herself. Colin had obviously forgotten her. For now, anyway. Why let Diana ruin something they both wanted? This was just a casual affair, she reminded herself. It wasn't going to hurt anyone, least of all Diana.

Determinedly she made herself move forward.

During her relationship with Curtis, she had always hated the moments just before making love. Curtis had always wanted to take off her clothes himself and had usually done it too hastily, tearing a seam here, losing a button there. It had seemed churlish to complain that he might be a little more careful. After all, passion was supposed to be unrestrained, wasn't it? Then she had always worried about which of them would provide protection. She had no patience with women who felt such a discussion took all the spontaneity out of sex. A mature woman needed to know she was taken care of.

There was no such awkwardness with Colin. When he reached the bed he took a small package from his nightstand and laid it ready. "I went shopping at lunchtime," he said lightly, looking so boyish and carefree and sexy her heart thudded against her ribs. "Does that make me seem to be taking too much for granted?"

"Yes," she said with a forced grin. "But thoughtful with it."

They both laughed, which relieved her tension a lot. Then they removed their clothes, two adults able to take care of their own preparations, looking at each other from opposite sides of the bed in the large dim room, the blinds closed against the last of the daylight. Her breath caught in her throat when she first saw him nude. His athletic body was so beautifully formed, the line where his suntan ended emphasizing the tender white of the flesh below. There was a mat of tawny hair on his chest and more golden hair glinted on his arms and legs.

She heard the swift intake of his own breath when she removed her bra and felt her nipples tingle to life as his gaze fell to them. His glance moved lower then, slowly returning to linger on her face. "You are so beautiful," he said softly.

She shook her head in remonstration. No one had ever called her beautiful. Striking, yes. Lovely, yes. Even pretty, as Taylor had said. But "beautiful" was a word reserved for those few fortunate souls whose features and measurements were all in perfect harmony. People like Diana.

"So beautiful," he repeated as he reached for her. She hadn't even noticed he'd stripped the bedcovers back, but suddenly, inevitably, she was in his arms, lying down in the middle of the enormous bed, feeling his body pressing against hers from head to toe. When his lips trailed kisses across her throat, she let her head fall back. Excitement was racing through her veins, clamoring for release from the deep aching rhythms he had set in motion. As his lips moved to her breast, her arms clasped him close and she moved with him in a gentle rocking motion as she looked beyond his shoulder at the ceiling and the huge chandelier hanging from it.

In the darkened room the antique bureaus and dressing table seemed to loom over them, stray fingers of light glinting on solid brass handles and knobs. Huge oil paintings in gilt frames gleamed darkly, mysteriously, against the dark paneled walls. Directly above them the shadowed canopy seemed lower than before, as though it were moving downward. Dimly she remembered reading a horror novel in which a murderer had engineered a four poster canopy that would lower itself inch by inch and eventually suffocate the victim sleeping innocently below it.

Quite suddenly she wasn't moving any more. Sensing her abrupt withdrawal, Colin lifted his head and looked at her. "Did I do something clumsy?" he asked, ready as ever to take blame.

"It's the room," she said, trying to keep panic from her voice. "I can't make love in this room."

"Why not? It's a bedroom." He kissed her forehead lovingly, gently. "People are supposed to make love in bedrooms."

"It's just that it feels more like a stateroom," she said apologetically. "There should be velvet ropes sealing it off from public view. I keep expecting a guide to come through with a group of tourists. 'And here ladies and gentlemen we have wax effigies of the master and his mistress dallying in the master's bed, which was handcrafted by Thomas Chippendale in 1775.'"

He raised his head and looked at her, his face still. "You're not joking, are you?"

She shook her head. "I'm sorry, Colin, I just can't. It's just too..."

"Another room?"

"Which one, the basement? Your workbench, perhaps?"

His arms had slackened around her and she pulled herself free and sat on the edge of the bed, reaching down for her tumbled clothing, feeling so mortified she thought she would die of embarrassment. "I'm so sorry, Colin."

He lay on his back, unself-conscious about his nudity, but with confusion and hurt showing clearly on his tanned face. "I'd hoped you'd spend the weekend," he said quietly. "I want you so much, Allison."

She stood up so that she could pull her cotton sweater over her head more easily. "Perhaps it's just as well," she said, feeling that if she didn't speak she would burst into tears. She certainly didn't want to inflict any more tears on him.

He looked up at her questioningly.

"I think mostly we feel sorry for each other," she said. "You're still grieving for Diana. I'm dreadfully worried about my mother. But we can't build a satisfactory relationship on mutual pity."

He raised himself on one elbow. "I wasn't aware that I wanted you because I felt sorry for you, or that I was the recipient of your pity," he said stiffly. "In any case, I thought we weren't going to analyze our feelings to death."

She sat on the edge of the bed, facing him. "Perhaps we should analyze them, Colin. I'll be in Bermuda for three more weeks—two if I can get my movie finished and find out what I need to know about Alys. I want to get back to my mother as soon as possible. It's hardly a good time to...start something."

"It's not just the house then?"

She wanted to be totally honest with him. He deserved her honesty. "The house is most of it," she admitted. "I'm sorry, but I don't feel I belong here." She attempted a laugh, which failed abysmally. "Maybe it's because I'm like Alys, one of the commoner sort."

"I'm one of the commoner sort, too, Allie," he reminded her.

"Not as long as you live in this...house you're not."
She had almost said *museum*, which showed how
much the place had affected her.

Colin had begun pulling on his own clothing. "Will
you at least let me fix you a drink, some coffee,
something, before I take you home?"

"Thank you, yes, coffee would be nice." How could
she refuse? She had obviously hurt him. His voice had
sounded stiff, though no stiffer than hers. "I'm sorry,
Colin," she said again. Time enough later to remind
him she had left her moped here and could take herself home.

It was impossible, of course, for them to be at ease
with each other. There wasn't anything more embarrassing than aborted lovemaking. Yet all the same,
watching him as he ground coffee beans and set up the
coffee maker in the kitchen, she wondered how she'd
found the strength to turn away from him. He was so
at ease in his masculinity that even when he was per-
forming a domestic task he made it look natural.
Curtis wouldn't have dreamed of making the coffee.
"Woman's work," he would have joked, but he would
not have been joking.

Go away, Curtis, she instructed him in her mind.

"I've had an idea," she said as she accepted a cup
of coffee, hoping to dissipate the awkwardness between them. "I'm going to see if I can hire Simon for
the weekend to go through Lionel's attic with me."

Colin raised an eyebrow. "What is this? Small talk?
You tell me you can't make love with me in my own
home and then expect me to indulge in small talk?"

"What else can I do?" she asked, flushing slightly. "I've told you how I feel."

"You were *almost* ready to make love with me."

But it was all too soon; it had all happened too fast. She was afraid it wouldn't stay casual...how could she tell him that? "The house—" she began.

"Again the house." His voice was stiff. "Diana and I rebuilt this house, Allison." He looked around the elaborate kitchen. "It's part of me and I'm part of it. So is she." He frowned, as though this were a new thought to him.

Allie remained silent. She had promised Mac she'd talk to him about the house and she had tried. But Colin had loved his wife. How could she advise him to leave the place he had shared with her? She met his gaze as sympathetically as she could, and after a while he took a deep breath and nodded. "All right," he said. "So you want to employ Simon."

He had evidently decided to postpone further discussion of their relationship. Wasn't that what she had wanted? Why, then, did she feel so disappointed? "Well," she said hesitantly, "I have another idea, an ulterior motive, I guess." She took a deep breath. Although the windows were open in the kitchen and it was the homiest room in the house—if dark paneling and crystal chandeliers could be called homey—she still felt stifled. "Could we possibly sit in the garden?" she asked. "It's warm in here."

He frowned again. "You really don't like this house, do you?" He held up a hand when she would have apologized again. "No, it's all right. I quite understand. Of course we can go into the garden."

How could he possibly understand, she wondered as she followed him out. He must think she was crazy, worse than crazy...totally insane. Still, she was glad he'd gone along with her suggestion. The air smelled wonderful in the garden. There was a stone bench where they could sit, with a small lantern beside it. It was cool now, but the breeze had dropped. The sky was dark, with only a few stars showing. No moon in view. The tiny whistling frogs that were so much a part of Bermuda's nightscape sounded like bells chiming in the trees.

"What ulterior motive?" Colin asked.

He sounded more relaxed, Allie thought. He was a different person outside the house. "Lionel told me the first day I met him that Simon was a good student," she said. "Celia told me the same thing. And Simon himself admitted he'd wanted to go on to college but couldn't afford it. His father drinks, did you know that?"

Colin shook his head.

Allie sipped her coffee. It was hot and strong, just the way she liked it. "There are eight kids in Simon's family. He's the eldest. When his father gets angry he throws Simon out. That's why he was in jail...he'd broken into a house so he'd have a place to sleep."

Colin was looking at her with an astonished expression. "You are an amazing woman," he said. "You've found out more about Simon's background than I have in all the years I've known him. I didn't even know he'd spent time in prison." He laughed shortly. "Come to think of it, you probably know more about *me* than anyone else does."

She felt a guilty twinge deep in her stomach, remembering that she did know one thing about him that even he didn't know. Damn Mrs. Tolliver. Damn Macintosh. Why had they told her about Diana's affair with Bruce Perry?

"What I thought originally," she said hastily, "was that if Lionel could get to know Si again, and if he knew that Si really wanted to go to college and become a teacher, just like him... Well, Lionel might encourage him to look into tuition loans or something. But now, well, Lionel seems to have plenty of money and he's a very kind man, so maybe..."

Colin laughed and set his coffee cup on the ground. "I seem to remember you became incensed when I suggested you might be an interfering woman. Why on earth should Lionel foot the bill for Simon's education? Si's a known troublemaker, Allison. I don't think you should introduce him into Lionel's house at all. Lionel has enough problems."

Allie put down her own coffee cup, prepared to do battle. "Si's okay," she said firmly. "He remembers the botanical names of plants."

"What difference does that make?"

"My father always knew the names of plants."

"Oh, well, then..."

"You don't have to be sarcastic. Anyway, Simon *admires* Lionel. When he and Celia talked about him, it was obvious—"

"No," Colin said. "I can't agree, Allison."

"That's too bad," she said.

He looked at her with narrowed eyes. "You're going to do it anyway, aren't you?"

"Yes. I'm going to take Simon over to Lionel's tomorrow if he'll go with me." She frowned. "I wonder if he works at the Botanical Gardens on Saturdays."

"What an unpredictable woman you are," Colin said.

"You think I'm crazy, too, don't you?"

"Crazy? No. Why would I think that?" He really did look surprised.

"All that in your bedroom," she said awkwardly.

"I think you're a very sensitive woman," he said. His voice was suddenly gentle, and he had reached over to touch her hair, winding a strand of it around his fingers. His face was close to hers now and she knew he was going to kiss her. "Unpredictable, sensitive and maybe a little afraid of getting in over your head," he murmured. "But I'm beginning to know you, Allison Bentley. It's against your principles to get involved in a short-term relationship, and you don't trust an attraction that develops too quickly, yet you were almost ready to get very involved with me. Which means your feelings must be pretty strong. Just as mine are. My house bothered you today, but perhaps you'll get over that when you become accustomed to it. Just wait and see, I'm a patient man. House or no house, you *are* going to make love with me before you leave Bermuda."

While she was still pondering that, his mouth met hers. He was not as gentle this time. Not that he hurt her in any way—she didn't think he had it in him to hurt anyone—but his mouth was demanding and she felt as though he were drawing her soul right out of her body. She wanted him. Oh, Lord, she wanted him. He was right about her feelings being pretty strong. The understatement of the year.

After a while he straightened and put her away from him. "If I don't send you home now I'll be carrying you back into that 'stateroom' you dislike so much," he said. He took a deep breath. "Do you want to be independent and ride that infernal machine home, or shall I drive you?"

What she wanted was not to leave, but how could she tell him that now? If he would just make love to her in this garden, with the moon gate gleaming whitely in the lamplight and the whistling frogs chiming in the trees and the air so heavily perfumed with flowers she would be tempted to stay with him forever.

CHAPTER EIGHT

ACCORDING TO A WORKMAN Allie came across in the Botanical Gardens on Saturday morning, Simon Leverett was no longer working there. The workman wasn't sure if he had quit or been fired.

Colin was possibly right about Simon, she thought. Probably he was the last person she should introduce into Lionel's house. Yet she wasn't often wrong about people, and after watching Simon with the children and talking to him about his dreams, she had felt he was basically a good person. He needed people to believe in him, to help set him on the right road. Celia had faith in him. There must be something there worth trusting in.

Celia was on duty at the Visitors' Bureau when Allie stopped by. Si would be ringing her up about noon, she said. He'd quit his job because it was boring. "I was so happy when he got that job," she said, her round pretty face strained with worry. She sighed deeply. "Happiness is always temporary, isn't it?"

She seemed relieved when Allie told her why she wanted to see Simon. "I'll tell him to meet you at Mr. Entwhistle's house," she said eagerly. "I'm sure he'll want to help."

Allie had been working for an hour in Lionel's attic, when Simon arrived. She was beginning to feel like an explorer hacking out a path through the jungle with her bare hands. Originally she had planned to be helpful to Lionel by trying to sort things as she went, but she soon gave up that idea. The only way to sort the contents of this attic would be to empty everything out through the windows onto the lawn outside and let the wind blow through it.

She was looking through a box filled with photo albums, when she heard voices below—Taylor's raised, Simon's raised higher. Lionel had been perfectly agreeable to Si's coming here, but she hadn't seen Taylor when she arrived. Evidently he wasn't happy with her bright idea. In fact, he sounded definitely truculent.

"I asked Simon to come and help me, Taylor," she called down the stairs.

Taylor appeared at the foot of the attic staircase, hearing aids in place, hair wild as ever, wrinkled face tinged pink with anger. "This young man is fresh out of prison, Allison," he objected. "I read about him in the *Royal Gazette*. I read all the newspapers, you know."

"He was looking for a place to sleep when he broke into that house," she said placatingly. "He had nowhere else to go. It was wrong, but he's paid for his mistake, Taylor."

Taylor snorted.

"Please, Taylor," she begged, smiling encouragingly at Simon, who kept looking over his shoulder as though he were ready to head back down to the front door. "Please stay, Simon," she said. "I really need your help. Lionel said it was all right," she added to Taylor.

"I certainly did," Lionel's deep voice agreed from somewhere below.

Taylor looked narrow-eyed at Simon, then at Allison. "You're responsible for him then," he said flatly. "Sue you he does any damage."

"Okay," she said with a sigh. "Simon, did Celia tell you what I wanted you to do?"

Si started up the attic stairs, edging carefully around Taylor, who glared ferociously at him. "Something about looking for some papers?" he said.

"Anything to do with Alys Thornley or Pruitt, or Penelope or William Pruitt," she told him. "Any reference to the seventeenth century, or the *Sea Venture*, or the *Deliverance*. Or something that says Joseph Entwhistle on it. A journal or a diary, perhaps. Joseph was Lionel's grandfather."

By now Simon had entered the attic. He whistled. "I thought this was going to be a one- or two-day job," he said, then laughed. "You might have to give me a pension when we get finished here, Allie."

She was relieved by the flash of humor. "You'll do it, then? Celia told you what I'd pay? Is it enough?"

"It'll do." He looked around, hands on his skinny hips, eyebrows raised. "Hooraw's nest, this is."

Allie wasn't sure what a hooraw's nest was, but she groaned agreement, anyway. "Lionel told me he and Taylor were pack rats," she said. "I think that was an understatement."

They worked together for a couple of hours. Allie was pleased to see that Simon first cleared a portion of the attic and then started setting things in orderly piles as he worked. Obviously he had more patience than she had. Colin had said he was a good worker, she remembered. Celia had said he liked tidiness as much as she did.

"Telephone for you, Allison," Taylor announced, appearing in the attic entrance around two-thirty. He sounded out of breath.

Remembering how he'd complained when Lionel had wanted him to go upstairs last time she was here, Allison immediately felt guilty. He was ninety years old; he shouldn't be running up and down stairs. "I'm sorry, Taylor. I can't imagine..."

"Colin Endicott," Taylor said, and her heart seemed to skip a beat. "Take it in my bedroom. Down the stairs, first on the left. I'll stay here till you come back," he added as she passed him.

Si looked up from an ancient trunk he was going through and smiled shyly at the old man, but Taylor's hostile expression didn't relax. He intended keeping an eye on Simon however long she was gone, Allie realized.

"I've been sorting through my records," Colin said when she picked up the receiver and greeted him.

Enjoying the sound of his voice, so British sounding, Allie didn't at first take in exactly what he had said, then she exclaimed, "I'm so glad, Colin!"

"I have you to thank, Allison," he said. "Once I got that particular monster out in the sunlight I realized just how ridiculous it really was. It was stupid of me to develop such a silly aversion to my own work."

"Not stupid," she protested. "Just a part of the grieving process."

There was a silence, then he sighed. "Yes. I think you're probably right." He was silent for another long moment, then he said, "I rang up to tell you I've found a mention of Alys. Only a bare mention," he added hastily when she exclaimed excitedly. "I was reading through the ancient records of the assizes. I hadn't gone through them before. Interesting stuff— someone indicted for stealing a potato valued at three pence, someone else for playing at unlawful games such as cards or dice. Quite suddenly, there was Alys Pruitt, sentenced to stand in church on the first Sabbath in March of 1626, wearing a paper on her breast detailing her crime."

"What did she do?"

"She called her neighbor an old bawd."

"What on earth is on old bawd?"

"I'm not sure of the precise definition, but I think it refers to prostitution. It wasn't a compliment, obviously."

Allie laughed. Somehow Alys had come to life with this revelation. In 1626 she must have been twenty-seven years old. Not with the sweetest disposition, evidently. "Proof at last," she said thankfully. "Is there anything there about her husband?"

"Nothing, I'm afraid." He laughed. "William might have been right there with her, insulting neighbors right and left himself, but he wouldn't necessarily be mentioned. Men and women are not always equal before the law, Allison. There's a story here of a man who beat his wife and they were both censured for divers discord, he to be bound to the good behavior and she to be ducked three times in the sea.''

Allie was horrified. "But he assaulted her!'' she exclaimed.

"Just one small example of seventeenth century justice," Colin said. "I suppose Alys was lucky to get off so lightly."

"She must have felt humiliated, though." She hesitated. "I don't know how to thank you, Colin. I'm so delighted that we've found some mention of her."

"Perhaps we'll find more. How is everything going over there?"

"Simon's working with me. We haven't come across anything yet, but he's very thorough. And neat, too. I'm sure he'll be a big help."

She had spoken quite challengingly, but Colin didn't comment, as she'd half expected him to. She decided not to tell him Simon had quit his job at the Botanical Gardens.

"May I see you tonight, Allison, for dinner, perhaps?" Colin asked. "We could go out somewhere."

He was being very considerate about her aversion to his house. Allie hesitated, wanting to accept, but not sure if it was a good idea to see him again so soon after yesterday's disaster. She still felt embarrassed over her reaction to his home, and maybe it would be best to slow things down a little, take a little more time to think. She suddenly remembered Mac quoting his grandmother, "When in doubt, do nowt."

"Maybe I should work here with Simon whenever I have any free time, Colin," she said. "For a few days, anyway. There's so much to go through."

"I did offer to help," he reminded her.

"I know you did, and I appreciate that, but I think maybe three of us—well, there's not much room to move. And I'm afraid I have a busy schedule ahead—Celia's arranged a glass-bottomed boat trip for me tomorrow out to the coral reef. I want to include that in my video. Then on Monday Celia and I are going to ride the bus to Somerset. Tuesday I have an interview with the minister of tourism. And Wednesday..."

"Of course. I understand." His voice was stiff. He knew she was making excuses. It was true she had all these things arranged, but there would surely be some spare time in there somewhere.

She was suddenly afraid she'd never see him again. "I'm going to shoot the King's Square ceremonies in St. George on Wednesday," she said carefully. "I'll be on my own then. I suppose you'll be working, though, so maybe you wouldn't be able to—"

"The program begins at noon, I believe," he interrupted. "I'll be there. In the meantime, I'll let you know if I find anything else about Alys."

He hung up before she could say another word.

Taylor was still standing inside the entrance to the attic, still squinting defiantly at Simon, who was working away without paying the old man any attention. "You're back," he said, when Allie reached the top of the stairs. "I'll be getting along then. Work to do. Can't waste all day up here."

He could have made it a little less obvious that he didn't trust Simon, Allie thought. "I'm sorry, Si," she said after Taylor had left.

Simon smiled at her in his usual shy way, but there was a bravado to the smile that didn't fool her one bit. He was hurt by the old man's lack of trust, obviously. Sighing, Allie knelt beside yet another unlabeled cardboard carton and started opening it. Wednesday, she thought, and immediately felt more cheerful. Not wanting to analyze her reaction she went to work with a will.

IT RAINED on Sunday, rather dampening Allie's enthusiasm for the colorful fish and wrecked ships she was recording that day. Monday in rural and beautiful Somerset was dry but cloudy. Tuesday brought ink-black storm clouds followed by forked lightning and thunder that sounded as though the gods of old were staging a pitched battle, complete with cannonballs. "When you live on a tiny slice of land in the middle of the Atlantic Ocean," one of the minister of tourism's assistants had told her, "you have to accept whatever falls on you."

Every evening Allie worked with Simon in the attic. It was, almost literally, a Herculean task. As they worked, Allie told Simon about the tasks Zeus had set Hercules so that he might achieve immortality. One of them was the cleaning of the stables of King Augeas, who owned three thousand cattle. "Those stables hadn't been cleaned for thirty years, either," she informed him.

Simon laughed. "What method did Hercules use?"

"He diverted a couple of rivers from their beds and flushed the stables out in a single day."

He nodded solemnly. "Good thinking."

Allie enjoyed working with Simon. He talked freely now of his unhappy and obviously underprivileged childhood, which contrasted markedly with Allie's own upbringing. Only two really good things had ever happened to him, he told her seriously. Lionel Entwhistle and Celie Jordan.

From the albums and letters and photos and clothes they were sorting, Allie was also learning every detail of Lionel's life. She knew what his wife, long since deceased, looked like, and what her favorite colors had been. She met their son, who had tragically drowned in a sailing mishap at the age of fifteen and remembered the pain that had clouded Lionel's face when he'd said he was the last of his line.

Through the headlines on Taylor's newspapers, she traced the history of Bermuda through two world wars and hurricanes and other disasters. But she couldn't find any trace of Joseph Entwhistle or Alys Thornley Pruitt.

Wednesday dawned clear and cloudless with a cool ocean breeze to keep the temperature bearable. By mid-morning King's Square in St. George was very crowded. A bunch of tourists were mugging for Allie's camera in the stocks and pillory, lines of people waited to go aboard the *Deliverance II* and so many men, women and children were standing on the bridge to Ordnance Island that Allie was afraid it would collapse before the ceremony even began.

Promptly at noon, the ancient cannon was fired, with a boom that resounded for quite a while. Then the town crier—a sturdy-looking man attired in knee breeches and long caped coat, a lace jabot, white gloves and a tricorne—called everyone to attention and announced in stentorian tones the news of the day...a day in the seventeenth century. There followed a skit in which a young man dressed in breeches and a striped shirt and with a kerchief tied around his head played the drunken fool, running in and out among the tourists, with the town crier in hot pursuit. When he was finally cornered, he was placed very firmly in the stocks and a couple of pretty wenches, dressed in long gowns and mobcaps, pelted him with tomatoes, much to the amusement of the crowd.

Allie had set up her camera early, wanting a good position on the waterfront near a guardrail that would protect her camera from jostling. Engrossed in taping the tomato throwing, she didn't see Colin approach. He didn't speak and it wasn't until she faded out, switched the camera to standby and stepped back that she saw him standing beside her. Her body responded with a flood of excitement that unnerved her. During the past few days—and nights—Colin Endicott had inhabited her thoughts with distressing regularity.

"Hi," she said weakly.

His smile dazzled her. "I've missed you, Allison," he said.

Oh, she did love the way he said her name. "Me, too," she answered stupidly, then tried to amend the statement. "I mean, you too, I've missed—" She broke off.

"Here we are then," Colin said.

"Yes."

"Deathless dialogue," he said, quirking one blond eyebrow. "Do you suppose we're both nervous?"

"Why would we be . . . yes, I guess I am, anyway."

"Me, too."

They looked at each other, Colin with a slight smile on his face, Allie feeling a definite acceleration in her heartbeat. He was wearing his Bermuda gentleman outfit: shirt and tie and Bermuda shorts and knee socks. She loved the way he looked in that outfit.

He was gazing at her very lovingly. Her breath caught in her throat. Surely he wasn't getting serious about her. She certainly didn't want that to happen. It *mustn't* happen.

She relaxed abruptly. Of course he wasn't serious. He hadn't known her long enough to get serious. He was attracted to her in the same way she was attracted to him. Sexually. He wouldn't be able to love any woman until he freed himself of his wife's memory and disposed of that museum of a house.

"I guess they're going to do the dunking ceremony next," she said, feeling better now that she'd worked everything out in her mind.

He nodded, pushing his hair back from his forehead with one hand. He was so tall, so fair, so handsome, so *golden*. She noticed a couple of female tourists aiming their cameras at him. How could she blame them? He was a perfect example of the healthy, well-dressed Bermudian male.

But it wasn't just his looks that attracted her, she knew. It was the way he was, the person he was. She remembered him talking about the soul of the wood, the compassion on his face when she'd told him about her mother, the way he'd held her. There were no shadows in his face today, she noticed.

"You've seen all this before, I guess," she said.

"Many times. It's very popular with the tourists. Gives them a glimpse of what the seventeenth century was like." He raised an eyebrow, a neutral expression on his face, a glimmer of teasing light in his eyes. "Did you read the plaque on the ducking stool?"

Allie had already taped the stool, which was rather like an extra long teeter-totter, braced at the middle on a wheeled cart and with a wooden chair like a small child's swing seat mounted on one end. She had also recorded the plaque, grimacing over the part that read: "Ducking was almost entirely reserved for the weaker, if not gentler, sex." She made a face at Colin and he laughed aloud.

The town crier was ringing his hand bell again and calling out, "Oyez, oyez!" Allie switched on her camera, conscious of the fact that Colin was watching her, conscious of the fact that his mere presence was enough to dry her mouth and make her fingers tremble.

"We have summoned you here at this time," the town crier said to the crowd of tourists, "so that you may witness the ducking in the harbor of a certain wench, who is to be punished for nagging her husband."

Much laughter from the crowd. A young white woman, one of the wenches in period costume, was dragged to the ducking stool by one of the town crier's assistants, a handsome young black man in a tricorne and breeches. "This wench," the town crier informed the crowd, "was tried and found guilty of nagging by a jury of six good and true *men*."

The young woman screeched penetratingly and convincingly that she was innocent, innocent.

"Duck her," the crowd roared.

The cart was immediately wheeled to the edge of the wharf, the end of the ducking stool was lifted high and the unfortunate wench splashed deep into the water. A second later she was brought up spitting and dripping, still screeching.

"Do you repent?" the town crier asked.

"Never," she screamed, bringing another laugh from the crowd.

The town crier rang his bell and down she went again.

"Worthies, please help me," she screamed when she came up once more.

"Duck her again," the crowd shouted.

"Do you repent?" the town crier asked when she was brought up again.

"Yes, yes, yes," she said in a pleading voice.

There was much laughter and applause, the cart was wheeled farther onto the wharf and the young woman helped off. The crowd began to disperse almost immediately.

"What do you think?" Colin asked as he helped Allie pack her camera gear.

"Everybody seemed to enjoy it," she said evasively.

He raised an eyebrow. "I asked what *you* thought."

"Well, it was all in fun, of course, and they all acted their parts very well, and it was really quite funny..."

"But?"

She sighed, stowing her equipment in the basket of her moped. He was going to think her terribly negative. First his house and now—

"The whole thing made me angry," she blurted out. "I kept thinking that once upon a time it wasn't done in fun. The crowd probably laughed just as much as this one and cheered on the procedure, but the poor victim wasn't having much fun at all. Think of poor Alys having to stand up in church with a paper on her breast, the object of ridicule and censure. Think of all the women who were ducked for no real reason. How terrifying to be dropped in the water and pulled out and dropped again. And the stocks that everyone plays around in over there," she added, pointing across the square. "Think of being fastened in those and pelted with rotten fruit and vegetables. There's a whipping post, too. What a cruel age it was."

"What a kind person you are, Allie," he said softly.

She smiled sheepishly. "I'm sorry, I know it's all just fun for the tourists, but I couldn't help associating it all with Alys." She hesitated, then made a face. "Don't take any notice of me, Colin. I'm not in a good mood, I'm afraid."

He was instantly alert. "Something's wrong? What is it? Your mother?"

She sighed and nodded. "I've been calling every day. Esther, the live-in nurse, keeps insisting Mom's fine, but somehow she doesn't sound convincing. Mom herself sounds...breathy. I wanted to go home, but when I told Mom what you had come up with about Alys and the assizes she asked me to keep trying to track down the full story. So I guess that's what I have to do." To her dismay, her eyes filled with tears. Again. "I'm sorry," she said.

He handed her a handkerchief that was as impeccably white as the last one he'd loaned her. American men didn't seem to carry handkerchiefs. It was a nice custom, Allie decided. The soft clean cotton was far more comforting than a piece of tissue paper. "Did I get mascara on it?" she asked, handing it back.

He shook his head slightly, studying her face. "Are you all right?"

"Fine. It's just that every once in a while..."

"I understand." He hesitated, then said in a worried-sounding voice, "Allison, I've done something and I have absolutely no idea how you'll feel about it."

He sounded so intense she was afraid to look at him. She glanced around, instead. The tourists had all left the square now. There was only the sound of an occasional boat horn or seabird. At the White Horse Tavern, where she and Colin had eaten dinner several nights ago, a waiter was feeding scraps to the fish in the harbor. The water was churning at that spot. She couldn't ever remember seeing someone hand-feed fish before. Bermudians were wonderful, she decided. Bermuda was wonderful.

"I've borrowed a cottage from a friend," Colin said. "It's mine until tomorrow morning. It's on the south shore."

Her gaze went directly, swiftly to his face. He was looking hopeful, sheepish and rather nervous all at the same time.

She laughed nervously. "You're very resourceful, aren't you?"

He raised an eyebrow. "I am of British ancestry, you know. We're noted for that trait."

"So this cottage you've borrowed...I guess it's supposed to be an alternative to your house, for my special benefit?"

"Are you angry?" he asked.

"No." She thought for a minute. "I'm flattered, I guess. Nobody ever provided me with a cottage before."

"We could go there now. I have the key."

They looked at each other. Desire was almost palpable between them. Allie's breathing had become erratic. Colin didn't seem to be breathing at all.

But then quite suddenly her breathing evened out and she was filled with the conviction that whatever this was between them it was right and good and she should stop fighting it.

"No strings?" she said.

"No strings."

"I like the south shore," she said faintly.

"You could ride your moped up to Aida Tolliver's," he suggested. "I could follow you, then drive you to the cottage." His hand touched her cheek briefly. "Dear Allison. Is this all right? Have I done the right thing?"

"I don't know," she said honestly.

"But you'll come?"

"I'll come."

THE COTTAGE WAS SMALL, with a neat little kitchen, a well-equipped bathroom, a king-size bed, table and chairs, dressing table and plenty of closets and a panoramic view of the ocean.

Allie had been afraid she'd feel embarrassed, but she wasn't at all. Once more, Colin had thought of everything. He had brought along plenty of food and fixed a light meal of fruit and cheese and some wonderfully fresh French bread, which they warmed in the kitchen's small oven. He had also provided a bottle of very good Chardonnay—Allie's favorite wine—and some beer for himself.

After lunch, he suggested they climb down to the beach, which proved to be a small cove, pink with coral, with a drop-off into turquoise water inhabited by bright blue fish. For a few minutes, she and Colin walked barefoot at the edge of the water, but desire was so strong between them that in no time they were climbing back up the steep path to the cottage.

They left the windows open so they could hear the constant splashing of the waves below, the cheery cries of the kiskadees, the occasional rattle of the tree branches shaking in the wind. The cottage was white outside and in, but so filled with sunlight, pouring in through a large skylight as well as the many windows, that the walls seemed golden. The draperies were golden, too, billowing like silken sails in the ocean breeze, and there was an arrangement of oleanders and hibiscus in a low oval dish on the small round dining table.

The bed was large and comfortable, with crisp yellow sheets and down-filled pillows and no canopy to make Allie feel claustrophobic.

Naked, they came together in the middle of the bed like starved and lonely pilgrims meeting in a foreign land, tangling fervently in an embrace and a kiss that heated Allie's blood to boiling point and made her realize she had never really appreciated a kiss before.

For a long time they were content to hold each other, kissing ever more deeply, their arms wound tightly around each other. His mouth tasted of the salty mist the ocean had sprayed over them as they walked in the shallows at the edge of the beach below. Possibly hers did, too. She could smell the salt—and the flowers on the table across the room. She could hear the muted cry of seabirds, feel the graininess of sand between her fingers and toes. All her senses were alert and heightened. All her emotions were centered on the man who was kissing her so thoroughly, so skillfully.

There came a moment when, as though by mutual agreement, they parted and looked deeply into each other's eyes. Their hands gently stroked each other's bodies. The calluses on Colin's fingers gave Allie a pleasant sensation as his hands played over her breasts.

She stole a glance at his face and saw to her surprise that he was frowning. Had his own personal shadows returned? Was he thinking of Diana? "Is anything wrong?" she asked him gently.

He looked startled and for a moment he seemed about to speak, but then he smiled vaguely, instead.

Lowering his head, he kissed each of her breasts in turn, taking his time, touching his tongue to each nipple until it grew firm with wanting.

She worried for a moment longer, but as he continued to caress her, trailing kisses across her throat, between her breasts, down across her abdomen, up to her breasts again, she let herself relax. Obviously she had imagined the shadows. He couldn't possibly be pretending she was Diana. That definitely wouldn't be healthy. "We could comfort each other," he had said earlier.

She raised her hands to touch and smooth his hair, finding it just as crisp and clean as it looked, then cupped his face and lifted it so that she could gaze at him again. "You seemed a bit nervous there," she said gently when his eyes questioned her.

"I am nervous. It's been a long time for me. I wasn't sure for a minute if I could..." He let his voice trail away into soft laughter. She joined in when she realized his pressure against her was so insistent there was no doubt of his ability to make love to her.

She let go of a breath she hadn't realized she was holding. If that was all he'd been frowning about, there was no need for her to be concerned. It wouldn't have mattered to her if there *had* been a problem, she thought. She would have been content to lie in his arms, tasting his kisses.

No, you wouldn't have, a small voice in her brain corrected her. Her whole body was tense with longing. Pressure was building within her, bringing that certain sweet pain that needed, *demanded* release.

Sensing her need, he lifted himself and touched gently between her thighs with the fingers of one hand. Immediately all feeling rushed to the place, pinning her to the bed with the power of her wanting. His fingers moving in a feather-light fashion, he looked lovingly into her face, watching the passion build in her, holding back his own passion so as not to diminish her feelings by one iota until she was ready for him.

Her tumble of dark curls was spread across the yellow pillow, her golden skin glowing, her eyes more green than brown in the sunlight pouring through the skylight above their heads. Her head was moving now on the pillow, back and forth, back and forth, slowly, and her mouth was parting, her breath quickening, her eyes shining. He wondered if she knew she was moaning, "Yes, yes, yes."

With exquisite timing, he stopped the slight feathery movement of his fingers, dropping his head at the same moment to kiss her hard, once, twice, letting the breath rush out of his mouth and into hers just as she stiffened. Her body was tense, uplifted, still for one long moment, returning the pressure of his mouth.

And then she moved her head to one side and cried out incoherently just as her body spasmed. Her hands held him tightly, and though he had wanted to thrust himself into her at the precise moment of her climax, he held back, letting her have this time to herself in all its powerful ecstasy.

Her wonderful eyes shone up at him from the pillow when the moment was over.

"I wasn't really wondering if I was capable of making love to you," he confessed.

"What were you frowning about then?" she asked.

He hesitated, then blurted out, "I was realizing that I love you, Allison."

Her eyes widened with shock and he wished he could bite the words back.

"You mustn't do that, Colin," she said quickly, sounding panicked. "You promised me no strings. I don't have any love to give. I'm committed to taking care of my mother. I can't take the responsibility. I don't have any energy left over."

He summoned a smile. "Seems to me you have energy to spare," he said as lightly as he could.

She frowned at him. "You know what I mean."

"Yes, I do," he said sadly. "But just for a little while I hoped it might be possible—"

"It isn't," she said firmly. "But we've got something better."

"What could be better than love?"

"Friendship. Affection." She grinned. "Lust." The grin faded, giving way to sympathy. "You aren't ready to love anyone yet, Colin. You're still tied up with..."

"With Diana?" He looked at her thoughtfully. "You know, this surprises me, but I don't really think I am. Not any more." He hesitated. "I'll never forget her, of course, but you see there were other influences at work." He shook his head. "How on earth did we get into this solemn discussion in the middle of such a joyous occasion?"

"You said you loved me."

Again he forced lightness into his voice, wary now, knowing he had to be more careful or he would frighten her away forever. She mustn't suspect the depth of his feeling for her, the depth of his love. He might be committed to her in his heart, but if he gave voice to that commitment he was in danger of losing her. "Of course I love you," he said brightly. "I love lots of things. Puppies and babies and sweet-smelling wood. Dark and stormies. Mac's fish chowder. Rain on the roof, swirling down to the water tank. The ocean splashing against rocks. Sunrise. Sunset. Fish and chips. Thunderstorms."

She was laughing now. "Is this list never going to end?"

"It's your fault," he said. "Just because I said I love you—that doesn't necessarily mean I *love* you. No pressure, all right?"

"Okay," she said, looking relieved. "Now...is it okay if I tell *you* something?"

"Tell away."

"I want you inside me. Now."

Her lovely eyes were laughing, glowing. He laughed with her. "Now who's being outspoken?" he asked. Then he reached over to the nightstand beside him, quickly readied himself with the protection he had brought and entered her with her tender assistance.

"Colin," she murmured, and then she was moving with him, holding him, finding his rhythm, adjusting herself to it.

Their mouths met and played teasing games as their bodies moved, touching, parting, pressing, brushing against each other, teasing each other. They turned on their sides, then Colin was sprawling on top of her, pressing her into the bedclothes. Then they rolled again and Allie was looking down at him, still moving with him, watching his eyes darken to cobalt as she alternately lifted herself and pressed herself down. Their hands moved over each other's bodies, gently at first, then roughly, urgently.

Pressure was building inside her again, building to an unbearable peak, but she wanted to wait, she wanted this wonderful lovemaking to go on and on in the golden afternoon and then on into the darkness of night. But she couldn't, absolutely couldn't wait. Her eyes asked the question and the pressure of his hands answered, pulling her down close to him, then rolling with her until he was over her again, barely moving now, teasing her again, making her wait, wait, wait.

And then there was no more waiting. Their bodies became one unit with one goal and the very air in the golden room seemed to shatter into a thousand particles of sunlight, spreading brilliantly in concentric patterns of light as passion exploded between them and lifted them. Looking up at the skylight, Allie felt as though she were soaring straight up into the endless blue of the sky in weightless, effortless flight.

Afterward he held her closer than ever. Tightly, as though he wanted never to let go. She felt heavier now, but it was a comfortable heaviness, like the tingling heaviness that comes just before healthy, restful sleep. She felt warm, cherished, happy.

"Happiness is always temporary," Celia had said.

Knowing that, agreeing with that, Allie thought that perhaps the thing to do was just to hang on to whatever happiness presented itself, for as long as you possibly could.

CHAPTER NINE

SHE LOST COUNT of the number of times she and Colin made love in the little cottage on the south shore. By morning, she barely even remembered the two of them working side by side in the kitchen around 10:00 p.m., fixing a chicken dinner because they had suddenly realized they were starving. Afterward, by mutual agreement, they had stayed the night, sleeping soundly in each other's arms, lulled by the sounds of the sea and the whistling frogs singing their little chiming song outside the open windows.

Around dawn they made love yet again, then Allie sorted through the groceries Colin had brought and made pancakes with blueberry sauce, accompanied by slices of paw-paw and freshly ground Colombian coffee. They ate on the terrace, looking out at the incredible blue of the sea, watching water splash high against the rocks below, watching the longtails soar.

They discussed their plans for the day like a married couple. Colin had customers coming in from the United States. He'd be tied up until five or so.

Allie was going to spend the day at Lionel's house, working with Simon in the attic.

Before they left the cottage, Colin drew her into his arms and looked at her tenderly. She stiffened for a moment, afraid he was going to speak of love again. But he said only, "It was a wonderful night, Allison." Then he kissed her.

Relieved, she kissed him back. She could handle this after all, as long as they kept it casual. If she plunged in too deeply, the thought of leaving Bermuda would be unbearable. And she had to go, she had to.

Colin drove her to Lionel's house. "Shall I pick you up here around five-thirty or so?" he asked.

She shook her head. "I'll take a bus back to the guest house. I have to change and pick up my camera gear. I'm going into Hamilton with Celia to film the Beating the Retreat ceremony."

He looked at her as though to check if she were making excuses again, then raised his eyebrows. "Am I permitted to accompany you?"

She grinned. "Sure. You can be a production assistant like Celia."

"Sounds impressive. What does it mean?"

"It means you get to carry the recorder."

He sighed. "Exploitation."

"No doubt, as Mac would say."

He kissed her on the cheek and smiled. "I don't seem to mind being exploited. I'll meet you at the guest house then. Outside," he specified.

She laughed. "Would you be avoiding Mrs. Tolliver? I wonder why. Meet me there around six o'clock, okay? I want to get a good position."

She started to get out of the car, gesturing him back when he would have come around to open her door for her. "I can manage to let myself—" she began, then broke off, listening. "It sounds as if Lionel and Taylor are having an argument," she said resignedly. "Maybe I should ride into town with you and come back a little later."

Colin got out on his side of the car, listening, too. "Not Taylor," he said after a moment. "That's Simon Lionel he's arguing with. Perhaps we ought to find out what's going on."

With a strong presentiment of trouble, Allie approached the open front door. Colin was right behind her. "I can't imagine Lionel being angry," he murmured as they stood inside the entry hall, neither of them sure if they should enter or not.

Once they decided to go on in, it took Allie a few minutes more to figure out what the argument was about. Lionel and Simon were both standing, facing each other stiffly, with almost identical expressions of outrage on their faces. Corded veins stood out on both their foreheads. Neither man acknowledged Allie's presence, though she was sure both knew she was there. They were shouting cryptic sentences at each other, snapping off the ends of their words. "Why would I come back today?" Simon demanded.

"To avoid suspicion?" Lionel said.

Allie still couldn't quite make out what was going on, but she didn't like the sound of it at all.

When she finally did understand, she wanted the carpeted floor to open up and swallow her whole. Lionel was pointing out hotly that the fact remained that Tallah's emerald necklace was missing.

"How could I even know there was a necklace?" Simon yelled back. "I never even heard of anyone called Tallah."

Colin touched Lionel's arm gently. "Simon wasn't here when you showed the necklace to Allison," he confirmed.

Lionel sat down heavily in his recliner, but he didn't lean back in a relaxed way. He sat on the front edge of the chair, holding on to his white cane as though it were the only stable thing in his world. "I'm not accusing you," he said to Simon in a grim voice. He turned his head toward Allie and Colin. "I haven't accused anyone. I merely asked Simon if he had seen Tallah's necklace and he started shouting at me. That necklace was in my dresser drawer yesterday morning. I wanted to keep track of it so I could give it to you at an appropriate time, Allison. Taylor and I were gone all day yesterday, visiting our sick friend. And when I went to get the necklace this morning, to take it into Hamilton for cleaning, it was gone."

"Did you ask Taylor about it?"

"Taylor stayed overnight with our friend. He would hardly take my jewelry with him, Allison."

"Then you *are* accusing Simon, Lionel," she said gently. "I wasn't here yesterday. You know that. If you're sure Taylor doesn't have the necklace, then there's nobody else left, is there?"

Lionel inclined his head toward Simon. "Just tell me straight out that you didn't take the necklace, Simon, and I'll believe you," he said flatly.

Simon gazed at him narrow eyed. Allie could feel how upset he was. He looked absolutely miserable, his liquid dark eyes dulled and without hope. She could almost read his mind. To think that Lionel Entwhistle—the whistler—his teacher, the man he admired more than any other, could suspect for one minute that he would steal from him...

"Did anyone else come to the house yesterday, Simon?" she asked gently, thinking that perhaps he'd called in a friend to help him and the friend had wandered around the house. Celia had said his friends often got Simon into trouble.

"I was here alone all day," Simon said.

Allie waited expectantly for him to answer Lionel, to deny all knowledge of the necklace. But instead he simply turned on his heel and walked out the front door.

"Perhaps I should go after him," Colin said, turning.

Lionel held out a hand toward him. "No, let him go," he said wearily.

"The police?" Colin suggested.

Lionel shook his head. "I'd rather give the boy a chance to bring it back."

"You really do think he stole it?" Allie asked, hearing Simon's moped start up.

"When I came back last night, I could tell that my bedroom had been tidied beyond recognition, Allison," Lionel related sadly. "This morning Simon said he'd done it to surprise me. It was an awful mess, he said. Which was true. However, he had even tidied the contents of my drawers."

"And the necklace was missing," Allie said with a sigh.

"Unfortunately, yes."

"Well, Allison," Colin began.

She turned to him. "Don't you dare tell me you told me so," she said hotly.

"I did, you know."

She was furious. "I will not believe Simon stole that necklace."

"You'll grant he's irresponsible? And a convincing liar? You do remember he convinced you he'd arranged an appointment with me."

"That was just a childish trick. He was trying to impress Celia." She turned back to Lionel. "You're sure the necklace isn't in your room? You checked in all the drawers?"

"Of course."

"Could I take a look?"

"Of course, my dear, but it's not—"

"Look, Allison, I'm going to have to leave," Colin said.

She nodded shortly, still upset with him, with the situation, with the day that had started out so promisingly. "Okay," she answered curtly.

"I really think we should call the police," he said. "That's a valuable—"

"You've already decided he's guilty, haven't you?" she said.

"Well, it certainly looks—"

"No police," Lionel said. "We'll work this out somehow."

Colin looked at them both, then sighed and turned away. "I'll see you at the guest house later," he told Allie.

Allie nodded, then headed up the stairs to Lionel's bedroom. Colin had sounded disapproving, but she wasn't going to let herself worry about him. She was going to make a thorough search, she decided. She was going to find that necklace.

But the necklace wasn't there. Allie searched for the best part of two hours, noting the thorough cleaning job Simon had done. Why had he done that, she wondered after she'd given up and resumed her work in the attic. Simon was supposed to be working in the attic yesterday. That was what she had paid him for. Was Colin right about him? Had Taylor been right not to trust him? Quite suddenly, she was remembering that she *wasn't* always right about people—she hadn't been right about Curtis Yost, for example.

Around noon Lionel went out. He was supposed to give a lecture at a local school, he said. He seemed very subdued, saddened. Allie felt guilty. She had brought Simon here. If he had stolen the necklace then she was responsible. No! She wouldn't, *couldn't* believe that Simon had stolen from Lionel.

She called Celia at the Visitors' Bureau to confirm their date for the evening and also to check on Simon. Simon had stopped by to tell her what had happened, Celia said. He was very upset. He was never going to live down his reputation, he'd said. He might as well live up to it.

"What did he mean?" Allie asked.

"I don't know," Celia said. "He was too unhappy to make much sense." She sounded so miserable herself that Allie's heart went out to her.

THE BEATING THE RETREAT ceremony took place on Hamilton's Front Street several times during the tourist season, beginning at 9:00 p.m. Allie had already taped the street in daylight, knowing tourists would love the row of quaint yet elegant shops and the horse-drawn carriages waiting serenely at the edge of the sidewalk. She had recorded most of Hamilton when she'd first arrived, enjoying the architectural medley of old wood and limestone buildings and small white roofed cottages mixed in with some very modern office buildings, a grand cathedral and some beautiful administrative buildings, one with a model of the *Sea Venture* serving as a weather vane.

Two huge ocean liners, blazing with light from bow to stern, were docked right at the edge of Front Street, towering over the city, making the town look as if it were tied up to the ships rather than the other way around.

The ceremonial parade itself actually dated back to before the Napoleonic Wars, where it had begun as a ceremony to mark the end of the day.

"It's a good thing we got here early," Allie said to Colin, looking around at the hundreds of sightseers lining the street. A very young policeman, pink cheeked and adorable in Bermuda shorts, shirt and tie and an English bobby's blue helmet had told her the corner of Front Street and Burnaby would be the best place from which to view the parade, and she had already set up her camera on its tripod.

"Are you going to have enough light?" Colin asked. The sun had already gone down.

"I checked on that first thing," she told him. She gestured at the buildings behind them. "The policeman told me all those floodlights would come on when the ceremony starts.''

"I don't know what I'm doing here," Celia said. She was wearing a cheerfully bright-red dress with a full skirt, but she looked as miserable as Simon had earlier in the day.

Allie glanced at her sympathetically. "You've no idea where Simon is, Celia. There's not a thing you can do for him. You might as well be with us.''

"I could be at the whistler's house, telling him he's mad to think Si would steal from him.''

"It didn't help that he ran away," Colin pointed out.

Allie glared at him. "He didn't run away. He walked out.''

"Same thing," Colin said. "He should have stayed and defended himself.''

"Simon gets frightened," Celia explained. "He expects people to think the worst of him, so he just disappears.'' She gazed at Colin pleadingly. "I know it looks bad, but Simon isn't a thief, Mr. Endicott. Really, he isn't. Please believe me.''

"I believe you believe in him," Colin said, which apparently satisfied Celia but didn't satisfy Allie.

However, just as she was about to reopen the argument, a hush descended on the crowd. In the darkness of the street a single staccato drumbeat sounded. Allie switched on her camera, feeling the hair on the back of her neck stand up. Along the street, in the place where a policeman usually stood in his "bird cage," directing traffic, another drumbeat answered.

From Allie's end of the street the invisible drummer played another roll. Then the floodlights the policeman had promised her came on and the Bermuda regimental band began to play a stirring march. Far down the street, the bagpipe section joined in with a loud wail. Then the two bands marched and countermarched, weaving in and out of each other, black faces, white faces, equally solemn and proud. One group wore band uniforms and pith helmets, the other kilts and full Scottish regalia.

For almost an hour Allie was kept busy recording the colorful ceremony. "You're going to shoot all of it?" Colin queried when there was a short pause in the action.

She nodded. "Cheapest thing I've got is tape. I can even use it over, remember. And I brought along a spare battery. I've no idea what I'll want to keep, so I'll just get all the footage I can. I'll edit a lot of it out later—most shots won't last longer than three seconds—but I don't want to miss anything potentially dramatic. Like that drum major's chin, for instance." She switched on the camera again as the man in question, who was clad in full Highland costume, stamped his feet directly in front of them and twirled a silver-headed baton almost as tall as he was.

She taped continuously until the Scottish sword dances had been going for several minutes. Then she decided a little of that was enough, and started panning the watching crowd. After a few seconds of that she panned one of the American ocean liners, focusing on the passengers hanging over the deck rails. Then she cut to the fairy lights strung between the ship's masts and zoomed in on a sole crew member or passenger watching alone from the observation deck, smoking a cigarette.

Simon Leverett!

Her exclamation was muffled in a burst of bagpipe music directly in front of her. She looked sideways at Celia and saw that she was completely engrossed in watching the kilted drummers whirling their drumsticks. Pulling on the sleeve of Colin's striped rugby shirt, she directed his attention to the viewfinder. He took a look and exclaimed as she had, then glanced quickly at Celia, who was still not paying attention to either of them.

"Stay here, all right?" he murmured in Allie's ear as he gestured in Simon's direction.

Allie nodded and went back to taping the bands, afraid that if she kept on watching Simon, light might flash off her camera lens and alert Simon to its position.

The ceremony was drawing to a close, with the pipers playing "Amazing Grace," a tune that never failed to bring a lump to Allie's throat. Then the bands massed right in front of Allie's camera—bless that helpful young policeman—and someone started lowering the Union Jack, which had been fluttering behind a dais full of dignitaries across the street. It was a dramatic moment, drawn out to its fullest suspense by the music, bringing spontaneous applause from the crowd.

Once this final ceremony was over, people started milling around, then pushing in different directions.

Allie stood her ground, packing up her video gear with Celia's help. "Where's Colin?" Celia asked.

Allie shrugged. "He was here a minute ago," she said truthfully, then caught sight of Colin, his head above most of the crowd, fighting the flow to get back to them. She couldn't see Simon, but Colin raised a hand, forming a circle with his thumb and index finger. "I guess he's found Simon," Allie said thankfully.

"What did you say?" Celia asked, but by then Simon was in sight, also. Colin was holding on to Si's shoulder, evidently not taking any chances of him bolting. "Si," Celia exclaimed, flinging her arms around him, her face radiant. "I've been so worried. Where on earth were you?"

"On the *Nordic Prince*," he said with a sheepish grin.

Celia looked unbelievingly at the ocean liner that dominated the other side of the street. "Si Leverett, are you saying you stowed away?"

He nodded. "It was easy, Celie. Nothing to it. I just walked on while everyone was walking off to go shopping this afternoon. Nobody even noticed me. I'll bet I could have gone clear to New York."

"Leaving me behind."

"I'd have let you know where I was. I need a fresh start, Celie," he said earnestly. "I need to go somewhere where nobody knows me, where nobody expects me to do wrong all the time."

"Running away doesn't help anybody," Colin said, placing a hand on Simon's shoulder again, looking as if he wanted to shake him. "First you have to clear yourself, then if you want to go to the States you can go with my blessing. By some more acceptable route. Did you steal that necklace, Simon?''

"Of course he didn't steal it!" Allie exploded. She glared at Colin. "Simon's been told all his life that he's a troublemaker. What he needs is for people to believe in him. Celia believes in him. So do I. You could at least give him the benefit of the doubt.''

Simon looked at her gratefully. Colin grinned at her. "Remind me to keep you on my side always, will you?'' he said. He glanced back at Simon. "Let me put my question another way, Si. You didn't steal that necklace, did you?''

Si looked up into his face and shook his head. "No, Mr. Endicott. I really didn't. But you know nobody's going to take my word for it. I was in the house alone. I don't have any idea what happened to the dumb necklace. I don't even know what it looks like. Is it diamonds? The way the whistler acted, I suppose it must be diamonds.''

Colin let out his breath. "Either you're telling the truth, or we should get you a job as an actor, Si," he said.

Allie smiled at him. "You believe him," she said. Then she hugged Simon. "I believed you all along, Si.'' She looked at him reproachfully. "You shouldn't have been in such a hurry to leave. Injured pride doesn't get you anywhere, Si. The circumstantial evidence was against you. You did tidy all of Lionel's drawers.''

Simon sighed heavily. "I got to the house early, and I wanted to do something nice for him. I wasn't going to charge you for the time, Allie. I just wanted to surprise the whistler."

"Well, you did that all right," Allie said. She shook her head. "Promise me, Simon, if someone accuses you unjustly of something or even seems to accuse you, just tell them very simply that you didn't do it."

"I wanted the whistler to trust me," he replied miserably.

"You have to earn trust," Colin pointed out, then he gripped Si's shoulder. "You've got my trust, Si. Now you have to earn the whistler's."

"Like how?" Si asked, looking suspicious.

"By coming to his house now, telling him straight out that you didn't steal the necklace."

"We'll all come with you, Si," Allie said as Simon shook his head.

"You have to do it," Celia said firmly. "If you don't, I'm never going to speak to you again."

Simon sighed. "All right. It looks like I'm outnumbered. I'll go, but what happens if Mr. Entwhistle doesn't believe me?"

"That's a chance you have to take," Colin said.

"We'll make him believe you," Allie promised, ignoring Colin's raised eyebrows. Okay, so it was a rash promise, but she had every faith in her ability to convince Lionel of Simon's innocence.

LIONEL WASN'T EASY to convince. "You stowed away on the *Nordic Prince*? Is that the act of an innocent man?" he asked, inclining his head toward Colin.

"Tell him, Simon," Allie urged.

"I did not steal the necklace," Simon said stiffly. "I'm sorry if you don't believe me, and I can't prove I didn't take it. I can only offer you my word."

If Lionel could only see the pain on Simon's face, Allie thought, he would know the young man was telling the unvarnished truth.

Even as she thought this she saw that Lionel's head was tilted, as though he were listening very intently to something no one else could hear. There was a moment's silence, then Lionel said with great dignity, "I'm sorry I ever believed otherwise, Simon. I believe you now."

Simon let out a long breath and gripped the older man's outstretched hand between both of his. But then just as Allie was letting herself relax, a frowning Taylor appeared in the doorway. "Why didn't somebody tell me it was Beating the Retreat night?" he complained. "I couldn't get out of Hamilton for an hour." He scowled at Simon, then looked at Lionel. "I see you still have that young man here. I'm telling you, Lionel, you're going to regret having him in the house. He's not to be trusted."

Simon immediately stiffened. So did Celia. "Mr. Entwhistle believes me," Simon said flatly. "He knows I didn't touch that necklace."

Taylor looked bewildered. "What are you talking about?"

"Tallah's necklace," Lionel said patiently. "It's missing, Taylor. I'm afraid I suspected Simon of taking it, but he assures me he didn't and I believe him. I just have to check again, I suppose. I must have missed it somehow."

"Tallah's necklace?" Taylor echoed. The most shamefaced expression Allie had ever seen had appeared on his wrinkled face. Lionel, of course, could not see it and went on explaining. As he talked, Taylor looked more and more uncomfortable. He was actually blushing—the most brilliant scarlet.

Finally Allie broke in. "You put Tallah's necklace somewhere, didn't you, Taylor?" she suggested.

He nodded, then started blustering. "Damn fool boy. How was I supposed to know he *could* be trusted? Knew his reputation. Always in trouble."

"You hid the necklace?" Lionel asked.

"Along with my pension check and your mother's pearls and your grandmother's silver cutlery," Taylor said gruffly. "Safekeeping. We were going to be away all day. Afraid the boy would take them. Put them all in the pantry, under the onions. Before we went out yesterday morning. Meant to tell you, but forgot all about it. You know how my memory is."

"Hell and damnation, Taylor," Lionel said with a rueful grimace. "I as good as accused Simon of stealing Tallah's necklace."

"I suppose you want me to get it out?" the old man asked.

"If you'd be so kind," Lionel said with heavy sarcasm. "I'm so sorry, Simon," he said when Taylor left the room. "This is what comes of two old men outliving their usefulness to society. We need a keeper, I'm afraid. I should have known Taylor was involved somehow. But it just didn't occur to me that he might have moved the necklace after I checked on it."

"It was easier to blame me," Simon said bitterly.

Celia shot him a worried glance and his face relaxed. "I suppose I can't hold that against you, sir," he said to Lionel. "I'm just glad you said you believed me *before* Mr. Rossiter came in."

Allie jumped in with a description of the Beating the Retreat ceremony, feeling that the subject definitely needed changing. She was aware that Colin was watching her, aware, too, that he knew why she was talking so much. His approval was obvious. How was it, she wondered, that he could read her intentions so easily? And how was it that *she* knew so clearly what *he* was thinking?

"I made a pot of coffee," Taylor said, coming back with a cardboard box and placing it on Lionel's lap.

Lionel's nose wrinkled immediately. "Onions," he snorted. "Why in God's name would anyone hide jewelry among Bermuda onions?" He laughed. "Wait till you try to cash that pension check, Taylor. They're going to turn their noses up in that bank, tell you to go home and take a bath."

"I'd love some coffee," Celia said tactfully, as Taylor's face purpled. "May I help you serve it, Mr. Rossiter?" she offered, getting up and ushering him out of the room, keeping his mind occupied with talk of ground coffee versus instant.

"Wish I could make up to you for all this, Simon," Lionel said gloomily, setting the box down beside his chair.

"That's not necessary," Simon said.

Allie leaned forward.

"Allison," Colin murmured, but she chose to ignore him.

"Poor Simon's out of work," she told Lionel. Colin looked surprised and she remembered she hadn't told him Simon had quit. "The job at the Botanical Gardens turned out to be temporary," she went on. Well, that was sort of true.

"Of course, Simon will be helping me in the attic," she continued, still managing to ignore Colin's pointed glance. "But that won't last forever. Do you know of anyone who might give him a job?"

"Allison!" Simon and Colin objected at the same time.

Perhaps that *had* been a little blatant, Allison conceded.

Luckily Taylor came in with the coffee tray at that moment. "That's a nice young woman," he told Simon with a smile, evidently trying to make amends for his earlier behavior. "She's scrubbing up the whole kitchen." He sighed. "Women are so much better at that sort of thing."

Allie opened her mouth to object to that statement, then closed it again. There wasn't much point in trying to reform a ninety-year-old male chauvinist. In any case a much better idea had occurred to her. "Celia likes things to be tidy," she said casually, accepting a cup of coffee. "Simon, too—it's one of the things they have in common. You should see the job he's doing in the attic, Lionel. You'll be able to find anything you want when he gets through. Poor Celia, though," she added, still studiously avoiding Colin's narrow-eyed gaze. "She has so many jobs, I don't see how she manages them all, and when she is at home she has to put up with a couple of untidy roommates. She and

Simon can't afford to take up housekeeping together, though they'd really like to get married. Did you know Simon wants to be a teacher?'' she asked Lionel, hoping some of the seeds she was so assiduously planting would germinate.

Colin was laughing under his breath, she saw. Laughing at *her*, Allie was sure. But she didn't mind. She had finally engaged Lionel's attention.

"Now why would you want to be a teacher, Simon?" he asked, gently. "Don't you know the pay is terrible and the hours are worse? You're never really off the job. There are always papers to grade, lessons to prepare."

"I used to take my littlest sister to nursery school," Simon said with a dreamy expression on his dark features. "I'd watch her...all those little children, looking so big eyed, so bright, all of them asking questions, questions. Now she's fifteen, could care less about questions, dropped out of school. All that brightness is gone. Seems to me—" He broke off, looking self-conscious.

"Go on, Simon," Lionel urged, sitting up straight in his chair.

"Well, I just wonder sometimes what happens in schools. People ought to keep that curiosity, that brightness. It shouldn't be squashed out of them with boredom. School ought to be fun, interesting." He looked directly at Lionel and Allie wished the older man could see the almost worshipful expression on his young face. "I remember when you taught geography, sir. It was like you took me to the top of a hill and spread the whole world at my feet and said, 'Hey, look here, Simon Leverett, this is all yours.' "

Colin's expression had softened, Allie was pleased to see. Lionel's face had crumpled in on itself. He hadn't needed to see Simon's face to be deeply moved. "Best compliment I ever had on my teaching, Simon," he told the boy after swallowing hard a couple of times.

Simon sighed. "That's the kind of teacher I'd like to be," he noted dreamily, then shook his head. "Whoever heard of a teacher who doesn't have an education himself?" He stood. "I'll go help Celie in the kitchen. That's probably where I best belong."

"I did that young man a profound disservice," Lionel admitted slowly after Simon had left the room. "He has the makings of a fine citizen."

"I think so, too," Allie said. "It's too bad he's never going to have a chance at a higher education."

"How old is he?" Lionel asked.

"Twenty-one."

"Hmm. Not really too late then," Lionel said softly, speaking more to himself than to Allie.

Time to let all those seeds germinate, Allie decided. She stood, too. "Maybe we should be getting along?" she suggested to Colin.

"Oh? You don't have any more tidbits of information to impart?"

Allie glanced at Lionel. He was frowning in a puzzled way. Allie turned back to Colin and put her finger to her lips. He was laughing silently and after a moment she joined in.

"You were shameless," he told her when they were alone in the car.

Simon and Celia had decided to take the bus home. Celia wanted to finish working in the kitchen. "Such a lovely big kitchen," she'd said wistfully. Lionel wanted to talk to Simon more about teaching.

"It's working, all the same," she said. "You watch, Lionel's going to offer to help Simon. And I wouldn't be surprised if he didn't invite Celia to try being his housekeeper. It would be perfect. She likes keeping house and she's so down-to-earth. She'd take good care of Lionel and Taylor."

"Little Miss Fix-it," Colin said as he'd said before. "Is it any wonder that I—" He broke off, leaning forward as though something in his driving required his full attention. Then he said, "Will you come home with me, Allison?"

An image of gilt-framed oil paintings looming out of the dark lodged itself in her mind. "Macintosh?" she said tentatively.

"Mac goes to bed promptly at ten. He won't even know you're there."

"It's pretty late, Colin. I don't think..."

He glanced at her sideways, then pulled the car to the side of the road and killed the engine. "Is it still the house?" he asked. "Even after last night?" He turned to face her, going on before she could say anything. "I can't come to the guest house with you. Aida Tolliver..."

"I agree," she said fervently. "Not a good idea at all."

Looking very frustrated, he put his arms around her, drew her close and began kissing her. She liked the way he kissed. His mouth was firm, confident and dry. He didn't press too hard or thrust his tongue in her mouth before she'd warmed up to him. Nor did he pin her head with his hands so that she couldn't move. His lips coaxed her, persuaded her... although she certainly didn't need any persuasion. One hand cupped the back of her head gently, his fingers tangling in her hair but exerting only minimum pressure. The other hand moved delicately across her back, then touched lightly on her breast, just resting against the soft fabric of her sweatshirt, his thumb grazing the nipple as though accidentally.

Her whole body was responding to him as enthusiastically, as eagerly as it had responded the previous night. Just as she had feared, she was no longer content with kissing. She wanted to make love. Now. Here in his car on the side of the road where someone else's car could pass at any time, headlights gleaming.

Her blood was racing through her body, her insides were melting, her heart was completely out of control—she could hear it beating erratically against her rib cage. She pulled him closer. Her lips hardened and parted under his. "Colin," she murmured against his mouth.

"Allison, Allison," he whispered back. Then his mouth moved delicately across her cheekbone, planting small kisses as it went. "We could go to a hotel, I suppose," he murmured in her ear. "I must say, though, I don't much like the thought of..."

She shook her head.

Abruptly he set her away from him and looked directly into her face. "Is it really the house, or is it Diana?" he asked.

She drew in a long breath, then let it out again. "Aren't they the same thing?" she said gently.

He frowned down at her, not answering for what seemed a long time, then he turned away and started the car. "Where are we going?" she asked.

"My house," he said, adding when she made a small sound of protest, "Dammit, Allison, it's time we had this out. Twice now you've made reference to my grieving. Remember the lecture you gave me about taking the monsters out of the closet? We're going to do it together, right now. You may think less of me when I'm done, but that's a chance I have to take."

CHAPTER TEN

IT WAS AFTER MIDNIGHT when they arrived at End Court. Taking Allie's hand, Colin pulled her with him into the house and along the hall to his study. She breathed a sigh of relief when they passed the staircase. She'd been afraid he intended taking her up there, and no matter how much she wanted to make love with him she couldn't, not in this house.

"Look here," he said, turning on the brilliant overhead lights. He was pointing at the portrait of Diana in riding clothes that hung above the marble fireplace. "This is my wife, the woman who helped me rebuild this house, the woman I lived with for six years. I keep her portrait there because she wanted it there and it seems to belong there, not out of any feeling that this room, this house, is a shrine."

"I know you loved her, Colin," Allie said gently. "I've no desire to trespass on your feelings or psychoanalyze them, but do you really feel comfortable in this house?"

He look bewildered. "Why shouldn't I?" he replied.

"Do you remember what Lionel said?" she asked him. "He talked about the feelings between people and how jangled they could be. That's how I feel here.

Jangled.'' She sighed. ''I guess it's just me. Maybe if you told me a little more about the house, it might change the way I feel.''

Frowning, he looked up at his wife's portrait. ''Diana found this house,'' he said. ''I had a house in Pembroke Parish, not too far from Hamilton, handy for my furniture company. It wasn't a big house, but it had a marvelous view of the harbor and all those little islands—have you seen them?''

She nodded. ''From the Belmont Hotel.''

''Diana wanted a bigger house, a classier house,'' he explained. ''She looked for weeks, every day, driving every lane and alley and street in Bermuda. And eventually she found this place.'' He shrugged. ''I've never cared much about where I lived, as long as it was in Bermuda and I had a roof that would collect rainwater. And the restoration work was a challenge. I enjoyed doing it. So did Diana. We were very happy working on the house, and I grew to love it as much as she did.'' He sighed. ''I'm afraid I was a sore disappointment to Diana in most other ways. The only thing we did agree on was this house.''

Diana was a wee bit of a snob, Mac had said. She wanted Colin to socialize more, then to go into politics.

''Anyway, as I told you before, when the house was finished, Diana didn't have enough to keep her occupied. Having brought the house up to snuff, she decided to start on me. She was going to turn me into a gentleman of leisure.''

He raked his fingers through his hair as though remembering former impatience. ''Oh, she didn't state

it in so many words, but she started urging me to sell
the company, to invest the profits and live on the interest. She thought my 'lectures' about my work, as
she called them, were boring. She didn't like the calluses on my hands. She didn't like my plebian habit of
working nine to five. That was *her* word, plebian—
lower class." He sighed. "The more I resisted all her
suggestions, the more she grew to hate Bermuda. She
began a campaign to get me to move to England—to
be with my parents, supposedly."

Shaking his head, he put an arm around Allie's
shoulders and led her to the kitchen, where he started
preparing coffee. "I love my parents, Allison, but I
don't need to live with them. They manage just fine by
themselves. I visit them every year. Diana, of course,
enjoyed our annual jaunt—she was able to keep up
with all her friends and see her family." He smiled
wryly. "If I wasn't enough gentleman for Diana, who
loved me, you can imagine what her family thought of
me." He laughed shortly. "Diana ignored all that. If
I didn't want to live with *my* parents, then *her* parents
could give us an apartment in Blade Hall. We could
ride to hounds, play polo, sail, go to London for the
theater season, live like real people."

Allie brought cups from the cabinet, remembering
where they were stored. He nodded thanks, but she
had the feeling he wasn't really noticing what she was
doing; he was watching the coffee water gurgle
through the grounds as though fascinated by the sight.

"Diana would not have made this coffee," he said
abruptly. "She would have rousted out Mac or one of
the maids—we had two when she lived here. She

would certainly not have considered it suitable for me to prepare food in my own kitchen.''

He turned around, leaning back against the kitchen counter, looking apologetically at Allie. "I sound as if I'm whining. I'm sorry. I did love her, Allie. We loved each other, but not quite enough, I'm afraid. I certainly didn't realize before we were married, or even in the early days of our marriage, that I was entirely the wrong husband for Diana Blade of the Sussex Blades.

"She died about the time I did realize it," he went on heavily. He was silent again, for a couple of minutes, looking down at the tiled floor. Then he raised his head and met Allie's sympathetic gaze directly. "You talked about me grieving," he said. "The trouble was, I couldn't grieve enough. We had grown so far apart I didn't have enough to grieve for. I could only feel guilty, because I had buried myself in my book, I hadn't tried to help her, I hadn't offered to go to England with her. I hadn't even driven her to the airport. I hadn't loved her enough to become the man she wanted me to be.''

He held up a palm as she exclaimed. "Oh, I know, Allison, I could never have become that person even if I'd wanted to. I no longer blame myself for staying true to myself. I just blame myself for ignoring the problems we had.''

He shook his head. "After she died, it seemed a terrible thing that we had wasted so many years. We started out so happily, with such good intentions. Perhaps if we'd had children... well, it just didn't happen. All there was left of six years of marriage was this house. Don't you see, I have to stay in this house. I owe it to Diana.''

Allison shook her head. "I'm sorry, Colin, I'm afraid I don't see that.''

"The day she left, Diana came into my study," he said as if she hadn't spoken. "I was writing. She said she just wanted to tell me she loved me. Whatever might happen I should always remember that she loved me. There were tears in her eyes.'' His own eyes met Allie's, shadowed, haunted. "It seemed to me afterward," he said slowly, "that she must have had some kind of premonition. Somehow she must have known she was going to die.''

It was perfectly obvious to Allie that Diana had not intended coming back. She had intended staying in England with her lover, Bruce Perry. "It wasn't necessarily a *premonition*," Allie said carefully.

She hesitated. No, she couldn't possibly tell him, even though she felt he should be told. If only he'd reached some realization himself. "You said to me once that there was some talk when Diana died," she ventured. "You wondered if Mrs. Tolliver had told me anything.''

He nodded. "There was some talk about the fact that Diana was going off to England without me. Someone started a rumor that we were getting a divorce.''

"But you weren't.''

He shook his head. "We should have probably, but the subject hadn't even come up. We didn't talk about *anything*, Allison.'' He smiled ruefully. "We didn't have Allison Bentley around to make us take the monsters out of our closets. We were just terribly well-bred about our failed marriage. We accepted it as it was, with stiff upper lips and all that.''

''You didn't even fight?''

''Never. We resolved our differences quite traditionally. I buried myself in work. Diana began going out more and more, meeting friends, going to parties—there are always parties in Bermuda, Allison. Diana was out night after night. I didn't like it, but I didn't try to stop her. It was a relief in a way that she'd found something to do. Later I realized exactly what she was up to, of course, but I was rather ostrichlike at the time.''

Relief swept through her. ''You do know about Bruce Perry then. I told Mac you probably did, but he—''

The words had barely even left her mouth before she knew she had made a terrible mistake. He *hadn't* known. He *hadn't* even suspected.

There was no way to call the words back. ''Colin,'' she said tentatively, trying to come up with some explanation that would change what she'd said, make it sound more innocent, less deadly.

But it was too late. Colin might not have known or suspected that his wife was having an affair with Bruce Perry, but the moment Allie as good as told him what had been going on he had recognized it as truth in one blinding flash. All color had left his face. ''Good Lord,'' he said. ''How stupid of me not to have seen...'' He was looking at Allie as if she were a stranger.

"You said you knew what she was up to," she whispered.

He seemed to be making an effort to remember. "I meant—I thought that she was probably trying to wake me up to what was wrong with our marriage, she was trying to force me into doing something about it. Truly, I had no idea that she and Bruce . . ."

He rallied a little. "Mac told you, you said."

"Not really," she answered miserably. "He hinted at it, and I told him I already knew. Mrs. Tolliver . . ."

"Mrs. Tolliver," he echoed heavily. "So then everyone knew. Except me. I really believed it was a coincidence that Bruce and Ian were on that airplane. As much of a coincidence as Johnny Barlow's nephew. Lots of residents make regular trips to England or the U.S. or other places. Bruce Perry. He was my closest friend. I grieved for him, too, when he died."

He looked her in the eye, but his own eyes were cloudy. "She was leaving me forever, wasn't she? She wasn't coming back. That's what she meant when she said 'whatever happens.' And I thought she was clairvoyant." He laughed shortly, but there was no humor in the sound. Then he turned abruptly and headed for the door into the hall.

"Colin," she began.

He stopped but didn't turn around. One hand gripped the doorjamb, gripped it so hard his knuckles turned white. "You must excuse me, Allison," he said in a voice that was scrupulously polite. "I just can't . . ."

A thickness had come into his voice now and his shoulders were uncharacteristically bowed. She had an idea that if she could see his eyes there would be moisture in them. There was an answering moisture in her own eyes, prickling behind her eyelids, threatening to spill over.

She didn't know what to do. She wanted to go to him, to hold him, to tell him how sorry she was, how she would rather have cut out her tongue than cause him a second's grief. But the formality of his voice had built a wall between them that she couldn't possibly scale.

"Would you mind terribly if I asked you to phone for a taxi to take you back to Mrs. Tolliver's?" he said. "There's a number on the bulletin board above the telephone, I believe."

Without waiting for an answer, he left the kitchen, moving uncertainly, as though he weren't quite sure if the floor was level. A moment later she heard his footsteps on the stairs.

Feeling desperately sorry for him, Allie started to follow, but then thought better of it and veered off toward the telephone. Just as she picked up the receiver, Mac came into the room. "I'll take you home, lassie," he said quietly. He was wearing a soft velour robe over his pajamas, which somehow made him look less erect than usual.

She slammed the receiver onto its base and ran across the kitchen into the old man's waiting arms. "Oh, Mac, I've done a terrible thing," she blurted out. "I misunderstood something Colin said and I told him about Diana and Bruce. It just came out."

"Aye, I know," he said, reaching to pat her shoulder awkwardly. He was a couple of inches shorter than she. "I was eavesdropping in yon dining room. I was in there drinking a mug of hot milk when the two of you came in here. A wee bit of indigestion tonight for some reason, so I couldn't sleep. I didn't want to make my presence known and embarrass you, and there was no way out without you'd see me."

"What am I going to do, Mac?" Allie asked, extricating herself gently from the old man's arms. "He looked so hurt, so shocked...devastated. Do you think I should go up and try to talk to him?"

He shook his head. "I don't know what's right, lassie. I do know when he gets over the initial shock he's going to be powerful mad with yours truly. I believe you also let it out that I knew all along?" His voice was dry, but his eyes showed sympathy.

She winced. "I did, didn't I? I'm sorry, Mac. I can't imagine why I was so stupid."

"Love does strange things to people, lassie."

She could hardly explain to him at this moment that he had misread the situation, that it was Colin who had talked about love, not her. Though it was almost certain that Colin was no longer in love, if he ever really had been.

"I'm thinking it's best to let him be for a while," Mac said. "I'll take you home and we'll see what a good night's sleep will do for us all."

"You really think he'll sleep?"

He sighed. "I don't know. He's been awfully dense about this situation. There's no telling how he'll react."

ALLISON LAY AWAKE most the night, staring up at the dimly shadowed ceiling of her bedroom. She hadn't meant to hurt Colin and she had no idea how to go about improving the situation. It was beyond improving. She kept seeing his face, so white, so bleak, so stricken. Mac seemed to think it would be best for her to leave Colin alone to recover from the shock, to let him get in touch with her when he was ready. She didn't know if his advice was sound or not, but she certainly didn't want to chance calling Colin and having him refuse to speak to her.

She would wait, she decided sometime just before dawn. With that decision she fell into an uneasy sleep.

When she awakened, she felt exhausted. She realized she hadn't really taken any time off since she'd arrived in Bermuda. She'd hardly even gone out unencumbered by video gear. Surely she could spare one day to lie on the beach.

She chose a public beach on the north side of St. George that wasn't much frequented by tourists. It was quiet, almost deserted, and she lay on a beach towel and tried not to think about anything for a while. Occasionally she drifted off to sleep.

On Saturday, feeling refreshed but still very worried, she telephoned Colin's house from a pay phone. She certainly didn't want Mrs. Tolliver overhearing anything she might say.

No one answered the phone. She remembered that Macintosh spent weekends with his lady friend. Did that mean Colin was alone, not answering, or was he gone, too?

She rode her moped to Lionel's house, feeling a need for human contact. Celia answered the door, wearing a brilliant yellow dress with a crisp white apron over it. Lionel and Taylor were visiting their sick friend in Hamilton, she said. The friend was recovering, Taylor had told her.

The change in the house was astonishing. There was a sheen of polish on all the furniture; every piece of Victorian bric-a-brac had been dusted and thoughtfully arranged. The patterned carpeting looked freshly vacuumed. There were fresh flowers everywhere.

"You've been busy," Allie commented as Celia brought her a mug of coffee.

"Not as busy as I wanted. I had to baby-sit yesterday, but I came in last night for a couple of hours and again this morning early." She beamed at Allie. "I want to thank you. It was you who gave Lionel the ideas about me and Simon."

"He acted on them?"

"Did he ever! Simon has already moved in. He's going to start working on the grounds for Lionel and Taylor as soon as he gets finished going through the attic for you. I'm going to move in, too. I'll keep a couple of my jobs, but mostly I'll take care of this house. Si is going to look after the garden."

Allie felt disappointed. "He's still going to be a gardener?"

Celia's round pretty face was wreathed in smiles. "I haven't told you the best part yet. In September, Si will start classes at Bermuda College. Lionel is going to pay tuition. In return Si will do garden chores and take over the driving. Taylor's getting too old for driv-

ing—he's had a couple of near accidents recently."
Her smile widened even more, showing all her beautiful white teeth. Her dark eyes were glistening with happiness. "Best of all, Si and I are going to be married at Christmas."

Allie jumped to her feet and hugged her. "I'm delighted, Celia. I'm so glad everything turned out so well."

Celia hugged her back. "It's mostly your doing. You're our fairy godmother. Do you think you could come back for the wedding?"

Allie managed to hang on to her smile. She had talked to her mother the previous night after her day on the beach. Patricia had sounded happy and comfortable, but there had still been, underlying every word she'd spoken, the sort of breathiness Allie had noticed before. Patricia and her nurse both insisted the breathiness existed only in Allie's imagination—or in some disturbance on the line, perhaps—but there was something about it that made Allie uneasy. "I'd love to come to your wedding," she said, "but I'll have to see how my mother is doing by then." She took a deep breath. "I haven't told you, Celia, but—"

"Lionel told us," Celia said. Her face showed sympathy, but she was so happy with her own good fortune it was difficult for her to hold back her smile for long. "Your mother is going to be fine, Allie. I just know it. Everything is so wonderful and it's all because of you."

Allie hugged her again. "Simon had something to do with it, you know. Lionel wouldn't finance his education if he didn't know Simon has a high IQ. And you are so special Lionel could probably sense how good you'd be for this old house."

"Lionel says I light it up like a thousand candles glowing in the dark," Celia said with a fond smile. "I'm getting to love that old man all over again, Allie."

"What about Taylor?" Allie asked with a grin.

Celia laughed. "I can handle Taylor," she said firmly. "Don't you worry about that. Listen," she added as Allie sat down again and picked up her coffee cup. "Let me call Simon down—he has something he wants to tell you. He rang you up at Mrs. Tolliver's yesterday, but you were out. He left a message for you. Did you get it? Is that why you're here?"

Allie shook her head. "I haven't seen Mrs. Tolliver since Thursday morning. She's not around much on weekends. I guess she must be off socializing. I came to help Simon. Why don't I just go on up?"

The attic had also undergone a transformation. Simon had acquired a few boxes somewhere and had sorted through about one-third of the attic already. He was tying a bundle of newspapers together when Allie reached the top of the stairs. He glanced up, smiling from ear to ear. All his former moodiness had been banished from his expression. He looked young and eager and bright and very, very attractive. It was easy to see why Celia loved him. "Allie," he exclaimed. "I thought I heard a moped. Did Celia tell you our news?"

"She certainly did. Congratulations on all counts. Will you get to go on to university, do you suppose?"

A small cloud of uncertainty crossed his brow, then lifted. "I'll manage it somehow." He shook his head. "Did you get my message?"

"No. Celia told me you'd called, but..." It suddenly occurred to her that he wouldn't have called her just to say hello. "You've found something?" she exclaimed, her voice squeaking with excitement.

He nodded, beaming, then picked up a tiny package from on top of an old chest of drawers. Not Joseph's journal then. Allie felt a spurt of disappointment.

"I didn't pay much attention to it at first," Simon explained, handing over the tissue-wrapped package. "It was just sitting in a little box, inside a bigger box with all kinds of odds and ends. But then I took a good look at it and knew you'd have to see it. Lionel says you must take it home with you."

He was smiling very mysteriously. Allie struggled with the last of the tissue paper, not really expecting anything very much, and then saw that she was holding an old-fashioned miniature painting in a narrow oval frame. A head-and-shoulders painting of a woman of about forty years of age.

The woman had large dark eyes with a glint to them, a full mouth whose unsmiling stiffness could not disguise its generosity and, a strong straight nose. She was wearing Puritan dress—a neat little white cotton cap on her head and a plain white kerchief tied in front as a collar to her dark dress. She wore no ornament or decoration at all, and needed none—her hair itself was ornament enough. Though pushed back and evidently tied in a knot behind her head, it had a life of its own; curling tendrils had pushed out under the edges of the severe cotton bonnet, softening her face and the line of her collar. Her hair was as dark as the stuff of her dress, as dark as the night, as dark as Allie's own.

Allie drew in her breath. She might have been looking at a portrait of Patricia Bentley in costume dress, fifteen years ago. Or a portrait of herself twelve years into the future.

She became aware that Simon had said something to her. Feeling dazed, she looked at him enquiringly. "I said, she looks like you, doesn't she?"

Allie nodded mutely and returned to studying the miniature.

"She'd have to be Alys or Penelope, wouldn't you think?" Simon asked. Allie had told him the story of her ancestors—and Lionel's—as they worked together earlier in the week.

"Alys," Allie said firmly. There was no doubt in her mind at all. This was Alys. She could hardly wait to show the miniature to her mother.

Feeling greatly encouraged by Simon's finding of such a treasure, she went to work with a will and didn't give up for the day until Lionel called her down to have tea.

Riding back to the guest house on her moped, it occurred to her that if Mrs. Tolliver had neglected to give her Simon's message, she might have forgotten to give her a message from Colin. Accordingly, she went right up to Mrs. Tolliver's rooms the moment she arrived. But Mrs. Tolliver was not in her drawing room and there was no reply when Allie knocked on the door to her private apartment.

In the morning Allie took her camera out early to tape local people going to church. She had noticed the previous week that they dressed in their best and went together as families. She got some terrific shots, she felt, but she didn't attend church herself; she was too anxious to return to the guest house and see if any messages had arrived.

This time she heard footsteps as soon as she knocked on Mrs. Tolliver's door. "I'll answer it," a man's voice said. A familiar voice with a pronounced Scottish accent.

It was hard to say who was more embarrassed, Allie or Macintosh. After he opened the door he stared at her in silence for a full minute, looking totally at a loss. At last he smiled rather sheepishly. "Well, now, it seems I'm found out."

"It would seem so, indeed," Allie teased.

"It's no a real secret, you understand," Mac said earnestly. "Colin knows, of course, and a few others, but when I found out you were staying here I thought it best to keep a low profile, as they say in your country. I was afraid you might be shocked."

Allie grinned. "I'm not shocked, Mac," she assured him. "And I'm sorry I disturbed you. I wanted to check with Mrs. Tolliver to see if I had any messages."

He nodded, then turned his head. "Aida, did anyone telephone Miss Allison Bentley?"

"Simon Leverett, yesterday," Aida replied from somewhere in the nether regions of her apartment. Her voice sounded soft, lazy, as though she might even still be in bed.

Allie smothered another smile. "I know about Simon," she said, trying not to sound disappointed. About to turn away, she turned back. "I was hoping Colin might have called," she admitted.

Mac gave her a sympathetic smile. "I thought it was like that," he said.

She didn't want to argue with him, so she simply nodded. "I'm worried about him, Mac. Is he okay?"

He shook his head. "It was a great shock to him. He's not taking it well at all. He looks like a man that's taken a mortal blow to the stomach and he's not sure he'll ever breathe again." He sighed. "I was going to bide at home, but he insisted I keep to my regular schedule." He actually blushed when he realized what he'd said, endearing himself to Allie more than ever. "He said he was going to work. Likely he's in the basement, sanding away at a piece of furniture. Good therapy for him."

"Do you think I should go to see him?"

He hesitated, clearly not wanting to hurt her feelings. At last he said, "Give him a day or two more, lassie. When I get home this noon I'll see how the land lies and give you a jingle on the telephone tonight or tomorrow."

She smiled gratefully. "Thanks, Mac." Turning away, she couldn't resist adding, "Tell Mrs. T. hello for me. I haven't seen her in a day or two."

"I'll do that," he replied gravely, with only a hint of a blush this time.

When Mrs. Tolliver came down to tell Allie there
was a call for her at nine o'clock that night she was
sure it must be Mac calling, or Colin himself. But the
minute she held the receiver to her ear she heard the
hollow wavelike sound that meant an overseas call.
Immediately her heart skipped a beat and her breath
caught in her throat. She was barely able to force out
a greeting.

"Allison," Esther Denham's brisk no-nonsense
voice said. "I think you'd better come home."

CHAPTER ELEVEN

ON MONDAY MORNING, Allie ate breakfast at a restaurant on the wharf in St. George, then used a public telephone to check on her mother's progress and to let Esther Denham know she couldn't get a flight out until the following day. Esther had told her the previous night that Patricia had been admitted to hospital. She had been having some difficulty with her breathing for several days and had suddenly begun running a fever, so Dr. Sotero had decided to hospitalize her. Patricia had instructed Esther that she wasn't to alarm Allie, but Esther had felt it was best for Allie to return to Seattle.

This morning there was no change in Patricia's condition. Which meant she was no worse, but no better, either. "Don't tell your mom I called you yesterday, okay?" Esther said.

"I won't," Allie promised.

After she'd made the call, Allie leaned her forehead against the side of the booth for a moment, then fumbled in her shoulder bag for a tissue to wipe her eyes and blow her nose. Patricia's attitude was not quite as positive, Esther had told her. And Esther had sounded very sad.

She had to hang on, Allie told herself. She mustn't expect the worst. She must hope for the best. Patricia had experienced setbacks before, but she had always rallied. Always.

Allie straightened her shoulders and sniffed determinedly. Her mother was going to be just fine. She would see her tomorrow.

Forcing control into her fingers, she dialed Lionel's number and explained that she had been called out of town. She gave Lionel her address and phone number in Seattle and requested that he tell Celia she had to leave and to ask Simon to carry on looking for Joseph's journal until he was through with the attic. Lionel assured her he would also press Taylor into service. Taylor and Simon were getting along much better now.

Lionel's voice softened. "Your mother?" he asked.

Allie had to swallow twice before she could answer. "The news isn't good, I'm afraid."

"I will pray for her," Lionel said gravely. He hesitated. "Will you come back to Bermuda, Allison?"

"I don't know." She took a deep breath to still the tremor that was distressingly apparent in her voice. "I can't make any decisions right now," she said. "Eventually, yes. Of course. I do want to see you again."

"And I you."

His dignified, warm voice was comforting. Allie promised to stop by the house if she had time. Otherwise she would write to him from Seattle.

After she hung up the receiver, she stood looking at the telephone for a minute or two, trying to decide if she should call Colin or not. Her mind kept vacillating. Probably he would be at work this morning. Unless he was still in a state of shock. Would he want to hear from her? Probably not. He had enough on his mind. And he hadn't called her. But how could she leave Bermuda without at least telling him she was going?

In the end she decided to wait until the afternoon. She would call Macintosh and ask him to let Colin know what had happened. She tried not to think about how she would feel leaving Bermuda without seeing Colin again. How quickly he had become important to her. If only she hadn't blurted out...

She shook her head as she climbed onto her moped. There wasn't much sense in having regrets at this stage.

Mrs. Tolliver was cutting flowers in the front flowerbeds when Allie arrived at the guest house. She was wearing a purple-and-yellow blouse, wide-legged green slacks, a straw hat with a drooping brim. "I'll be coming up to see you shortly, when I get through packing," Allie said. "I couldn't get a flight today, after all, but I'll be leaving early in the morning. I'd like to pay my bill today and—"

"Freda will take care of you," Mrs. Tolliver told her airily with a dismissing wave of one gloved hand. Allie had forgotten her hostess wanted to pretend her paying customers were graciously invited guests.

"I'm getting very forgetful, I'm afraid," Mrs. Tolliver continued, putting down her basket and delicately mopping her forehead with a lace-edged handkerchief. "There were two telephone messages for you last evening after the one from your mother's nurse. It was late and I was about to bathe when they came and afterward they quite slipped my mind. I do apologize. One was from Mr. Macintosh." She blushed prettily. "The other was from Colin Endicott." She bestowed a rather arch smile on Allie. "Both gentlemen wanted you to return their calls."

Relief washed through Allie. Colin *had* wanted to get in touch with her. She wouldn't have to leave Bermuda without seeing him again.

"AIDA TOLD ME about your mother," Colin said without preamble when Mac called him to the phone. He had been at home when she'd telephoned, working in the basement. According to Mac, he'd spent the whole weekend down there.

There was so much sympathy in Colin's voice that Allie had trouble speaking for a few moments.

Into the silence, Colin said, "Are you all right, Allison?"

"I'm going to be," she managed, then hesitated. "Are you?"

"Let's not worry about me," he answered ambiguously.

There was another short silence, then he said in a strained voice, "You're leaving today?"

"Tomorrow. I couldn't get a flight out today. They told me it wasn't even worth going out to the airport on a standby basis. They have a long waiting line. I wouldn't have got a flight tomorrow if it hadn't been an emergency. I feel so . . . helpless. I feel as if I want to start swimming."

"Was the news really bad, Allison?"

She sighed. "It wasn't good. Esther didn't say much, but she doesn't seem the kind to panic, so if she says I should come home, then Mom must have had a major setback."

"What are you doing today?" he asked.

"Packing. Checking my tapes. I might go to to see Lionel if there's time. Simon found a miniature painting of Alys, by the way. I'm going to take it home to show Mom."

"I'd like to see it. I'd like to see you."

"Yes," she said with a sigh of relief. She had hated the thought of leaving with her last memory of Colin one of him walking away from her.

"I could . . . I'm sure I could get the keys to the cottage. Would you like to meet me there?"

"Yes," she said again. Probably, she thought, after they'd agreed on a time and hung up, she should have suggested they meet at a restaurant, or at Lionel's house. But she hadn't hesitated. She wanted to see him alone. Alone, she could apologize to him for blurting out gossip and hurting him so much.

Colin arrived at the cottage first. Allie parked her moped at the bottom of the hill, next to the Renault, left her safety helmet in the basket and climbed up the steps slowly, not sure what kind of reception she would get. She still had no idea how Colin was feeling in the wake of the shock she'd given him.

His smile at the door was welcoming, sympathetic and so full of affection that when he opened his arms to her she went right into them and began sobbing on his shoulder just as she had done before.

"I'm sorry, Colin," she apologized when she finally regained control of herself.

He smiled at her, his blue eyes fond. "I wore my crying shirt," he said, and she saw that he was indeed wearing the blue-and-green striped rugby shirt he'd worn when they'd first met. And she was wearing the green nylon windbreaker and blue jeans she had worn that day.

"A new beginning," she said, making use of the handkerchief he'd handed her.

He shook his head, then took her hand and led her into the sunny little cottage. Sitting her down on the flowered sofa that was set in the bay window, he gently unzipped her windbreaker and slipped it off over her shoulders. "We don't need to begin again," he said. He smoothed her hair into place, but it popped right back into its springy curls.

"I did an awful thing to you, Colin," she said. "I had no business—"

He placed one finger over her mouth. "I should have been told earlier," he said. "I should have known. The evidence was all around me, but I refused to see it." He looked at her ruefully. "It was a shock, of course, and it took me a few days to begin seeing straight again. I really regret losing that time with you, Allison. Especially now that you have to leave."

She nodded. "I missed you." She looked at him directly. "Are you feeling okay? Really?"

He returned her gaze steadily, taking both of her hands in his. The past few days were almost a blank to him now. At first he had raged at his own stupidity,

then at Diana and Bruce's perfidy, then at Allie for
bringing such a cruelly bright light into the darkness
of his ignorance. At some time on the second day he
had gone down into his basement workshop and se-
lected a piece of Bermuda cedar that was particularly
fine. After examining it carefully, he had begun to
carve, knowing that if he made something with his
hands he would feel as though he were once more in
control. Sure enough, working with the wood had
soothed him, and gradually his mind had calmed. The
past was past, he had told himself. It was no use raging over something that could not be changed. Sitting
there in his workshop, inhaling the cedar aroma of the
wood, he had visualized a door in his mind, a closed
door.

"I'm fully recovered," he said firmly. "I dislike
clichés, but they do seem to convey truth, so I'll use
one just this once. What's done is done."

Allie didn't seem quite convinced, so he smiled at
her to let her know he really was just fine. His smile
didn't feel too convincing to him, either. Allie looked
wan, pale under the tan she'd acquired in Bermuda.
The expression on her face was severe, as though she
were holding tightly to her self-control. The flesh under her glorious eyes looked bruised and her eyes were
strained. He could sense the tension, and the fear,
emanating from her body. Though sunlight was
pouring into the cottage through the skylight and he
had closed the doors against the strong ocean breeze,
her hands felt cold in his. She was looking directly at
the brightly wrapped package he had brought with

him, his farewell gift to her, but he was fairly sure she wasn't seeing it at all.

"I've been doing some thinking about your mother," he said. "My mother has a doctor in Harley Street. He might know of someone..."

She was shaking her head. "Mom's been seen by many specialists. In Texas, in California, at home in Seattle. She's been treated in every way possible. With progressively more discomfort. And with disappointing results each time. All the doctors say the same thing—she has relapsed so repeatedly and so rapidly after each treatment that there's no hope anymore of complete remission. I don't know what the specific problem is this time, but because of her low leukocyte count, she's highly susceptible to infection."

Letting go of her hands, he cupped the side of her face with one palm and gently rubbed the skin above her nose with his thumb in the place where a frown line was developing. "I wish I could tell you everything was going to be all right," he murmured.

"So do I," she said with a sigh. She met his gaze again. "Could you please just hold me, Colin?" she asked.

He drew her into his arms and for a long time they sat there, not speaking, not moving. Colin could feel the shape of her breasts against his rib cage every time she breathed. It wasn't long before he began feeling a response other than sympathy, but he refused to acknowledge it. He didn't want to do anything that would send Allie away from him in anger, even though, at this moment, he wanted her more than he had ever wanted a woman in his entire life. As soon as he had come out of his state of shock, he had known that Allison Bentley was the only woman for him. He loved her. He was in love with her. It was the sublimest of torture to sit here with her voluptuous body in his arms, her wildly curling hair against his cheek, so alive, so fragrant. All the same, he wasn't about to move or speak or reveal in any way the agony of his wanting, the depth of his love.

When she spoke, her voice was so low he didn't at first take in what she had said. When she repeated it, he felt his heart, which had seemed so dead during the past few days, jolt back to life.

"Colin," she had murmured. "Could we possibly make love?"

She kissed him on the mouth, a long full kiss. Then she took his hand and led him to the bed. She looked very solemn still, but not quite as sad. Her eyes were glowing. She was seeing him—there was no doubt about that. All the same, he was afraid that subconsciously she wanted only to reaffirm life, or to forget reality for a while. He decided not to discuss these possibilities with her. He didn't really care why she wanted to make love. He was only glad that she did.

TIME NEVER REALLY stood still, Colin thought. It moved along inexorably on invisible feet, skipping over seconds, minutes, hours, weeks, months, years. But still, in the mind of a man or woman, time could seem elastic. An hour spent waiting for a telephone to ring could seem like seven; an hour spent in the arms of a loved one could shrink to five minutes. For Colin,

making love to Allison, time had ceased to exist, outside concerns had ceased to exist.

"Time out of mind," Allison murmured, and he
knew that she was sharing his thoughts. The sun struck
brilliance from the gently rolling water in the bay below and was reflected into the windows of the cottage, glinting on Allie's dark hair, on the sheen of
moisture coating her lovely body, on her glowing lustrous green-brown eyes. She looked happy—for
now—the dread gone from her expression. Time out
of mind. She was living this day as a fantasy, he realized. When the fantasy ended she would return to
reality. She would leave Bermuda. She would leave
him. And under the circumstances, he couldn't even
ask her to stay.

But for now, she turned when he turned, moved
when he moved, and often instigated a turn, a move
of her own. Making love to Allison was like taking
part in a ballet, Colin thought, a ballet that had been
choreographed by an artist. The rhythm was fault-
less, even though the music was audible only to the
two people taking part.

His hands traced every line of her body from her
neck to her shoulders and arms, over each breast,
down over her abdomen, behind her to stroke her hips
and thighs, down her legs to her ankles and feet, back
again to her hips. Allie remembered how he had
stroked the lines and curves of the Queen Anne highboy in his basement workshop, remembered the
expression on his face as he'd spoken of the soul of the
wood. Was he seeking *her* soul?

She felt her breath catch in her throat when he kissed her breasts. He was gentle, almost reverent, yet everywhere he touched she could feel heat rising from her body to meet him. Her own hands moved over him, absorbing into their memory the feel of his skin and the muscles beneath the skin and the veins and arteries that carried his blood.

Somewhere not too far away a car horn blasted the silence with a raucous sound, startling them, making them laugh. And then, abruptly, they became frenzied, as though suddenly conscious of time passing and opportunities lost, their hands and mouths frantic, seeking, searching. And at last he was inside her and she was able to surround him. She ached to hold him forever imprisoned, while at the same time she was impatient for the release that would lead to his breaking away from her. She watched his face above her and suspected it reflected her own expression, a complicated mixture of yearning and pain and joy.

They climaxed together and cried out, then held on to each other tightly for a long time, as though they were afraid to break the spell. But eventually limbs cramped and bodies required space and they loosened their hold and looked with deep affection into each other's faces.

"I didn't realize until this weekend that I was only half a person before you came into my life," Colin said softly. "I had cut myself off from so much. I didn't want to feel, because if I felt at all I would feel pain. Subconsciously, I suppose, I had known about Diana and Bruce. I certainly must have suspected my marriage was over long before Diana left for England. But I didn't allow myself to know it as a fact."

He stroked her hair. "For the past two years of my marriage I didn't want to look below the surface because there was chaos there and I'm a man who appreciates order. Now, when I'm with you, everything seems to make sense. I feel as though I've found my proper place at last."

Allie shook her head, feeling alarmed. "I don't want that kind of responsibility, Colin."

He smiled. "Too late." He kissed her gently. At the same moment, outside the window, there came a shrill cry, "Kiss-ka-dee."

Allie laughed. "Perfect timing." She sighed. "I love Bermuda. I'm going to miss the kiskadees."

"Nothing else?"

"The tree frogs, the turquoise water, the pink sand, the exotic flowers, the sugar-white roofs on the houses."

"Nothing else?" His face was alight with tenderness.

"Lionel and Celia and Simon and Macintosh and Mrs. Tolliver and even Taylor," she listed, teasing him. "You did know about Mac and Mrs. Tolliver, I suppose?"

"I knew, yes. Mac told me you looked a bit surprised."

"An understatement. What an ill-matched pair. And yet if it works, why not?"

He narrowed his eyes, then lifted himself over her and kissed her hard until she had no breath left. "Who else will you miss?" he demanded.

"You," she finally admitted.

His eyes held hers. "You will come back, Allie?"

She couldn't look any more at those fiercely blue eyes. They were asking an additional question that she wasn't ready to answer. "Sometime, yes, of course, but..."

He put a finger over her lips. "No buts." He kissed her again, lightly, almost inquisitively, as though he had never kissed her before. Incredibly, she felt him growing hard against her and felt a corresponding ache deep within her that lifted her away from the mattress and into his arms.

"I DIDN'T KNOW it could be like that," she murmured a long time later.

"Nor did I. But I always suspected it."

Easing himself away from her, he took her hand and pulled her with him into the bathroom. Together they showered and shampooed, soaping each other, laughing and playing like two undersea creatures, reveling in the cool freshness of the driving spray and soap that smelled of the sea. Naked, they stood for a while in the bay window, arms wound around each other's waists as they looked out at the blue-green ocean and the endless horizon, until they decided they were ravenously hungry. After they dressed, Colin grilled fish in the small kitchen while Allie tossed a salad and made coffee and poured wine. Food had never tasted so good.

"I have a gift for you," Colin said, after they had washed and dried the dishes. Ceremoniously he led her to the flowered sofa and sat down very close to her, then handed her the small but bulky package he had brought with him.

She felt the outline under the paper but couldn't decided what it could be. "Lumpy," she commented.

"Open it," he growled.

But first she wanted him to look at the painting of Alys. She pulled the package from her shoulder bag, still wrapped in its tissue paper. He studied the miniature for a long time, holding it up to the light. "It's so uncanny," he said at last.

"The resemblance."

He nodded.

"You should see my mother. They could be twins." Carefully she packed the painting away, then picked up Colin's gift again. "Shall I do it?" she asked.

He sighed. "Please. The suspense is killing me. I'm so afraid you won't like it."

Allie pulled off the bright paper and exclaimed with pleasure. "It's a friendship goblet! I saw one like this in the straw market. It wasn't as beautifully finished as this one, though."

The graceful object had been carved out of cedar. Friendship goblets, the lady in the straw market had explained, had originated generations ago in the highlands of Scotland. The ancient craft had been handed down and brought to Bermuda by Scotsmen many years ago. Each goblet always had a loose wooden ring looping the stem. Ring and goblet were turned from a single piece of cedar, a tricky procedure.

This particular goblet was perfectly carved, perfectly proportioned, so smooth it felt like glass. "It's beautiful, Colin," she said softly. "You made it yourself, didn't you?"

He nodded. "I haven't done any carving in years. I used to do a lot when I was a boy, but then I began working with furniture and it got away from me. I made the goblet this weekend from a piece of Bermuda cedar I'd been saving for something special. It started out as therapy. I didn't really know what I was going to make—it just sort of formed itself. When I saw what it was I realized it was exactly the right thing." He hesitated as though he were going to add something, but then apparently changed his mind. He simply said, "I'm glad you like it, Allison."

He was looking at her expectantly, with a slightly wry smile at the corner of his mouth, as though there were something about the gift that had not yet become apparent to her. She examined it again, marveling at the craftsmanship that had gone into its making. And then she saw that there were two rings looping the goblet's stem. She glanced quickly at Colin. Was this what he had been waiting for her to discover?

"But this isn't a friendship goblet—it's a marriage goblet," she exclaimed. "The lady at the straw market told me about the custom of the double rings, though she didn't have one in stock at the time. She said they're traditionally given as wedding gifts." She frowned. "I don't quite—" She broke off. "Oh, Colin," she said.

His fingers touched the wooden rings. "A ring has been recognized since time immemorial as the symbol of eternity," he said slowly. "It has no beginning and no end." He hesitated, taking in a long slow breath.

"It's my way of asking you to marry me, Allison. I love you. I want you to be my wife."

"Oh, Colin," she said again.

When she didn't say anything else, he tilted his head and smiled ruefully at her. "One of the things I've loved most about you," he said lightly, "is that you're such a tremendously good conversationalist. Don't tell me I was mistaken."

"You don't know me well enough," she pointed out. "How can you want to marry me after so short a time?"

"Don't tell me it's too soon," he said flatly. "Don't tell me I don't know what I'm talking about. Just listen. I love you. I want to marry you. Not now—I know you can't handle even the thought of marrying right now—but I want you to hold the thought . . . for sometime in the future." He lifted her hand and kissed the palm. "I don't know you well enough? I think we were meant for each other from the start. When you were upset, under the moon gate, and I put my arms around you to comfort you, there was a rightness between us. It happens that way sometimes. Some people call it fate." He looked earnestly into her face. "Have you run across the motto of Bermuda yet— *Quo Fata Ferunt*?"

"Whither the fates lead us," Allie murmured.

"Exactly. Couldn't we just follow along? Why fight it? I know you felt it, too, the rightness between us, when I first held you. You did, didn't you? Admit it. Don't worry about whether it's possible or not, just admit that it *is*. You love me. I know you do."

"Oh, Colin." She couldn't seem to get away from those two words. She had no idea what else to say to him.

After a moment he laughed and gathered her close in his arms and rested his chin on her hair. "Don't look so worried, Allison. You don't have to answer now. You can consider my proposal when you're back in Seattle. Write to me. You will write to me?"

She nodded.

"Let yourself feel, Allison," he urged. "What are you feeling right this minute?"

"Confused," she admitted with a sigh. "And enormously moved. I'm sorry, Colin," she said carefully. "You're very special to me, you must surely know that, and it's obvious that I'm strongly attracted to you, but I just can't make any decisions now. I've got so much on my mind right now, so much that isn't...it's just not a good time for..." She drew a little away from him and looked down at the goblet. "For something like this." She looked back at him. "Our timing is off," she added sadly.

He touched her cheek lightly. "Promise me you'll tune in on your feelings when you can?"

She nodded.

His smile seemed to require a lot of effort. Gently he took the marriage goblet from her unresisting fingers and set it down on the coffee table in front of the sofa. At once she felt relieved, and lighter somehow, as though the symbolism of the goblet had been too heavy a load for her to carry.

As she looked at him, Colin stood and drew her to her feet. Putting his arms around her, he pulled her against him, his hands tightening across her back, pulling her closer, ever closer, his legs braced apart as he eased her into the angle of his hips. "In the meantime," he murmured, "we have the rest of the evening and the night."

CHAPTER TWELVE

"THERE MUST BE something else we can do," Allie said. She had been home for a week now and had felt progressively more helpless.

Esther Denham, her mother's nurse, an angular, bespectacled woman with graying auburn hair and competent-looking hands, sat down next to her in one of the hospital lounge's molded plastic chairs and patted her arm. "Everything that can be done is being done, my dear."

"I shouldn't have left her."

"She wanted you to go to Bermuda. She was worried about your health."

Allie sighed. "I thought that was her main reason."

"Not the only one, though." Esther smiled. "She was surely delighted with that painting of Alys Thornley. It was nice, considering how she'd identified with Alys, that they should look so much alike. She surely did rally when you brought that painting in."

"I still can't understand why you didn't call me home sooner," Allie continued, hardly registering what Esther had said.

"Patricia wouldn't let me. She wanted to know more about Alys and she liked the sound of this Colin Endicott. She was hoping something would come of it." Esther looked at her sideways. "If there's anything you could tell her about that, she'd surely be pleased to hear it. Anything at all. You know how important attitude is."

"There isn't anything to tell," Allie replied. She certainly wasn't going to tell Esther she missed Colin Endicott far more than she had even expected to. Only yesterday, walking back to the condo after consulting with Marty and Linda about her Bermuda video, she had seen a tall blond man strolling ahead of her, wearing a knit shirt and shorts, and her heart had caught in her throat for a moment. He had been a poor excuse for a double, too—slump shouldered and flabby around the middle. All the same, even after she realized he was nothing like Colin, she continued to watch him until he rounded a corner and was lost to her.

She missed Bermuda almost as much as she missed Colin, though she loved Seattle and had never imagined she would want to live anywhere else. She shook her head. She mustn't think about Bermuda and Colin, or she'd start yearning again. And when she yearned to be back there she was being a traitor to her mother.

"Do you suppose they're through with the blood work?" she asked. "I really don't see why they have to kick me out every time they want to stick a needle in her."

"Hospital policy," Esther said soothingly, patiently. She stood up with a rustle of starched dress. "Come along, we'll gate-crash."

Allie squeezed the other woman's arm affectionately as they walked together along the hall. "Thanks for being so patient with me, Esther," she said.

The lab crew was packing up, ready to leave. Patricia was lying flat on her back, her head turned to look out the window at the view of Mount Rainier shimmering in the distance. She appeared exhausted. "Hey," Allie said softly, taking one of her hands between her own.

Patricia's smile was more incandescent than ever. It seemed to Allie that as her flesh grew weaker her spirit shone ever more brightly. "Hey, kid," she murmured.

"Tired?"

"Mostly I feel like a pin cushion."

"Hang in there, Mom."

Always before Patricia would have grinned and said, "I'm hanging, honey. I'm hanging," but this time she just smiled weakly and said nothing at all. Allie was suddenly filled with fear. There was no color in Patricia's face or body. Allie tried not to look at the contrast between her own hands, browned by the Bermuda sun, and her mother's, which were almost translucent enough for light to shine through.

"How's the video going?" Patricia asked.

Grateful for the change in subject, Allie suppressed her worry. "It's coming along. I've got the tapes logged and indexed and we've made the final changes in the storyboard. I'll go in on Monday and start work on the actual editing. After that I'll lay in some narration and put some music behind the whole thing.''

"I liked what I saw.'' Allie had shown parts of the raw tape to Patricia on the hospital TV a few days ago.

Patricia smiled. "For all the time I worked in the store, it still seems a miracle to me that you could tape all that thousands of miles away and have it here for me to see so quickly. I guess that comes of belonging to a generation that wasn't nurtured on television. I feel as though I'd been to Bermuda myself. You do a terrific job, Allison.'' Her voice was slurring slightly and her eyes closing.

"Go to sleep,'' Allie murmured. "I'll sit here and keep you company for a while.''

Patricia rolled her head from side to side on the pillow. "You should be outside, darling. It's a lovely day. June was always one of my favorite months. There are still rhododendrons in bloom. Why don't you drive over to the arboretum?'' Her eyes had closed, her voice faded to a murmur. "Your father loved the arboretum...the Japanese garden...the waterfront trail.'' She chuckled softly. "I can just see him, striding along in that restless way of his, reeling off the names of all the plants—he did so love...''

Allie sat with Patricia all afternoon, watching the faint rise and fall of her mother's chest under the ruffle-edged yoke of the bright red flannel nightgown she insisted on wearing. She needed all the color she could get, Patricia had pointed out. Why were hospitals such drab places, she wanted to know. Sunshine yellow paint didn't cost any more than insipid green; red plastic chairs were surely as readily available as brown.

In her next life she was going to return as a hospital decorator, she told all the nurses. She was going to take them out of their white piqué and put them in scarlet or royal blue. She was going to have great artists paint the ceiling of all the corridors like Michelangelo's Sistine Chapel so patients would have something to look at when they were being trundled around on gurneys.

Patricia slept for a long time. She seemed very weak in her sleep. Allie had to concentrate to hear her breathing. She didn't move, not once. Allie remembered her father complaining that Patricia always hogged all the blankets. "She just rears up in her sleep, grabs a double handful and yanks away," he would say.

As day followed day, Allie kept vigil at her mother's side as often as Patricia would allow, concentrating her energy on her to keep her from slipping away.

Two weeks after Allie had returned from Bermuda, Esther came quietly into Patricia's hospital room and tapped Allie on the shoulder. Watching her mother, Allie had fallen into a light doze and was startled, disoriented, when she was first awakened. When she realized Esther had deliberately woken her, she looked immediately at her mother, her heart skipping a beat, and found that Patricia was awake, also looking at Esther, with curiosity. "You have a visitor," Esther announced.

"I can't see anyone now," Allie said at once. Friends had been calling or coming by ever since Patricia had been admitted to hospital. She had confessed to Allie that she found visits much too exhausting. "People will insist on being jolly," she'd explained.

"Tell whoever it is to leave a name and number and I'll call later," Allie requested.

Esther didn't move. There was a singularly arch smile on her somewhat plain face. "It's not Marty or Linda, is it?" Allie asked. "There's nothing wrong at the store?"

Esther shook her head. "Not as far as I know." Her smile widened. "This visitor claims his name is Colin Endicott."

Allie sat up abruptly. "Colin? *Here*? Are you serious?"

"Would I joke about a man like that one?" Esther asked. She grinned at Patricia. "Did you see her blush when I said his name?"

Patricia chuckled. "I certainly did. Go on, Allie. Go see him. And bring him in here. I have a certain curiosity about Colin Endicott. I discovered him first, remember." As Allie started toward the door, Patricia called after her. "Don't bring him in right away," she warned. "Take your time. Greet him properly—give me time to put my makeup on. My face is fish-belly white, Esther. We have to do something."

Allie exchanged a delighted glance with Esther. Patricia's asking for makeup was an excellent sign. Maybe...

Colin was carrying a garment bag and a soft leather suitcase. He must have come to the hospital straight from the airport. How had he known which hospital? Of course—Allie had written him on hospital stationery from the nurses' station. In his rugby shirt and white chinos, he looked wonderful to her, so tall and tan and fair, incredibly healthy, out of place in the intensive care ward, yet so much in the right place . . . definitely in the right place.

He set down his bags the moment he saw her and held out his arms. She went right into them without hesitation and he held her very close, as though he didn't ever intend to let go. She heard the slight snick of her mother's door and realized Esther was probably peeking around it, reporting back to Patricia. "Oh, Colin," she murmured.

He put one hand under her chin and lifted it, smiled at her tenderly and kissed her, then assumed a wounded expression. "Are you still stuck in that track? Is that all you can say, 'Oh, Colin'?"

She grinned at him. She felt like a flower that had wilted, but had been placed in water in the nick of time so that all its leaves and petals had lifted themselves up toward the sun. Her hands clasped the back of his neck, her fingers making contact with his wonderfully crisp hair. "I can't believe you're here," she exclaimed. "Is that better?" she asked with a grin.

"It's an improvement," he conceded. Then his face sobered and he said very seriously, "I've missed you terribly, Allison."

"I've missed you, too," she told him.

His smile was dazzling. "Really?"

"Really. I saw a man downtown a while back who looked a little like you and I almost attacked him."

He didn't comment, but he kept on smiling. Then he kissed her, gently but very thoroughly. A couple of nurses went by chuckling audibly, but Allie didn't care.

"Your mother?" Colin asked when they finally came up for air.

Allie shook her head, but managed a smile. "She's anxious to meet you."

"I've brought her something," he said.

"Another goblet?"

"Better."

There was such mischief in his smile. Allie realized that all the shadows had left his face. She wondered if that was because he was away from his house. A memory of gilt frames and dark canvases flickered in her mind and she shivered involuntarily.

"Allison?"

"Nothing. I'm fine. A goose walked over my..." She shook her head. "What did you bring? I can't stand the suspense."

He was still holding her in his arms. "First, I must tell you that everyone sends you their love. Everyone misses you. Especially Celia. She said to tell you everything with her and Simon is cool-cool."

"I know—she wrote me. She wanted to tell me you'd set up a scholarship fund for Simon so he could go on to university in the U.S. after he graduates from Bermuda College. That's pretty terrific of you, Colin."

"Not just for Simon," he said. "My company did have a policy of helping students who want to work in cabinetmaking, but hearing Simon's story persuaded me that our efforts were too narrow in scope. Many of our young people can't afford higher education. So we're creating several scholarships for those students who are willing to work hard." He shrugged. "It's not such a virtuous idea. Bermuda will benefit from it."

"Well, I think it's magnificent of you," she said, reaching up to kiss him again. "And if you don't tell me what you've brought my mother I'm going to scream right here in the hospital corridor and bring everyone running."

He grinned, then tapped his suitcase with one foot. "It's in here. I also have to tell you," he added, ignoring her groan of protest, "that I spent some time working with Simon and Taylor in Lionel's attic." He rolled his eyes. "I was beginning to feel as frustrated as a miner who knows the gold is in there, but can't quite manage to find it, but then Taylor and I lifted a box off another box and we both let out a whoop." He frowned. "That must have been on Wednesday evening. Anyway," he went on hastily when Allie curved her hands around his neck as though she were about to throttle him, "what we found was Joseph Entwhistle's journal."

"Joseph's journal? I don't believe it!" Allie flung herself at him, hugging him, laughing and crying at the same time. "I don't believe you found it. It really was there. Oh, Colin, my mom will be so pleased. I just hope—" She broke off, looking at him. "You brought it all the way here."

He nodded.

She kissed him, meaning at first to show her gratitude, then forgetting all about gratitude in the rush of sensations throughout her body. She had known that she missed him, but now that he was here the past two

weeks seemed, in retrospect, to have been even lone-
lier. "I'm so glad you're here," she murmured.

PATRICIA WAS SITTING UP against her pillows, her face
flushed with pleasure as much as from the rosy blusher
she'd carefully applied. For one brief moment, Allie
saw her as she had looked before she'd become sick
and she wished . . . oh, how she wished . . .

"Colin Endicott," Patricia said warmly as he took
her hand and held it between his own. She flashed him
a grin that made her appear like her old mischievous
self. "Allie told me you weren't an old curmudgeon,
after all. She was certainly right."

Colin sent a startled glance Allie's way, then his face
cleared and he grinned at Patricia. "My original letter, I suppose. I'm sorry about that."

"Allie explained that to me. To tell the truth," Patricia added, "I saw you in Allison's video, walking
under the moon gate in your garden, so I already knew
you didn't deserve the nasty thoughts I'd had of you."

"Don't worry, Colin," Allie said hastily. "I'm
going to edit that section out."

"I should hope so," Patricia said. "You'd have
lonely women pouring into Bermuda by the plane-
load."

Colin smiled at her. He was still holding her hand.
"I'm delighted to meet you, too," he said, and they
exchanged a look of complete understanding. There
was no doubting the immediate rapport that had
sprung up between them.

"Colin's brought us Joseph's journal, Mom," Allie said eagerly.

Patricia closed her eyes momentarily, then looked gratefully at Colin. "I can't tell you what this means to me," she said. "Is there any mention of Alys?"

Colin nodded. "Oh, yes. According to the journal, Joseph went to Bermuda to trace Alys's story. He'd been fascinated by it since he was a little boy. He didn't intend to stay forever. He just wanted to get away from his very strict father for a while. He wrote that he was thirty years old and still in thrall to that righteous old man. But he fell in love with Bermuda immediately, and when he met Tallah he decided never to leave."

"He'd found his place," Patricia murmured.

Colin nodded, looking surprised. "That's exactly what he says in the journal. It seems Alys had a theory that everyone has a place in this world and if they don't find it they can never be happy." He intercepted a delighted glance between Patricia and Allison. "I see you're familiar with that part of the legend."

Patricia nodded.

"In any case, Joseph's family would not have welcomed him back," Colin continued. "Tallah was black and they wouldn't accept her. That was their loss, Joseph wrote. There's a picture..."

He dug into the suitcase and pulled out an old battered photograph, which someone had dated on the back. 1888. Joseph and Tallah had been married ten years, Allie calculated. Joseph, more dignified and distinguished-looking than handsome, with a beard and mustache, was seated, awkwardly holding a baby who must have been his and Tallah's son. Tallah, slender and breathtakingly beautiful in a low-necked, full-skirted floor-length gown with a bustle, her ebony hair pulled back and tied with a ribbon, stood behind him, one fine-boned hand resting on his shoulder. She was wearing the emerald necklace.

"My aunt Jenny never mentioned Joseph and Tallah," Patricia murmured. "Her own prejudice, I suppose."

She sounded strained and Allie looked at her alertly. "Maybe you need to rest, Mom. We can look at the journal later."

Patricia shook her head. "I'm okay, dear. If Esther will order me in a shot of magic medicine I'd like to go on with this. I'm very excited about it. And after all, I don't really know how much—" She broke off, and Allie wondered miserably if she'd intended to say she didn't know how much time she had left.

A few minutes later, Patricia had been given a shot of painkiller and professed herself ready to journey through her family's history.

It was a fascinating journey, chronicled in Joseph's fine handwriting in a beautifully bound book whose pages were only slightly yellowed. Joseph's own grandfather had had access to a journal kept by Alys herself, it seemed, but it had disappeared. However, Joseph had put together everything his grandfather had told him.

The story began with the wreck of the *Sea Venture* and ten-year-old Alys's arrival in Bermuda. "So early in my life I have found my place," she had written in that original journal. "Alone and orphaned, living with people who care naught for me but only for the duties I can perform, I can yet present a cheerful face to the world, knowing that I have found my home in Bermuda.''

But then, when the *Deliverance* and *Patience* were built, Sir Thomas Gates had insisted that the passengers and crew of the *Sea Venture* go on to Jamestown as originally planned. Alys had declared her intention of returning to Bermuda as soon as she possibly could. And she had done so at the age of seventeen as the wife of William Pruitt.

"She married William *before* she went to Bermuda!" Allie exclaimed.

"She married him so that she *could* go to Bermuda," Colin said.

Alys, it seemed, had originally been engaged by William to care for his infant son Douglas after his wife died in childbirth. She had not admired Mr. Pruitt greatly, she had written, for he had a choleric nature and he looked at her in a strange brooding way that worried her mightily. But William Pruitt had been offered a position in Bermuda by the Somers Island Company, an offshoot of the Virginia Company, which had financed the original journey of the *Sea Venture*. He was to advise on the growing of tobacco, which had been decided upon as the prime product of the colony. Before he left for Bermuda, however, his baby son died of a fever. Alys begged Mr. Pruitt to take her with him, anyway, and he agreed to do so if she would become his wife. Evidently Alys had weighed her fears and dislike of Mr. Pruitt with the prospects of returning to Bermuda and Bermuda had won.

Unfortunately her fears had proven well-founded. Mr. Pruitt was a cruel and unjust man, unhappy that his new young wife did not at once provide him with an heir to replace Douglas. He was also angered by Somers Island Company complaints about the inferior quality of the tobacco they were receiving.

William Pruitt must indeed have complained of his wife, Allie thought as she read Joseph Entwhistle's journal aloud to Patricia and Colin and an entranced Esther Denham. Alys had suffered through several miscarriages and had not given birth until she was thirty years old. And then she had presented her husband with a daughter, Penelope, rather than the son he had hoped for.

However, Alys had never regretted coming to Bermuda. Always interested in helping the sick, she had become expert with remedies for various illnesses, concocting "simples" from Bermuda's indigenous plants. She was known to all as a kind woman, Joseph had written, albeit a woman of some temper when crossed, as witnessed by her appearance before the assizes in 1626, where she was chastized for calling her neighbor an old bawd. On that occasion, William had been much provoked by her behavior.

Allie exchanged a glance with Colin, elated by the way this account was meshing with everything they had been able to find out about Alys. Colin looked a little tired, she thought. Probably he was suffering from jet lag and here she was keeping him at the hospital. "I'm fine, Allison," he said, evidently reading the concern in her expression. "You can't stop now."

She smiled at him gratefully and he smiled in return. How incredibly blue his eyes were, she thought, then realized that Patricia was looking from her to Colin with great interest. "Mom?" she asked.

"I'm okay, dear," Patricia insisted. "I'll have plenty of time to rest later." She smiled ruefully. "Isn't that the truth!" She looked at Colin apologetically. "My humor tends to be rather grim, I'm afraid, Colin. It's the one way I've found to make my situation livable. I forget how it must seem to strangers. Not that you're a stranger, of course. Why, you're almost one of the family." She glanced rather slyly at Allie.

Colin laughed. "I can't think of a better family to belong to," he said.

Patricia tilted her head to one side and regarded him solemnly for a moment. "Is that a fact?"

"Don't encourage her, Colin," Allie said firmly. "She's been trying to marry me off for years. Give her an inch and she'll be knitting baby bootees before you know it."

"Nonsense," Patricia said. "You two wouldn't make a good match, anyway. Your babies would be utterly gorgeous, but mix blond with dark brown and you've got mud-colored hair. Who wants a grandchild with mud-colored hair?" She paused dramatically, then added, "Of course, most likely, Allie's darker genes would be dominant, Colin. So your babies would likely have her eyes rather than yours. It seems a shame to lose those beautiful blue eyes."

"I wouldn't mind a bit," Colin said.

"Truly?" Patricia asked with another sidelong look at Allison.

"Mother," Allie warned, aware that a lot more was being said by these two people than appeared on the surface.

Patricia sighed. "Okay. Back to Alys. Poor thing, imagine having to stand up in church with your crime posted on your bosom. Shades of the scarlet letter."

"There's worse to come," Colin said, then looked a little sheepish. "I scanned most of the journal on the plane, I'm afraid. I just couldn't resist."

Patricia patted his hand where it rested near her on the bed. "Don't give it another thought, Colin. You'd naturally want to know what kind of ancestors your future children might have."

"Mother!" Allie exclaimed again.

"I'm sorry, dear," Patricia said without a trace of apology in her voice. "We're just speculating, of course. Joking. Aren't we, Colin?"

"Of course," he replied smoothly, but the two of them exchanged a glance of such understanding that Allie marveled that the two people she loved most in the world had become so close so fast.

Loved? Wait a minute, she instructed herself. She loved her mother, yes, but since when had she decided she loved Colin Endicott? She glanced at him in a way that was meant to be surreptitious, but found he was looking at her, directly and lovingly. Meeting his gaze, she felt such a rush of warmth and love that her breath stopped in her throat. It didn't matter when she had decided she loved him, she thought. The fact remained that she did, and when he looked at her like that she didn't want to turn away.

"I thought we were going on with the story," Patricia complained.

Allie felt herself flush, felt rather than saw that her mother had noted the flush, and forced herself back to Joseph's journal.

It was Alys's kindness to the sick that had been her undoing. William Pruitt had become a prominent man in Bermuda, and fairly prosperous. He had inspired some jealousy among his neighbors, but perhaps, Joseph wrote, as William was known to be an ill-humored man, they had been afraid to attack him in any way. Instead they had attacked his wife.

In 1650, Scottish prisoners who had been captured in battles between British royalists and Cromwell's soldiers, were dispatched to Bermuda as slaves. Many of these, uneducated and superstitious, told colorful stories of the witch-hunts going on in England and Scotland. These tales captured the imagination of the governor of the colony and he began searching for signs of witchcraft among his islanders. Signs there were aplenty. Turkeys and cows had died after being "overlooked." A child had died after a visit by a family friend.

From this small beginning, hysteria had taken over in Bermuda as it had elsewhere in the world. It was easy to see that a woman such as Alys, skilled in herbal lore, already noted as a troublemaker, who had insulted a neighbor, was a likely target. In 1651, she was accused of casting an evil eye and of administering love potions. She was sentenced to be ducked five times in the harbor.

Horrified, Allie looked at Colin. "I knew there was nothing entertaining about that ducking ceremony."

He nodded. "All the same," he pointed out, "Alys was lucky to get away with her life. There were twenty-two such trials and five of the victims were hanged."

"She didn't live long," Allie said, looking back at the journal. "She died in 1652, just one year later. She was only fifty-three years old."

William Pruitt, that upright citizen whose virtues had been extolled on a plaque in St. Peter's Church, had, according to Joseph, denounced his wife right after the trial and insisted she leave his house. Through the "goode offices of his friends," he had caused all mention of Alys Pruitt nee Thornley to be stricken from the community's records, so that it would be as if she never existed.

Alys had felt sick at heart over this, as well she might. She had become persona non grata in her beloved Bermuda. She had instructed her daughter, Penelope, twenty-three at the time of her mother's death, to tell her children, should she have any, the whole story of their grandmother's life so that William's efforts to erase her existence should fail. Bermuda was her place and her memory deserved to be kept alive there, she had written. "I can only hope that time will be merciful and such wrongs as have been done me shall be redressed," Alys had said before she died.

Penelope had subsequently quarreled with her father over his treatment of her mother and had emigrated to Virginia, where she had married a man named Walter Cummings and given birth to two children, a boy, John, and a girl, Elizabeth.

There was a silence in Patricia's hospital room. "Poor Alys," Patricia said softly.

"I promise you," Colin said, leaning over to take her hand in his again, "when I complete my history of Bermuda, Alys's entire story will be included."

"Thank you, Colin," Patricia said gravely. She looked at Allie. "Is that all of it, darling? I must admit I'm a little tired."

Allie had been flipping forward through the journal. "That's all there is about Alys," she replied. "There's a little about Penelope, then Joseph tells what he knows about the rest of the family, then there's his own story, most of which we know. We can get back to it tomorrow."

Patricia nodded. She did appear very tired, Allie saw, and there was a brittle look to her, as though if someone breathed too heavily on her she might break. She felt a rush of alarm, quickly suppressed. No, Patricia wasn't going to die yet. Not for a long time yet.

CHAPTER THIRTEEN

"YOUR VISIT did my mother a world of good," Allie told Colin over dinner. He had taken her out to a nearby seafood restaurant. Allie wouldn't go far from the hospital now. When she did she felt too anxious about her mother to eat.

Colin looked at her sympathetically. "She's very ill, isn't she?"

Allie nodded, on the brink of tears but managing to hold them back. She wasn't going to mar Colin's first day in Seattle more than she already had. "We mustn't let her see how worried we are," she warned. "Her doctor said right from the start that a positive attitude can work miracles."

"Has he said that lately?" Colin asked.

Allie looked down at her clam chowder, which had suddenly become tasteless. "What do you mean?"

He reached across the table, picked up her hand and kissed it lightly. "I mean, darling Allison, that your mother is barely holding on to life. And I think she's only holding on for your sake. I think she's very, very tired and I think she needs you to let go."

"How can you make such statements?" Allie said hotly, pushing her chowder bowl away. "You just got here. What do you know about her condition or what she wants?"

"I can make such statements because I love you," he said. "And perhaps the fact that I just got here makes it easier for me to see the reality of the situation."

"I let go of her months ago," Allie said.

"In theory, perhaps. But what about in practice?"

"This is just a setback, Colin. She could recover and live for months yet."

He shook his head. "I'm sorry, Allison. It doesn't look like a setback to me." He gazed at her tenderly. "You don't think you are keeping monsters locked in the closet?"

She took a deep shaky breath. "Maybe I am," she admitted. "But this is the worst monster ever. I'm not ready to let him out. Not yet, Colin."

Colin set her hand gently down on the table. "Eat your chowder, Allison, darling. You need your strength. And don't take any notice of me. I probably don't know what I'm talking about. But lean on me if you need to, all right? Don't try to go through this alone."

Obediently she picked up her spoon and began eating again. "I didn't ask—how long can you stay?" Her voice had recovered its strength, she was pleased to discover.

"As long as you need me," he said.

ALLIE GAVE COLIN a key to the condo and insisted he stay there while he was in Seattle. She planned on staying at the hospital and no one was going to argue her out of it. She had done all the work she was going to do on her video for a while. Now she was going to concentrate on willing her mother to get well.

Colin didn't raise any objections. But he arrived at the hospital early the next morning, soon after the hospital day began. Over the next three days, Allie read aloud the rest of Joseph's journal, which told of *his* grandfather's, Hal Costigan's, investigation into his family's roots and the details he had uncovered and had incorporated into the family tree in the family Bible. Then Joseph went on to tell about his marriage to Tallah, the birth of their son, Edward, and the details of their life in Bermuda. They loved playing tennis, which had become immensely popular in Bermuda. They had even built their own court. They owned a sailboat and bicycles and a horse and buggy. When Edward, an outstanding cricketer, graduated from an English university, Joseph was delighted to record that his son was going to marry Sara Lowe, a girl Edward had known and loved since they were children. Toward the end of the account there was a joyous entry dealing with the birth of Edward's son, Lionel, and the sadness that followed when the baby was discovered to be incurably blind. Tallah had died soon after Lionel's birth, but Joseph had found comfort in helping to care for the boy and in watching him grow into an intelligent, useful, happy young man.

"You have to meet Lionel, Mom," Allie said softly. "As soon as you're recovered from this setback, we'll try to arrange for him to visit. He's a wonderful man."

Patricia smiled wistfully at her. She had spoken very little this day, but she had listened with great interest to the rest of Joseph's story. She looked at Colin now, then at Allie. "I'd like to talk to Colin for a few minutes, darling," she said. "Why don't you and Esther go and have a cup of coffee in the cafeteria."

Allie frowned.

"Please, dear," Patricia urged.

When Allie and Esther came back from the cafeteria, Patricia and Colin were poring over a chart of the family tree, which Colin had copied from Lionel's family Bible. Propped against her pillows, Patricia looked tired, but serene. She carefully rolled up the chart when Allie came into the room. "Now I'd like to talk to you, darling," she said.

Allie's heart began beating erratically at the serious note in her mother's voice.

After Colin and Esther left the room, Patricia patted the side of her bed. Allie sat down. "What are you and Colin up to?" she asked.

Patricia smiled mysteriously. "No good, you can be sure of that," she said ambiguously. "My what a lovely man. Not just in looks, though his looks are certainly impressive, but the way he is inside...so sensitive, so caring. If I were twenty years younger..."

She looked lovingly at her daughter. "Sweetheart, I'm never going to meet Lionel. You have to accept that. I'm never going to leave this hospital, not on my own two feet, anyway."

"Mom," Allie protested.

"Hear me out, darling." She took a deep but shaky breath. "I'm tired, Allie. I'm tired of hurting. I'm tired of living only a minute fraction of a life. I'm tired of lying around being useless. I'm tired, period. I don't want to fight any more."

"But you have to. You said you'd fight to the last breath."

She moved her head wearily. "This is my last breath, Allie." She smiled. "You know," she added softly, "I've always been intensely curious about what happens after you're dead. When Mark died, he looked so... empty. Whatever it was that made him Mark—the essence that was Mark—had obviously gone away. Where had it gone? I've never been a churchgoing person, but I've always had a strong belief in God. And I don't see how anyone can give birth to a baby, or watch a flower grow, or a tree, or look at the stars, and not believe in *something*. I think of death as just another adventure, like going through a door into a room you haven't seen before and finding it to be so beautiful you wonder why you were ever afraid to venture into it."

She took Allie's hand in hers and looked at her very directly. "If I'm sure of anything in this world, it is this—whatever awaits me on the other side of that door, your father will be there to share it with me. My place was always with him and it always will be."

"Mom," Allie said softly.

Patricia moved her head slightly again. She hadn't yet finished what she wanted to say. "I'm so glad you found Alys for me. And I'm even more glad that you found Colin for yourself. No, don't interrupt, darling. I knew the minute I saw him look at you that he loves you. I remember that look from when Mark used to look at me. And I asked him right out what his intentions were—Colin, I mean, I was never in any doubt about Mark's intentions." She smiled faintly.

"And he told you he'd asked me to marry him."

"He did." She tapped the back of Allie's hand and glanced at her with mock indignation. "You didn't quite get around to informing me of that little fact. Are you going to marry him?"

"Oh, Mom, I don't know. I love him. I've admitted that much to myself, if not to him. But marriage? When he lives so far away? He loves Bermuda. He'd never leave it."

"For you, he might. Or you can go to him."

"But my home is here. The business..."

"You never cared for the business side of the business. Sell it. Follow your heart, my darling."

"But I'm not even sure if my heart is telling me the truth. What if I'm not really in love? What if Colin just came along at a time when I was vulnerable and—"

"You'll know when it's right," Patricia said. She sighed. "I told Colin I thought it would make things very tidy if you were to marry him and go to live in Bermuda. History would have come full circle." A glimmer of her old mischief appeared in her eyes. "By rights I should extract a deathbed promise from you that you'll marry Colin. Deathbed promises are very binding, you know."

"Mom!"

"I'm sorry, darling," she said, without looking at all penitent. "I'd much rather go out with a witticism than a whimper." She gazed at Allie very solemnly. "Speaking of my imminent departure...Colin agrees with me that you're having trouble letting me go."

Allie had to swallow a couple of times before she could speak. "I can't," she managed.

"You have to, dear." There was so much love, so much certainty in Patricia's voice.

"But I love you, Mom," Allie protested.

Patricia's smile was dazzling. "You think I don't know that?" She was solemn again. "I love you, darling. You love me. Because you love me, you have to let me go."

Allie leaned over to hug her, careful not to hug too hard. All the same, she could feel the bones in her mother's body. Embracing her, feeling how insubstantial she really was, Allie was finally able to accept the inevitable. She sat up and looked steadily into her mother's much loved face, knowing her mother would be able to read her acceptance there.

"Thank you, darling," Patricia murmured.

The end came three hours later, just as the setting sun was beaming strawberry-colored light onto Mount Rainier's snowy upper slopes—one of the sights of Washington State that Patricia had always loved.

Colin and Allie were both sitting beside Patricia's bed. Esther was puttering around in the adjoining bathroom. Allie was holding her mother's hand and felt her grip tighten suddenly. She glanced at Patricia quickly and saw that Patricia was looking at her in a meaningful way, as though she wanted to communicate something to her. "Mom?" she queried.

Patricia smiled at her, then at Colin, then at Allie again. There was such love in her smile.

A moment later, she made a small sound deep in her throat, like a sigh, and all the life that had animated her features disappeared. The pressure of her fingers on Allie's ceased.

Allie stood up. "Mom?" she said again, uncertainly this time, then raised her voice. "Esther?" Esther came bustling into the room, took one look at Patricia and pressed a call button. At once there was a flurry of activity and Allie and Colin were eased gently but firmly out into the hall.

Allie stood looking out the window at her mother's much loved view of the mountain, hugging herself with both arms against the sudden chill that had come upon her. She felt as if she were made of some fragile porcelain that would shatter in a thousand pieces if she didn't hold on tightly to herself. After a moment, Colin slipped one hand under one of hers and she gripped it, so tightly that later he showed her the crescent marks her nails had made in his flesh. But at the time he didn't complain. Nor did he speak, sensing that she was just barely hanging on, hoping, afraid to hope, not really wanting to hope.

Esther came out of Patricia's room. Tears were standing in her eyes. "Such a dear sweet lady," she said softly.

Allie's ears felt as though they had been stuffed with cotton. She could hear her own heart beating, nothing more. She felt numb, as though every bit of emotion she'd ever felt had dried up and gone away, leaving no residue behind. Going into her mother's room, she noticed only peripherally that the medical crew was silently packing up their equipment. Patricia looked so small, so still, so insubstantial. Allie looked down at her mother's face for a long time. Colin stood with her, his arm around her shoulders. She was so grateful to him for being there. She remembered what Patricia had said about her father's body looking empty. But it seemed to Allie that the essence of Patricia was still there, inside that motionless white body. Any moment she might open her eyes and smile mischievously and make one of her outrageous remarks.

"Are you okay, Mom?" Allie whispered, repeating the childhood litany that had soothed away her night-time fears. "You're not scared or anything, are you?" Her voice seemed to echo in the still room. The entire hospital seemed hushed, as though its usual bustle had come to a complete halt. "Don't be afraid, Mom," Allie murmured, not really sure if she was trying to comfort her mother or herself. "Please don't be afraid."

COLIN HELD HER in his arms all night, while she talked compulsively about her mother and father and happy childhood memories. Toward three o'clock in the morning the reality of her loss struck and she sobbed it out against Colin's chest, noisily at first in great jagged bursts of weeping, then more quietly, until at last she was overtaken by a kind of numb languor that eventually became healing sleep.

She had remembered the period after her father's death as one of endless attention to detail, endless searching for papers, for addresses, for names. But Patricia had been preparing for death for a long time and everything was in order. All the same it was a nightmare to have to handle the details of the funeral, the will, the disposal of Patricia's personal belongings to the many friends she had named.

It was Patricia's total physical absence that was so hard to believe in. It seemed to Allie sometimes that if she were to turn suddenly she might just catch her mother smiling at her, looking lovingly at her, with mischief never far from her eyes. But when she did turn, no one was there. When she struggled through Pike Place Market, jostled by tourists and local shoppers, she could almost see her mother reaching over the slanted counters and the neat piles of apples and tomatoes and leeks, money in hand. "Look at the size of those carrots," she'd be exclaiming. "Give me a couple of pounds, will you? And a pound of those lovely looking mushrooms. And a head of romaine. Look at that broccoli, Allie, and those beets. Don't you just love all this stuff? God, we're going to be so healthy."

So healthy.

All the time, Colin was with her, asking nothing of her, helping her, giving her his strength and his comfort without question. Without really realizing she was doing so, Allie began leaning on him more and more, relying on his advice, his help, his attention to detail.

So it came as a shock to her when he told her one evening that he was leaving the following day.

"Oh, Colin," she said, then laughed shortly because she'd used the same helpless-sounding exclamation he had objected to before. The laugh sounded strange to her ears . . . foreign. Hadn't she laughed at all since her mother had died? How long had it been now? Two weeks?

They were in the kitchen washing dishes after dinner. Allie had cooked fresh-caught salmon, bought that morning in Pike Place Market. Her appetite had returned for the first time since the day of her mother's death. She had lost weight, she knew. Normally she would have celebrated that fact, but it seemed to her she had lost too much weight. Her face looked haggard on the rare occasions when she caught sight of it in a mirror or a darkened window. She remembered Patricia's saying, "Be careful what you wish for.

It may come true." For once, remembering Patricia, she didn't wince from the fact of her loss. Her mother's words would probably come back to her for the rest of her life, she thought. Surely it was a comfort to know she would always be able to recall a phrase, a sentence, a witticism.

She glanced at the calendar that was fastened to the refrigerator with a small magnet. July 11. Yes. Two weeks. She had missed July 4 altogether, didn't even remember hearing any fireworks. How inward-turning grief made us, she thought.

Patiently waiting, Colin had watched the play of emotions on Allie's face. "Is that all you're going to say?" he asked at last.

She leaned tiredly on the edge of the sink, her head hanging. How fine-drawn she looked, almost fragile, he thought. But there was strength in her, too, underlying the fragility. He had seen it surface several times during the past two weeks. She might bend in a storm, his Allison, but she would never break. "I'm sorry, Colin," she said. "I guess I resort to 'Oh, Colin' when I don't know what else to say." She straightened and looked at him pleadingly. "I don't want you to go. You said you'd stay as long as I needed you."

"You don't need me any more. You are perfectly capable of standing on your own two feet. Your independent nature is one of the things I love about you." He hesitated, then continued, "You could always come with me."

She took a deep breath and shook her head. "I can't, Colin."

He felt empty, as though he had suddenly become a hollow shell of a man.

"Not yet," she added, and he breathed again.

"When then?"

"I don't know." She looked at him, her eyes miserable. "I wish I had met you at a happy time when everything was good in my life and I could tell for sure how I feel about you."

"You love me—you know you do."

"Yes, but..."

He didn't allow her to finish her sentence. Pulling her into his arms, he kissed her thoroughly. "You said it—you finally did." He set her away from him and looked at her as sternly as he could. "Say it again," he ordered. "Properly."

"I love you, Colin," she said, "but..."

"No buts. I love you. You love me. That's all that's important."

"The fact that I live in Seattle and you live in Bermuda counts, too," she pointed out.

"Don't you know I'd move here like a shot if it was the only way... except for the business."

"I have a business, too. My mother and father built it up together. How can I just hand it over to strangers?"

"You're saying you don't want to marry me." His voice sounded leaden in his ears.

"I'm saying I can't give you an answer right now," she amended. "I don't know what to do. It's too soon after..."

The hollowness was back. "Allie..." No, he wasn't going to plead with her, reason with her. It was too soon. Hard as it was to do so he was going to leave with his proposal still unanswered. He was afraid if he pressed her too much now, while she was still vulnerable, she'd tell him no just to end her confusion.

Taking her hand, he led her into the living room, then sat down with her on the white sofa. "Allie," he said again, but more tenderly. "Do you realize we've been sleeping together for two weeks and we've yet to make love to each other?"

She nodded, smiling. "I suppose you expect me to congratulate you on your restraint? I was just as restrained, remember."

"You mean you wanted me, too?"

"The past few nights, certainly. I'm a normal healthy human being. Your body against my body. Why wouldn't I want you?"

He shook her slightly. "Why didn't you tell me?"

She was solemn suddenly. "Because it felt so good just to lie in your arms."

He held her close. "I love you, Allie."

She didn't reply, but he sensed her pleasure over his use of her nickname. She disliked formality. Even at Patricia's funeral she had refused to let the occasion become too grim and ritual. She had greeted everyone who'd attended herself. She had chatted about past memories with old friends and had arranged for a pianist to play Patricia's favorite show tunes, instead of the usual somber organ music.

Tonight she was wearing an apple-green linen dress that suited her wonderfully. No mourning clothes for her, she had insisted. Patricia had expressly forbade it. Colin had noticed earlier that the apple-green dress buttoned all the way from hem to open shirt collar. Now seemed an appropriate time to exploit that fact. "All right," he said in his best British 'this meeting is about to begin' fashion. ''We still have the rest of this evening and tonight.''

She laughed, obviously recognizing the words he'd spoken to her on her last night in Bermuda. She stopped laughing when his fingers released the first button, but she made no effort to stop his busy fingers. By the time he'd reached the fifth or sixth button—he had lost count—her wonderful eyes had begun to glow. ''Therapy,'' he said, as he unfastened her lacy bra and lowered his head to nuzzle the soft rosy nipple he'd uncovered.

''I wish I had your video camera,'' he added a few moments later as he lifted the dress out from under her. The sun was going down, sending streaks of gold blazing across the sky. The living room of the condominium was filled with the glow of it. The flawless skin on Allie's body seemed dipped in gold dust. Her hair shone. ''I could make a movie just about the way you look at this moment,'' he said reverently.

''It would never get past the censor,'' Allie murmured, lifting her hair from the back of her neck in a gesture that was so graceful, so unconsciously sensual, that his breath caught in his throat. She had no idea of her own sensuality, he felt sure. Walking with her through the crowded market this morning, he had seen male heads turn time after time. But Allie had walked on, unaware of the interest she'd aroused.

''It's going to be an art movie. For private screening only. It won't even be submitted to a censor,'' he suggested with a movie villain leer. ''One of the best things about video . . . no one has to see it but the cameraman.''

She aimed a mock punch at his shoulder, but changed it into a caress, then began unbuttoning his shirt. She had thought when she was seeing Curtis Yost that she would prefer to undress herself, but she had enjoyed it when Colin stripped her. Obviously it was the man who mattered, not the act itself. "I don't think it's allowed in movies for the hero to stay clothed while the heroine is naked," she said as she pulled his shirt off him. "It's too erotic."

"You'll be telling me next I have to keep one foot on the floor during the love scene," he grumbled as she started fumbling with the fastening of his belt.

"There's going to be a love scene in your art movie?"

"All great movies have love scenes in them," he said solemnly.

"Very profound," she started to say, but his lips were on hers and she wasn't sure the words had emerged. They certainly didn't seem worth worrying about now.

Every time he kissed her it was like a new experience. This time his lips were like velvet, brushing very lightly over the surface of her lips in a way that caused tiny electrical impulses to come to life between their two mouths. She wanted to deepen the kiss, to explore the surface of his mouth with the very tip of her tongue, yet at the same time she didn't want him to stop that sensual, gliding motion, so she relaxed and let him set the pace.

When his lips trailed gentle kisses down her neck and then hardened against her throat she was unprepared for the surge of sensation in her body. She almost felt faint, it was so acute. She thought for a minute that she was falling, and then found that he was easing her down from the sofa onto the hearth rug.

"What is this?" she heard him mutter.

She laughed. "It's my mother's favorite rug. She saw it in a magazine and ordered it. She didn't know it would be so coarse. But she loved the clean lines of the geometric pattern, so she kept it, anyway. One has to be prepared to suffer for beauty's sake, she said."

"It scratches," he complained.

"I know."

In spite of all their complaints, neither of them made any attempt to go anywhere else. And in spite of the harshness of the rug's fibers, they moved across it constantly as their hands found each other and caressed each other and their bodies twisted to surround each other. After a while it was hard to tell, Allie thought, where he ended and she began, and they had both obviously forgotten about the coarseness of the rug.

His mouth had sought the cleft between her breasts and he was tracing a line down it with his tongue, awakening nerve ends as he went. Then he raised his head and his eyes, incredibly blue in the light-filled room, locked with hers in a gaze so intense, so searching, so filled with passion, that Allie felt he had seared her soul.

"My turn," she whispered, and he obediently turned on his back and let her explore the wonderfully firm contours of his golden body. Without any feelings of shyness, such as those she had experienced with Curtis Yost, she was able to move over him with fingers and lips, touching and kissing him everywhere, even his most intimate parts. He didn't lie still under her ministrations, but turned and twisted with her, giving her access, taking advantage of her positions to kiss and caress the hidden folds of her body. He kissed her abdomen while his hand smoothed her hips and thighs, then his lips traveled on a searching journey that culminated in the most hidden place of all. Gently his lips nuzzled and kissed and all the while the sweet pressure of passion built up inside her, stilling her hands and her body and her breath.

She could hear the soft moans coming from her own throat, echoed by incoherent murmurings of his own. She gripped his head, holding him close, closer, straining toward him as the pressure built and built to an unbearable pitch, and then exploded into a rolling wave of purest joy.

Before she could come down from the heights of her ecstasy, he was inside her, thrusting deeply, holding her, enfolding her with warmth and love and security, bringing her up with him to the heights again, so that when his own immense shuddering climax began she was able to match him with another of her own.

Afterward, lying in his arms, overwhelmed with emotion, she remembered the other occasions on which they had made love, in the cottage on the south shore.

She missed the kiskadees and their impudent chirping calls, she decided. Here in the condo there was always the roar of the city, together with police and ambulance sirens and the squealing of automobiles coming to an unscheduled stop. It was hard to rhapsodize about the roar of the city when you'd experienced kiskadees and waves swishing over coral, and warm perfumed breezes rattling the sea grape leaves.

To live in Bermuda. Could she do it, she wondered. Could she live in Bermuda with Colin?

Once again the image of gilded frames around dark ancestral oils flickered in her mind. Living in Bermuda with Colin meant living in Diana's house. And she didn't see how she could ever even consider doing that.

She drove Colin to the airport with his proposal unanswered. They would continue to write to each other, of course. She would finish the editing on her Bermuda video.

"And after that?" Colin asked in the last second before he boarded the plane.

"I don't know," she whispered, then watched him walk away.

CHAPTER FOURTEEN

THE STORE WAS EMPTY of customers. It was the hour when afternoon shoppers had gone home to dinner and evening shoppers had not yet arrived. Working away in the editing suite at the back of Northwest Video, Allie realized the only voices she could hear were Marty's and Linda's. They were quarreling again. Linda had broken up with yet another man just two days earlier, so she was feeling aggressively grouchy. This affair had lasted less than a month.

"You really think this new labeling system of Linda's will work?" Marty asked, poking his head around the door five minutes later. So that's what the quarrel was about this time.

Allie swiveled her chair and summoned a smile. "Give it a try, okay, Marty?" she suggested wearily.

His expression changed from aggravation to concern and he came forward and put his hands on her shoulders and looked closely into her face. "You okay, babe? You getting enough sleep?"

Marty was a big, extremely handsome balding man who was self-confident enough to let his hairline recede without adopting unusual hair arrangements to disguise it. Allie thought he was quite good-looking—he had a warm outgoing personality similar to her own—but there had never even been a hint of attraction between them in the ten years since he had come to work for Allie's father. She thought of him as a replacement for the brother she'd never had and had always wanted.

"Eight hours a night," she said firmly. That wasn't strictly true. She spent eight hours in bed, but her mind kept going around and around trying to decide what to do about the business, what to do about Colin. Colin. She couldn't believe how much she missed him, longed for him.

"I didn't keep you up too late last night?"

Allie had spent the previous evening baby-sitting Marty's twin daughters.

She shook her head. "I was home by eleven." She grinned, suddenly feeling mischievous. "How did the date go?"

He shuddered and rolled his eyes despairingly at the ceiling. "Isn't there a woman left in Seattle who likes kids?" he demanded.

Allie laughed. Evidently the second half of his evening hadn't gone any better than the first. She hadn't really expected it to. Usually Marty's daughters were amenable, easygoing little girls, but last night their devilish streak had predominated and they had absolutely refused to go to sleep until their father came home. When he did arrive, with his latest lady love, they had flung themselves upon him, climbing him as if he were a tree, both complaining at the top of their voices because he had deserted them. Allie had noticed as she let herself out that the lady love looked fairly grim around the mouth and eyes.

"Keep looking, Marty," she advised him sympathetically. "You'll find Ms Right one of these days."

Marty snorted and went back into the store. Allie turned back to the editing system. A moment later, she heard him arguing with Linda again.

"Men are impossible," Linda said from right behind Allie's chair.

Allie jumped. She had become engrossed in her work and hadn't heard Linda come into the editing suite. "Marty had a bad night last night," she said soothingly.

"Who didn't?"

Allie sighed and turned around. Sure enough, Linda had draped herself against the doorjamb, and looked as though she were prepared to stay for a while. Her freckled face was set in doleful lines and her usually flyaway red hair appeared limp.

"Men troubles again?" Allie asked.

"Is there any other kind?" Linda answered. "You wouldn't believe the blind date I had last night. Gourmet cook and wants the world to know it. You know the kind? Always knows where you can get the best sausage. Or mushrooms. Wouldn't dream of using anything but durum flour for pasta. Owns a spaghetti-making machine. Knows every spice that was ever grown and grinds them himself with a pestle and mortar. So there we were in an Italian restaurant. He kept up a running and very audible commentary through the whole meal, criticizing everything. There were four of us, so I ducked out while he was lecturing the waiter on the *proper* way to make fettuccine Alfredo. I went to the ladies' room and never came back." She sighed explosively. "My friend Cathy swore he was a sophisticated man about town. Mister know it all, more like. What a bore."

She smiled wistfully at Allie. "You sure your friend Colin doesn't have a brother?"

Allie shook her head.

Linda looked at her curiously. "You hear from him, Allie?"

"He writes frequently, yes."

"What are you going to do about him?"

Allie sighed. "I don't know yet, Linda."

"Well, I wouldn't wait around too long if I were you. Men like that don't grow on trees. Believe me, I've been looking for a man long enough to know that."

"What kind of man are you looking for, Linda?" Allie asked.

Linda made a face. "The kind that doesn't exist. A man who is macho and sexually aggressive, but kind and sensitive and thoughtful at the same time. There's no such animal unfortunately."

I know a man like that, Allie thought, but she certainly wasn't going to say so.

After Linda left, she found herself thinking about Marty again. Marty was certainly macho, but he also had his sensitive moments. He had offered Allie his sympathetic presence on numerous occasions since her mother's death a month earlier, content just to be there for her without necessarily saying anything, knowing she was grieving, grieving himself, but not needing to talk about it. The only thing he had said at the funeral as he'd taken her in his arms and hugged her to his barrel chest was "I really loved that woman, Allie." There had been tears in his eyes. She wished he could find a woman who liked children.

Linda liked kids, she thought suddenly. More to the point, she liked Marty's kids. Linda had done some baby-sitting for him when she was between dates.

Marty and Linda?

Allie's fingers paused on the search dial of the editing controller as she stared blankly ahead at the source and editor monitors and the audio equalizer.

A second later, she shook her head. It would never work. Listen to the two of them now, arguing over Linda's new labeling system again.

Allie tried again to concentrate on the images flickering across the source monitor. Marty and Linda. It was a crazy idea, but it wouldn't go away.

Abruptly she caught her breath. She had reached the place on the raw tape where Colin was walking beneath his moon gate. Colin. She missed him so terribly. Her days seemed incomplete, her nights empty, without him. Her fingers reached involuntarily for the pause button and she sat gazing at him for the longest time, forgetting all about Marty and Linda.

But later, when she was back at the condo, she remembered them again. After a long hot dry spell, Seattle was enjoying some much needed rain, so there wasn't much to look at from the windows. There didn't seem to be anything she wanted to watch on television, either. Allie sat on the white sofa and gazed into the empty fireplace, intrigued by her mind's coupling of these two people who had been part of her life for so long.

Linda wanted a sexually aggressive man, she had said. Marty was sexually aggressive; she'd seen him in action.

Linda had remarked once that she found bald men sexy.

Well, then...

Probably such thinking was an exercise in futility, Allie decided. But without Patricia the condo always seemed unbearably empty in the evenings, so she welcomed something to think about. The condo had always been more Patricia's than Allie's, anyway. The furnishings were all hers, and the linens, the colors her choice. Everything in the place spoke of Patricia. Allie hadn't even lived in the condo until her mother had become ill. Then she'd given up her apartment and stored her belongings away.

She had to face facts, Allie decided. Marty and Linda had worked together for several years without developing an interest in each other.

Maybe that was because their timing had been off, like hers and Colin's.

Now that she thought about it, Linda had usually been deeply involved with someone when Marty was between women friends, and vice versa. But right now, they were both alone—unhappy about it, as their irritation with each other attested—and both of them were unattached.

Supposing, just supposing, she gave them something other than themselves to think about, something that might even force them to look at each other in a different light. Wouldn't that even help to solve her problem?

The shot of Colin she had watched earlier flickered again through her mind. Colin. Yes. Something had to be done. Quite suddenly she heard a couple of voices in her mind—Patricia's saying, "Go for it, Allie, go for it,'' and Celia's saying wryly, "A woman's gotta do what a woman's gotta do."

Plumping up the pillows at one end of the sofa, Allie settled herself into a comfortable position and fixed her gaze on the ceiling. It just might work, she thought, as she stared upward. It was certainly worth a try.

COLIN STOOD in the middle of one of the paths that divided the formal garden into separate areas, looking around aimlessly. He had left work early today, feeling restless, conscious that he had a great deal to do at End Court. He had put the house up for sale soon after his return from America, but certainly hadn't expected it to go so fast. Now he had promised the prospective owners that he would vacate the premises as soon as possible. He should be indoors, helping Mac pack stuff in boxes. Not that there was a lot to pack. He had sold most of the furniture along with the house, saving only those pieces he had made himself.

It was a beautiful day. The breeze blowing through the trees that surrounded End Court kept it from being too hot and the humidity was lower than usual. How had he ever let Diana talk him into planting this formal garden, he wondered. Flowers should grow in clumps, not rigid rows...there should be suggestions of wildness, of riotous joy in their groupings. The only thing he really liked in the garden was the moon gate, which had already been there when he'd acquired the house.

He wished he could take the moon gate with him. It was also the one thing at End Court that Allie had liked. He could construct a new one, of course. Which Allie might never see.

He walked over to the bench and sat down, sighing. Allie's last letter had been a confusing one. She had written about some plot she was engaged in that involved the people who worked for her. Marty and Linda. He'd met them at Patricia Bentley's funeral. He'd met so many people that day. Allison had a lot of friends. Probably she wouldn't want to leave them. Certainly she had said nothing in her letters about reconsidering her decision to stay in Seattle. He shouldn't have left her as soon as he had. He'd hoped his leaving would force her into making a decision. The right decision. Evidently she wasn't going to reply right away to his latest letter, the one in which he'd told her about disposing of End Court. He'd thought that might just make the difference.

Lost in thought, it was a moment before he heard the high-pitched buzzing sound that was growing louder as it came closer, a moment more before he identified it. A moped. Someone was riding one of those infernal machines on his property.

He stood up, irritated, and strode toward the moon gate, intending to reach the front of the house before the trespasser so that he could give whoever it was a dressing-down. Imagine shattering the stillness of this lovely day with that objectionable racket.

The truth of it hit him a second before he saw the rider. Allie, of course. It had to be Allie. Who else would ride in here in the middle of a workday? He started to run toward the moped even before he'd fully determined that it was indeed Allie, hidden under one of those ridiculous-looking safety helmets. She barely had a chance to cut the engine and set the stand in place before he had her off the bike and in his arms. Together, both exclaiming and laughing—she with surprise that he was home—she'd intended waiting with Mac for Colin to come—he with amazement and not very convincing annoyance that she'd come without warning him of her arrival—they struggled to get the helmet off her head, their fingers made clumsy with impatience so that the task became impossible.

Finally Colin lovingly set her hands aside and said in a very masterful way, "Let me do it." Once the helmet was off, and put away in the moped basket, he studied her face. "How are you?" he asked carefully. "Truly."

She smiled faintly. "As my mother used to say, I'm hanging." She sighed. "Well, you know, it still hurts, I still miss her and always will. But it gets a little less painful each day. I'm going to be okay."

"Stable Mabel?"

She nodded, and he drew her close and kissed her long and thoroughly, feeling like a man who had crossed an endless desert and had just discovered water. He felt as though his thirst would never be quenched, but eventually curiosity overcame his other yearnings and he released her and drew her with him to the bench in the garden where they had sat together before.

"First," he said firmly, "you must tell me this. Are you here forever?"

"I don't know," she replied hesitantly, and his heart felt as though it had contracted with pain. "It's up to you," she added, and his heart expanded again and beat more strongly then it had ever done. He was suddenly so happy he couldn't even speak.

She frowned. "My idea was that I could make Bermuda my headquarters," she said carefully. "It occurred to me that in this technological age Bermuda is really very central. I can easily get to Europe from here. I've always wanted to do travel videos there. And now that I've solved the problem of what to do about the business, I can take the videos back to Seattle, do the editing myself, then let Marty and Linda see to the copying and distribution."

It was his turn to frown. "You mentioned Marty and Linda in your last letter. I couldn't make head or tail . . ."

"I don't blame you," she said with a short laugh. "I wasn't sure where I was going with that project myself." She flashed a mischievous smile. She had gained back some of the weight she had lost, he was glad to see. She looked like his Allie, radiant with good health and happiness.

"I've been interfering again," she admitted, then briefed him on what the situation had been between Marty and Linda before she decided to get involved. "There they were," she said. "Two attractive, intelligent, lonely people, always dating people who weren't suitable for them."

"And I suppose you've now convinced them they are perfect for each other," he said lovingly.

She shook her head. "Not yet. It might take a little time. What I did was offer to sell them the business, under very reasonable terms, on the condition that they buy it as partners. Equal partners. That way I didn't feel I was letting my parents down. It's as though the business is still in the family. I've lifetime rights to the editing suite, according to Marty."

"But Marty and Linda had already been managing the business between them, hadn't they?"

"Yes. Ever since my mom got sick. But not for themselves. You know as well as I do that once you get into business for yourself you work twice as long and hard. They won't have time to get mixed up with anyone else for years. It seems to me that sheer loneliness will make them come together before too many months have passed.

"Perhaps," he said doubtfully.

She laughed. "At least I gave Cupid a push. If it doesn't work, nothing's lost. I've gained my freedom, and they've gained a lucrative business."

He looked at her directly. "Is all this—getting Marty and Linda settled, getting rid of the business, deciding Bermuda was central enough to work from— is all this your only reason for returning? Or did you come in response to my last letter?"

Allie looked puzzled.

"What letter? I had one about ten days ago, but I don't think . . ."

"I wrote again a week ago. I thought perhaps it was that letter that brought you."

She shook her head. "I booked my flight a week ago, when I leased out the condo. The letter probably went on to Linda. I gave her address to the post office for the time being." She laughed. "She's probably been too busy to check her mail. I just dumped the whole business in their laps. It was such a wonderful solution as far as I was concerned. I wanted to get out of town before they could change their minds." She looked at him gravely. "You haven't changed *your* mind, have you?"

"Never," he said, hardly breathing, finally daring to hope. "But I would like to know exactly what changed yours."

She met his gaze steadily. "I was working on the video in the editing suite one afternoon and I came across the shot of you walking through the moon gate."

He nodded, remembering.

"I realized when I looked at that shot that I wanted to spend the rest of my life in Bermuda. With you. Especially with you. Bermuda is my place. You are my place. As soon as I worked that out everything else seemed to fall into place." She smiled. "My mother told me I'd know when the time was right. And I did. I do."

She didn't get to breathe again for quite a while. Colin seemed intent on establishing some kind of record for kissing longevity and she certainly had no objections to assisting him.

But at last he released her. "You're going to marry me then," he said.

She nodded, smiling radiantly. "I've even brought the marriage goblet along. I left all my stuff at Mrs. Tolliver's until I could make sure you still wanted me, if you wanted me to stay with you here."

"We'll pick it up later," he said. There was a small frown shadowing her smooth forehead, he noticed. He thought he knew its cause. "Since you didn't get my letter before you left, Allie, you don't know that I've sold the house."

She shook her head, her eyes shining as though candles had been lit behind them. She hugged him tightly. "Oh, I'm so glad, Colin. I had decided I was being silly about the house and I could live anywhere as long as I was with you, but I was still worried about it, my feelings about it." She drew back and looked at him levelly. "You won't regret selling it, will you? I mean, if you did it just for me..."

He placed a finger over her lips and wouldn't let her continue. "When I came back here," he said, "I went wandering through the house. I guess I was able to look at the place more objectively than I had before. Even before I met you I had realized it didn't hold the serenity for me that I had thought. It came to me that I had been wrong to close a door on the past, so I forced myself to really look at the house. And I saw that a duplicate of the Blade family home in Sussex had been imposed on a traditional Bermudian home. No wonder you felt jangled. I also realized that if Diana could walk away from this house as easily as she did, there was no reason for me to cling to it. I think I hung on because I felt so guilty about her dying without me. When I finally let it sink into my wooden skull that she was leaving me for another man when she died, I was able to forgive myself for not going with her. She obviously didn't want me to go with her."

He drew in a deep breath. "I've already sent Diana's portrait and the photo of her at Gibb's Hill Lighthouse to the Blade family."

He grinned at her and shrugged as though a great burden had been lifted from his shoulders. "Since you didn't get my letter before you left you don't know the best part," he said happily. "I've bought a new house.

It's on the south shore, not far from Lionel's house, with its own beach, almost a duplicate of the one below my friend's cottage. The water is shallow for a long way out, so it's a very safe place to raise children. And the house is full of light, Allie, no shadows anywhere. There's a magnificent view." He hesitated, then frowned a little. "I haven't signed the final papers yet. I wanted to wait and see if you'd come in response to my letter. I wanted to let you look at the house first, to see if you'd like it."

"Can I open all the windows and let the wind blow through?" she asked.

He nodded. "Of course you can."

"Then I'll like it. I'm sure of that."

He pulled her close again. "We don't have to delay our marriage for any reason, do we, Allie? We can get married soon, really soon?"

She nodded, her lovely eyes luminous. "Are you working on your history book?" she asked.

"I am. I've already written Alys into it."

"I'm glad." She looked at him with a shy but loving glance that entranced him. "Don't you think Alys would be pleased that I've come to live in Bermuda?" she asked.

"She'd be as delighted as your mother was at the prospect," he assured her. "She'd feel the same as Patricia, that everything had come full circle at last."

"Like the moon gate," Allie whispered.

"Like the moon gate," he agreed. And then he stood and took her hand. "Come along," he said, and tugged her toward the moon gate. Solemnly he stood under it with her, then lowered his head to kiss her tenderly. "Now we'll be sure of a long and happy life," he said with satisfaction.

"I love you, Colin," Allie murmured.

"I love you." He took her in his arms and kissed her again, gently, lovingly. Above their heads a small yellow-breasted bird landed on top of the moon gate and cried out raucously, "Kiskadee."

Harlequin Superromance

COMING NEXT MONTH

ATTRACTIVE, SPACE SAVING BOOK RACK

Display your most prized novels on this handsome and sturdy book rack. The hand-rubbed walnut finish will blend into your library decor with quiet elegance, providing a practical organizer for your favorite hard-or soft-covered books.

Only $9.95

Approximately 16" x 8" when assembled

Assembles in seconds!

To order, rush your name, address and zip code, along with a check or money order for $10.70* ($9.95 plus 75¢ postage and handling) payable to *Harlequin Reader Service*:

> Harlequin Reader Service
> Book Rack Offer
> 901 Fuhrmann Blvd.
> P.O. Box 1396
> Buffalo, NY 14269-1396

Offer not available in Canada.

BKR-1A

*New York and Iowa residents add appropriate sales tax.

HARLEQUIN SUPERROMANCE BRINGS YOU...

Lynda Ward

Superromance readers already know that Lynda Ward possesses a unique ability to weave words into heartfelt emotions and exciting drama.

Now, Superromance is proud to bring you Lynda's tour de force: an ambitious saga of three sisters whose lives are torn apart by the conflicts and power struggles that come with being born into a dynasty.

In *Race the Sun*, *Leap the Moon* and *Touch the Stars*, readers will laugh and cry with the Welles sisters as they learn to live and love on their own terms, all the while struggling for the acceptance of Burton Welles, the stern patriarch of the clan.

Race the Sun, *Leap the Moon* and *Touch the Stars* . . . a dramatic trilogy you won't want to miss. Coming to you in July, August and September.

The Welles Family Trilogy

LYNDA-1A